Dead
Ringer

Also by this author

Dead on Account

Death Duties

Death Benefit

Salvation Hall

Dead Ringer

A Rose Bennett Mystery

MARIAH KINGDOM

~ Perceda Press ~

To my parents, Doreen and Brian, for opening my eyes to books

1

It was ringing again.

He put down the mug, adding another coffee ring to the collection that already stained the faded floral coaster, and stared at the ringing phone. It was out of its cradle, left idly on the coffee table amongst all the other detritus, dancing with the vibration of the incoming call. Perhaps if he left it there long enough, he mused, the battery would run flat as it had on the other handset, and then he needn't worry about phone calls at all.

For a moment the ringing stopped and he closed his eyes, savouring the peace. It was short lived, as he knew it would be. The person on the other end was a persistent bugger. They weren't going to give up until he answered it.

He sighed and looked away, lifting his eyes upwards towards the ceiling so that he could avoid looking at what once had been a sanctuary. If he looked at the room, at its component parts, he would have to think about it. Think about why the once pale blue velour of the sofa was now grey with ink smudges from a growing pile of unread newspapers. Why the mahogany sideboard was littered with dirty crockery and the tell-tale tin-foil trays of take-away food. Why the air hung stale with the aroma of long-eaten curry, and grubby carpet, and unwashed flesh.

But looking away didn't stop the thoughts from coming. He closed his eyes, but he couldn't shut them out. *It was because she was gone.* Because she was gone, she was gone and she was never coming back. He sniffed back the snot of tears, opened his eyes and looked down at the phone.

It was still ringing.

He glanced at the clock. Five thirty, the same time as last night. And the night before, and the night before that. The night before the night before that he had picked it up and answered it, and instantly wished that he hadn't. The caller had only managed a few words before he placed the handset back on its cradle, disconnecting the call. He didn't want to talk about it. Not right now. Right now, he couldn't handle it.

But he couldn't avoid it for ever. He knew that. Sooner or later, he was going to have to speak to him, going to have to deal with it. Deal with all of it.

For God's sake, Robert, pull yourself together. He's your brother. Laurence is your brother, and he's only trying to help. He keeps calling because he's trying to help you.

His eyes took a turn about the room and lighted on Kate's picture, a shot of her laughing gaily into the camera as she leaned back against the ship's railings on that last cruise. *Oh Katie, what have I done? What haven't I done? Didn't I always say I wouldn't cope without you?* He closed his eyes again and took a deep breath, then opened them and picked up the ringing phone.

'Robert Donovan speaking, how can I help you?' It was almost a whisper, the words unnecessarily formal anyway given that his brother would be on the other end.

The caller was less reticent, and his voice was strong and steady. 'Good evening Mr Donovan. Thank you for answering my call.'

Not Laurence, then. The unknown voice took him by surprise. 'May I ask who is calling please?'

'Your bank, Mr Donovan. I'm calling from your bank. You know, those people you take money from. Without paying it back.'

Without paying it back? His eyes moved to the bureau in the corner of the room and a pile of unopened mail. Bills, of course, in that pile. And bank statements. And

8

credit card statements. There must be. He took another deep breath and tried to pull himself into the real world. 'May I ask which bank?'

'Which bank?' The caller was almost incredulous. 'You mean there's more than one?' He laughed. 'Well I suppose there would be. There always is with your sort. You're not fussy whose money you filch, are you?'

'Filch?'

'Yes, you know. Filch. Steal. Thieve. Rob. Help yourself to … without any intention of paying it back.' The caller paused, and then said 'mind you, I must admit you don't spend it like most people do.' He laughed again. 'Have a nice time at the garden centre, did you? I had no idea you could spend so much on that sort of thing. Two topiary bay trees? Three hundred quid a pop?'

Donovan was struggling to keep up. Who the hell was this, and how did he know what …? He glanced out through the French windows into the darkness of the garden where he knew that two sculpted bay trees stood proudly in their hand-crafted pots, flanking the Lutyens bench that had been his last gift to Kate. He spoke into the handset and this time his tone was a little stronger. 'Who is this, please? Who is calling?'

'I told you, Mr Donovan. It's your bank. The people who gave you a credit card. That's the credit card you've been hammering to buy crap for your garden.' The caller blew out a breath. 'Over four hundred quid for two plant pots? That's a hell of a habit. Is there any chance you might pay some of it back? Or doesn't that figure in your plan? Eh? D'you think you can just spend the money and not give it back?'

Donovan put a hand up to his face and rubbed at his brow. 'I know I've got a little behind with things.' He glanced again at the unopened mail. 'I'm sorry. I can only apologise.'

'Apologise?' The caller was indignant. 'I think you need to do more than apologise. I think you need to start repaying what you owe. Three months, now. Three friggin' months and you haven't paid a penny. You know your credit file's screwed, don't you? You know we're going to come knocking every day until you pay it back?'

'I don't think you're meant to speak to me like this ...'

The caller's tone, so far almost jocular, took on a hardened edge, low and menacing. 'I'll talk to you how the fuck I like. People like you make me sick. You're quick enough to spend it, but you don't give a shit about paying it back. Something for nothing, that's what you all want. Usually it's holidays. Or clothes. That I can understand, everybody likes to treat themselves. But you, your type, you're the worst. Spending it on crap, poshing up your garden, showing off to the neighbours, pretending to be something you're not, and all at the bank's expense? What's that all about?'

Donovan's face crumpled. 'I didn't do it for the neighbours. I did it for Katie. I did it for my wife. She loved the garden, I ... I ...' He began to weep. 'She died. She died in August, I ...'

'You *what*? You buried her in the garden? The posh plants mark the spot?' The caller snorted. 'To be honest, Mr Donovan, I don't give a shit about your wife. All I want to know is this – how much are you going to pay back, and when? Because you know what? Until you start paying, you and me are going to have these little chats every single day.'

Jodie Pearce paused in the hallway, her overnight bag still weighing heavy in her right hand. She glanced almost longingly at the door to her right, quickly brushed a thought from her mind, and then pushed gently on the door to her left.

It wasn't a bad size of bedroom for a modern flat and yet Chris, with his habitual untidiness, had still managed to make it look too small. The work clothes he had just changed out of lay crumpled across the double bed, blue shirt thrown on top of grey trousers, and his black duffel coat thrown on top of both. The coat was cheap, the fabric milling on the shoulder where he always carried the rucksack containing his packed lunch and morning newspaper.

Shoes littered the floor. Five, six, seven pairs she counted in all, not neatly lined up side by side but pitched carelessly against the skirting boards as he had pulled off each shoe in turn and thrown it to the side of the room. All of them needed cleaning. Black work shoes, scuffed and water-marked from the walk to work. Grubby trainers never cleaned after playing squash. Football boots encrusted with dried grass and mud. A pair of brown suede hiking boots with a broken lace had unwashed socks poking out of them, malodorous from their last use, but not considered soiled enough by their owner to make it to the washing machine.

Once inside the room the view didn't look any better. She dropped her bag onto the bed and took in her surroundings. One bedside table bore an alarm clock and a small lamp, its plain cream shade soiled with fingerprint smudges. On the other a bottle of cheap aftershave and an aerosol deodorant jostled for space with a canister of fungal foot powder.

She winced and took hold of the corner of the duvet, pulling it back tentatively to inspect the colour of the inner sheets. Thankfully they looked clean enough. She let it go and watched as it fell back onto the mattress. Best not to dig too deeply. Her mother said that all blokes were messy, and blokes living together were the messiest of all. But she knew from experience that just wasn't true.

She glanced at her watch. It was ten past six and he'd only been gone five minutes. In another fifteen he would be back with the take-away and a bottle of cheap wine, ready for their cosy evening in together. The first cosy evening in they had spent in this flat. They had been going out for four months now, four long months, and this would be the first time they had slept together in his bed. She hadn't been able to put it off any longer.

It wasn't the sex she was avoiding, of course. They had made love before, she and Chris, many times in those four months, but not here. She had always insisted on it being at her place, in her bed, comfortable in her spotlessly clean room, soothed by the scented candles she always lit when he came to stay over, safe surrounded by her welcoming flatmates and their amiable boyfriends. She gently sniffed the air and wished she had remembered to bring a scented candle with her. The room could use one, and not just to create a romantic ambience.

Another few minutes had passed. In ten minutes he would be dishing up Chinese food, opening a bottle of Blue Nun and choosing a DVD, not for them to watch after their meal but to create a background noise to his fumbling and snuffling and groping.

She shivered. It wasn't too late to leave. She could leave a note, tell him she didn't feel well, say she'd gone back to her mum's to be looked after for the night. Mild panic was rising in her stomach, and she grabbed her bag from the bed and walked out into the hall. In front of her, the door of another bedroom was tantalisingly ajar. Her stomach lurched and, drawn irresistibly towards it, she pushed it open. A gentle aroma of Gaultier cologne hit her nostrils.

In many ways the room was a mirror image of Chris's bedroom, same double bed, same bedside tables, same chest of drawers. But there the similarity ended. Lit by two candlestick lampstands, nothing too personal was on view. A row of books lined the top of the chest of drawers, a clock and a radio rested on one bedside table, a musky scented candle stood unlit on the other, a grey fur throw was draped across the bottom of the bed.

She dropped her bag onto the floor and stepped into the room. Sitting on the edge of the bed she worked her fingers into the soft pile of the throw, closing her eyes, breathing in the cologne and the candle and the smell of his hair, remembering the feel of his fingers straying gently down her back, the pressure of his mouth against hers. The warm, safe feeling as he wrapped her, naked, in the fur throw and held her until she went to sleep. An involuntary sob escape her lips and she began to shake.

This was the room she wanted to sleep in, not the room across the hallway. She couldn't do it. Not with him in the next room, not knowing he was in here with someone else. It was OK at her flat, she could bear it at her flat, but not here. Not like this.

She scrambled to her feet and grabbed her bag, and was barely out of the room when the front door to the flat crashed open and slammed shut, and the sickly sweet smell of lemon chicken wafted down the hall to block her escape.

The room was warm and the bed was comfortable, and the clean crisp pillowcase cool against his cheek smelt of lavender, and of love.

The thing Robert Donovan had avoided for so long, talking to Laurence, telling his brother just how bad it all was, had somehow lanced the boil of his despair and opened up the wound to heal. It went against the grain to ask for help, he'd always been so resilient, so self-sufficient. But Laurence understood this need as much as he understood his brother's pain, and the rescue had been a gentle one, casual without being uncaring. 'Come and stay for a few days,' he'd said, forgetting all the unreturned phone calls. 'Liz would love to see you. She has no one to mother now that Jake's gone to Uni. You'd be doing us a favour.'

Robert knew that the favour was all to his benefit. Showered, shaved, fed and now resting in their son's bed he felt human for the first time in months, human and ashamed. How the hell had it come to this? Was this what happened when the bottom dropped out of your world and you surrendered to the grief? You lost your love, you lost the will to live, lost the sense to deal with the mundane things in life, and then one day some shitty little lowlife from a call centre calls you up and abuses you because you're too immersed in your grief to keep your affairs in order?

He thought again about the call and frowned. Who was he to call the lad a shitty little lowlife? It wasn't much of a job, making a living by chasing unpaid debts. It was bound to have its stresses. Little wonder that the caller was aggressive, angry even. It wouldn't make for a happy life, would it, spending day in day out talking to people who borrowed more to spend on the luxuries of life than you earned in a month to keep a roof over your head and put food on the table?

He gave an involuntary sigh. Laurence was downstairs now, trying to put his affairs in order. Opening the bills that he had been ignoring, reconciling the bank statements, making notes on who to contact and how to put things straight. The money wasn't an issue, of course, it never had been. The unpaid bills couldn't amount to more than ten thousand, and there was at least thirty thousand in his deposit account. It was good of Laurence to deal with it. Well, to deal with the unpaid bills in any case. As to the caller …

This was a point on which they so far didn't agree. Laurence wanted to take the bank to task for the distress caused by the call, and Robert didn't want to make a fuss. There was no denying that the caller's behaviour had been improper. But then again, it had been the wake-up call that Robert had needed. He couldn't help thinking that rather than demanding an apology he should be shaking the lad by the hand and recommending him for "employee of the month".

2

A bitter, biting wind blew tiny flecks of November sleet onto DI George Mulligan's overcoat, where they melted into the coarse worsted. Collar turned up against the cold, his gloved hands thrust into his pockets for extra protection, he braced himself against the wind's chill. Thirty odd years at the job and it still didn't get any easier. He watched from a distance as a makeshift screen was erected around the body, a young lad, his whole life ahead of him, that life snuffed out by some nutter in a car. Mulligan tutted under his breath. What a bloody waste.

Somewhere up above him a window opened and he looked up at the culprit, a young woman in a pink dressing gown, leaning out for a better look at the unfolding drama. Nosy mare. He lifted a hand out of his pocket and flicked it in her direction, watching with satisfaction as she took the hint and slammed the window shut, swishing the curtains shut with a flourish of indignation.

He broadened his gaze from her window to the whole wall, the gable end of a renovated block of flats on the outskirts of Scarborough. *Bellevue Mansions*, he thought to himself. Didn't think I'd be seeing this again so soon.

It was a shabby block, barely renovated at all on the outside apart from new double glazing and a small porch built around the main entrance. He already knew what it looked like from the inside, with its cheap bland carpeting and magnolia walls. He knew what it smelled like, too, the heady aroma of trade paint mingled with freshly gutted herring, thanks to the close proximity of a fish processing plant. He sniffed at the air, and then at the sleeve of his overcoat. A north-easterly wind might be bitter, but at least it was odourless.

The sound of a car engine caught his attention and he turned to look down the car park. The driver flashed the headlights of his Audi in recognition, and then reversed cautiously into the only empty parking space. Mulligan shuffled across the car park and got into the passenger seat. 'Sorry to drag you out, Scottie.'

DS Scott sniffed. 'It's alright George, it's not like I had anything better to do. Anyway, I'd rather have the overtime than wallow in front of the TV.' There was a gentle Welsh lilt in his voice that was at odds with his name. 'What have we got? Hit and run, is it?'

'I'm not sure. The victim is a young man by the name of Andy Miller. He lives …' Mulligan paused and corrected himself. 'He *lived* in flat 2d. He was found by a young couple who live on the same floor. They were coming in from the cinema and nearly drove over the body. They were pretty shaken up, so I've sent them up to their flat for now.'

'Did he live alone?'

'No. He shared with a lad called Chris Kemp. But the flat's empty this evening. According to the Bishops – that's the couple who found the body – both lads spent a lot of time in the local pub, The Half Moon. I've sent someone up there now to see if Chris Kemp is there.' Mulligan frowned. 'The door to the flat is open, by the way. The lock has been left on the catch so that anyone could enter without a key. The outer door of the building had been left open as well, but according to the Bishops the outer door catch is faulty. There's an intercom system that lets residents open the outer door remotely, but it's been faulty for a week or so. Anyone who has a visitor has to come downstairs and open the door manually.'

'And you think that's what Andy Miller was doing?'

Mulligan shrugged. 'I can't think of any other

explanation. He was found out here in the car park in his shirt sleeves, no jumper or coat, and no shoes.'

DS Scott raised his eyebrows. 'He came down into the car park without his shoes on? In this weather?'

Mulligan nodded. 'In his socks. In this weather. Thin socks, lambswool maybe, not the thick, outdoor type.' He thought for a moment, then said 'I can see that he might come downstairs like that to let someone in, but to walk out into the car park?'

'Maybe the visitor couldn't park, or was having trouble with their car? Maybe he slipped out to help?'

'Maybe. The thing is,' Mulligan turned to face his partner, 'the body was found in front of a parked black BMW saloon, a 5-series. Keys in the ignition, engine turned off, about four feet forward out of its parking space. Its front bumper was just about over his knees, but you can see that the car went over him further than that, and more than once.' The DI flinched at the thought and looked away, out of the car's window, in the direction of the makeshift screen. 'He's a bit of a mess, poor lad. Whoever did it didn't like him much, that's for sure. I'd say they've driven over him deliberately, and repeatedly.'

'But they haven't driven off? The driver abandoned the car with the keys in the ignition? Have we run a plate check?'

'We don't need to, the Bishops were able to tell me who the car belonged to. But at this stage it doesn't help us much.' George Mulligan turned back to look at his colleague. 'Because the car belonged to Andy Miller.'

'It just didn't make a lot of sense coming home for the weekend if I didn't need to.' Rose Bennett shifted in her seat and moved the phone from her right ear to her left. The manoeuvre disturbed the West Highland terrier dozing in her lap, and he lifted his head to stare at her critically with his one good eye before curling his lip and hissing out a low growl of displeasure. 'Shush, Mac,' she whispered, nudging his back end with her free hand, shifting his weight to a more comfortable position.

'Did you tell me to shush?' The male voice at the other end of the line was unimpressed.

'No, I was talking to Mac. He's sleeping on my lap.'

'That bloody dog is spoiled.'

'There's no need to take it out on the dog. It's not his fault I had to work the weekend.'

'You could have worked the weekend here, at home. You didn't have to stay up there at Lu's.'

'Of course I did. You know Lu is away for the weekend. I've stayed to look after the dog. I couldn't leave him on his own.'

'That's just an excuse. You could have brought him home with you for the weekend, the girls would have loved to play with him.'

'He doesn't like being played with.' She pursed her lips and lifted her eyes heavenward, tiring of the pointless argument. Of course she could have taken Mac home with her for the weekend. Of course it was all an excuse. They both knew there had been a clear choice between the quiet comfort of her aunt's cottage or the brittle atmosphere created in her own home when Mike's daughters came to stay. They both also knew that her decision to stay away could set a dangerous precedent.

She tried to sound conciliatory. 'Look, it wouldn't have been fair. To any of us. I had to work. You wanted to spend time with your kids. They wanted your undivided attention and the chance to let off steam, and I needed peace and quiet to work on my investigation. I thought I was doing us all a favour.'

'They missed you.' His tone was reproving. 'Hell Rose, they only come once a month. It's not asking much. Alexa was particularly upset that you weren't here. She wanted to show you the project she's just done for school.'

Rose suppressed a smile. At least not being there had

given the girls the opportunity to feign disappointment at her absence, rather than their usual display of disappointment at her presence. 'The important thing is that they spent quality time with you. Isn't that what it's all about?'

'I would like them to spend quality time with *us*.' The air hung silent and cold for a moment, then he asked 'how is the investigation going, anyway?'

'Slowly.'

'Are you any closer to nailing who made that phone call?'

'Not really.' She glanced down at a small table to her left, and the notebook and pen waiting for her. 'I really ought to get back to it.' She forced a sigh. 'You know, there will be plenty of other opportunities for the girls to visit.'

'Of course there will.' His tone softened. 'We can talk about it when you get home. I've already asked Saskia and she's fine about them coming to us for Christmas this year. Isn't that great?' He didn't wait for her to reply. 'Rose, honey, I'll have to dash. The girls promised to call me this evening, and my mobile's going off in the hall. It's bound to be them.'

And he was gone.

Rose closed her eyes and savoured the relief. When the East and Northern Bank had approached her with a new assignment, one to be carried out at their Scarborough office, she'd jumped at the chance, and not because the assignment interested her. An assignment in Scarborough meant the opportunity to visit her aunt in nearby Market Melbourne, to stay in the comfort of her cottage, to enjoy evenings with a glass of wine and conversation about all the myriad things that she and her Aunt Lu had in common. She frowned, knitting pale brows tautly over tired eyes. *Face it, Rose. You'd rather be up here with Lu than down there with Mike.* She brushed the thought away. Now wasn't the time to think about it.

She dropped her mobile phone onto the table and picked up her notebook, balancing it on her lap. The back cover rested gently on the dog's hindquarters and he gave a murmuring growl. 'It's not heavy,' she whispered. 'And if you don't like it, you could always get off my lap and move to the sofa.'

The dog pretended he hadn't heard and went back to sleep.

She flicked back through pages of notes made on Friday afternoon, a summary of her scant findings so far. The basis of the assignment was simple. She was to investigate allegations of a threatening phone call made to a credit card customer by a caller claiming to be from the bank. Experience told her that she had no chance of finding the caller, but she knew that the ENB had to at least look as though they were taking the allegation seriously, and putting an independent investigator on the case mitigated any risk of the bank being accused of trying to cover up any malpractice on their part.

The ENB ran a small team of six people dedicated to chasing credit card arrears. There was a team leader, a deputy, and four standard recovery agents. Three males and three females. The call in question was made by a male, so if it was made by this team there were three possibilities. She had interviewed all six of them, and found no evidence of wrong-doing so far. All six understood the process they were required to follow when calling customers. All six of them understood their regulatory responsibilities.

And of course all six of them were wary, and who could blame them? Rose had been presented to them as a consultant engaged to review the bank's process for dealing with customers in arrears. They had been assured that theirs was not the only team to undergo the review. But she knew they weren't convinced. No one mentioned Robert Donovan by name, but Rose knew that secrets were rare within the East and Northern Bank.

Rumour and gossip spread readily across teams, across buildings, across towns, across business divisions, and although no one had said as much she knew they would be aware of the real reason she had been parachuted in to sit amongst them and observe their working practices.

She was looking for the person who made that call.

Over on the table her mobile phone beeped with an incoming text. She gave a sigh. She didn't need to look to know it was a text from Mike. She stared back at her notes, considered her lack of progress in a more positive light, and couldn't resist indulging in a momentary fantasy that if she could string this investigation out for another three weeks she could possibly stay up at Lu's for Christmas.

Chris Kemp sank down onto the edge of the sofa and rested his forearms on his thighs, twining his fingers loosely together. His head was forward and turned to the left, so that Mulligan could see his pudgy face in profile. He hadn't shaved today and carroty stubble covered his face and neck, blending into the close-cropped auburn hair that covered his scalp. Behind the stubble his skin looked raw from razor burn, above it foggy blue eyes had retreated into their sockets, the skin around them puffy and swollen.

Mulligan looked across at DS Scott, who registered understanding with an almost imperceptible nod before backing away into the hallway. 'I understand that you've lived here with Andy Miller since the summer, Mr Kemp, is that correct?' He watched as the young man nodded without looking at him. 'And you get on well together?'

'Yes.' Chris Kemp glanced in his direction then just as quickly glanced away, unable to make eye contact. 'Andy wanted someone to share the rent. He knew I was looking for somewhere.' He cleared his throat. 'We work together at the ENB, in the call centre. We're in the same team.'

'The East and Northern Bank? That's just up the road

isn't it?'

'It's about a twenty minute walk. That's why Andy chose this flat. Because it was close to work.'

Mulligan nodded. Chris Kemp was still avoiding his gaze, but his own eyes were fixed firmly on the young man's face. 'You must have spent a lot of time together?'

'Yes, we're best mates. At least, I mean …' It was still sinking in that Andy Miller wasn't anyone's best mate now.

'I realise this is difficult for you, Mr Kemp.' Mulligan nodded again in sympathy. 'He didn't go to the pub with you this evening?'

'No. I've been out with Jodie. That's my girlfriend. We just went to The Half Moon for a few drinks. I stayed on for a couple of pints after she'd gone home.'

'Is there anyone who can corroborate that?'

It was one of those questions that always got a reaction. Chris Kemp looked up at him now, a hint of defiance in the blue eyes. 'Yes.' He thought for a moment. 'I met Jodie at seven thirty and we were together in The Half Moon until just after nine. She left, and I went up to the bar to watch the darts match on TV. You can ask the landlord. He was watching it with me.'

Mulligan forced what he hoped was a reassuring smile. 'I'm sure there won't be any need for that.' He watched as Chris Kemp relaxed a little. 'Tell me, was Andy expecting a visitor this evening, someone who would need him to go downstairs and open the main door to the building?'

'No, not that I know of. His girlfriend's gone away for the weekend. I asked him if he wanted to come out to The Half Moon, but he said no. I sent him a text after Jodie went home, I thought he might change his mind and come down for a pint before closing time.'

'Did he answer you?'

'No. But I didn't think anything about it. I just thought he'd turned his phone off, or fallen asleep or something.'

Mulligan nodded to himself. 'You say his girlfriend is away. Do you know when she will be back?' He watched

Chris Kemp's eyes narrow with what looked like suspicion, and decided that the point might be worth pursuing. 'Is she a long-term girlfriend?'

'They've been going out together since the summer. She's gone to Cambridge to visit her aunt and uncle. I don't think she's due back until late tonight.'

'Is she likely to come here when she gets back?'

The young man looked momentarily panicked. 'I don't know. Andy didn't say.' He frowned, troubled. 'Who's going to break the news to her?' The frown deepened with an afterthought. 'And his family? Who's going to tell his mum and dad?'

'We'll do all that, Chris. Nothing for you to worry about. But it would help if you can give me his girlfriend's name and contact details, and the same for his family.' He watched as Chris Kemp began to relax again. 'And of course we'll have to talk to his employer. Can you tell me which department Andy worked for at the ENB?'

'Credit card recoveries.'

'Recoveries? What field of work is that?'

'We contact customers to recover money against unpaid credit card bills.'

Mulligan's interest was piqued. 'You mean you chase people for payment against outstanding debts?

'I suppose you could put it like that.'

'That sounds like a tricky job, Chris? Do people take exception to that, being chased by their bank?'

'Sometimes.' Chris Kemp thought for a moment. 'I don't know that it's that tricky. Someone has to do it. These people have borrowed the money, it's only right they should pay it back.

3

'Dead? But I only spoke to him on Friday. He was fine. I don't understand?' Rose rolled over and propped herself up on an elbow. She squinted at her phone and tried to focus on its clock. It was two minutes past seven.

At the other end of the line Clive Barden was still speaking. 'It sounds like an accident. He was knocked down, close to his apartment. A terrible thing, Rose, a young man building a good career with us. Very sad.' He coughed to clear his throat. 'Of course, I need you to complete your investigations today and tomorrow, but in the circumstances ... low key, I think. Very low key.'

Rose rolled back onto the bed and wrapped an arm around her head. 'I hate to say this Clive, but isn't this rather getting to be a habit? The last time I did an investigation for you out in the field a young girl was murdered. And that was down to the ENB's negligence.'

'I resent that remark.' Clive's nasal intonation became suddenly brittle. 'Pandora Mitchell's death was nothing to do with the bank. Her killer was a rogue individual acting out their own appalling agenda. It was purely coincidence that they both worked for the ENB.'

Rose sighed. He was still in denial, then. Pandora Mitchell had worked for the ENB, and died because of it, died because she discovered that two of her colleagues were selling fraudulent bank accounts to a crooked solicitor. One of those colleagues had murdered the girl to keep her quiet. Rose was in no doubt that if the bank's control on fraud had been tighter then Pandora would still be alive.

But it was too early in the day for an argument, and in any case Clive had probably suffered enough. The other colleague involved in the fraud was his own ex-wife, and the discovery had been a body blow for a man whose whole life centred around his role as Head of Risk at the East and Northern Bank. It had been a blessing that she hadn't been involved in the murder, but her prison sentence for fraud still hung around his neck like the proverbial albatross.

She softened her tone. 'I'm sorry Clive, it's just very early in the morning, and I'm not quite taking it all in. It's a bit of a shock.'

He clicked his teeth. 'Yes, well … I suppose I should ask if you interviewed Andy Miller last week.'

'Yes, I interviewed him. There's nothing to report there, if that's what you're worried about. He fully understood the bank's recovery processes, and he understood the regulations around them. If he was on the heavy side when he called customers to discuss repayment plans he was hardly likely to admit it to me, was he? I've asked the IT department for copies of all calls made by his team on the day that Laurence Donovan claims his brother was threatened. I'm hoping that Stan Wilkins will have those recordings for me today. If Andy Miller was the operative who made the call to Robert Donovan we'll soon know.'

'Thank you, Rose. I know you'll keep me informed.' He paused, and then said 'I'm due to speak to the police again at eight. The bank will be fully co-operating with any requirements they may have. I will make them aware of your investigation, it's possible they will wish to speak to you. You have no objections?'

'Of course not. You know I will help if I can.'

The call ended, Rose dropped her phone onto the bed, sank back into her pillow and covered her face with her hands. An unexpected death in the middle of her investigation? Dear God, here we go again …

George Mulligan placed his elbows on the desk and rested his chin in his hands. He blew out a long sigh full of the night's frustrations. Four hours' sleep hadn't done him much good, his eyes ached with tiredness, and his ears still rang with Mrs Mulligan's late-night opinions about early retirement from the force, and why husbands who didn't grasp the opportunity deserved everything they got.

At the other side of his desk DS Scott mirrored his posture, his chin resting on one upturned hand while the other hand idly stirred a frothy coffee with a long plastic spoon. Scottie was lucky in Mulligan's view. He didn't have a twittering wife at home to give him earache. At least not since his wife left him for her best friend's husband, taking the kids with her. If you could call that lucky.

He pulled the plastic lid off the top of his own coffee and sipped on it. 'So where are we now?'

'Up a gum tree without a paddle.' DS Scott stopped stirring and dropped the spoon into a waste bin under the desk. 'I interviewed the Bishops, but they can't tell me much other than how they found the body. They didn't see anyone near the car, but they can't swear that there was no one out in the street as they drove in. The family have been informed, and the father came down this morning and identified the body. I asked him if he knew of any personal conflicts, whether his son had any enemies, but he didn't think so. Chris Kemp concurs with that. According to him, Andy was a good old boy liked by everyone at work. When he wasn't at work he spent a lot of time with his girlfriend, and when he wasn't with her he was usually either at home or in The Half Moon, usually with Chris Kemp. They had some drinking buddies in the pub, but otherwise Andy Miller kept pretty much to himself.'

'Have we checked Chris Kemp's alibi?'

'We have, and it's good. The landlord at the pub has confirmed that he was in the bar with his girlfriend from 7.30pm until we picked him up just after ten. She left the pub just after nine, but he stayed on to have a drink with the landlord and watch the darts, just as he said.'

'Have we spoken to her? Jodie, is it?'

'Jodie Pearce. No, not yet. She's on the list for this morning.'

'And the girlfriend?'

'Annabel Halmshaw. She was informed of the death last night, and took it very badly by all accounts. She lives alone, so one of the uniformed officers stayed with her until she'd calmed down.' Scott sipped on his coffee and looked thoughtful. 'They all work at the ENB, you know. Andy Miller, Chris Kemp, and the two girls.'

Mulligan shrugged. 'It's not that unusual. Social lives tend to revolve around the workplace these days. Have we had confirmation of the time and cause of death?'

'Not yet, it's due later this morning.'

'So for now it's looking like sometime between 7pm, when Chris Kemp left home for The Half Moon, and 9.30pm when the Bishops reported finding the body. We assume it was caused by someone repeatedly running over him with his own car.' Mulligan blew out another breath. 'Not a nice way to go.' He picked up a ballpoint pen and began to tap idly with it on the desk. 'What about motive? Any thoughts yet?'

DS Scott shrugged. 'Theft of the car is the obvious one. He could have seen someone taking the car, and run out into the car park to stop the thief driving off. That would explain no shoes or coat?'

'Assuming they had stolen a set of keys first? How did the keys come to be in the ignition? Were they Andy Miller's own keys?'

'I dunno. They were taken away with the car. I'll get hold of them today and ask Chris Kemp if he recognises them.' DS Scott swigged on the last of his coffee and tossed the empty cup into the bin. 'What time are we going to Scarborough?'

'Ten o'clock. I've been speaking to the bank's Head of Risk this morning. They're offering full co-operation and a meeting room so that we can interview his colleagues, providing we keep it low key and don't distress anyone or disrupt business. And there's something else.' His face brightened at the thought. 'Andy Miller's team are currently being investigated for a possible breach of banking regulation. The ENB have an independent investigator on site looking into the breach. She's already familiar with Andy Miller's colleagues, so she should be able to give us some background before we conduct our own interviews.'

'If she's willing to help.'

'Oh I think she'll be willing to help us, Scottie.' Mulligan indulged in a wry smile. 'Rose Bennett and I have met before.'

Michael Spivey put a nicotine-stained finger up to his face and rubbed at the side of his nose. The air in Henry Campling's office was always stale, rank with tobacco smoke and the smell of decaying leather-bound books, and it irritated his sinuses.

He swivelled gently to the left in the leather chair, and then to the right, his eyes taking in the heavily-laden shelves of books and papers. In front of him Henry's huge mahogany desk, its wood polished to a high shine, was tidy by comparison, empty save for a desk diary, a phone, and a wooden box full of pens and pencils.

He'd been into this room so many times, and yet today was the first time he had really looked at it, really taken it all in. Probably because Henry didn't invite him to sit down. Usually he hovered nervously by the door, awaiting instructions or delivering some piece of information as required. Sitting down never entered into the equation.

Not for Henry.

He found it hard to think of this as anything other than Henry's office, even though Henry himself was now absent from it. George Mulligan had seen to that, alright. Henry was in Scotland now, out on bail, a disgraced solicitor hiding from publicity and awaiting trial for money laundering offences, thanks to Mulligan and that nosy mare Rose Bennett. He'd been lucky there himself, if you could call sixty hours of community service lucky. He'd opened a bank account with fraudulent documents stolen from Henry's desk, but he hadn't used it.

He rubbed again at the side of his nose. Lucky that, that he hadn't used it. Truth be told, he hadn't had time to use it before Rose Bennett had discovered his crime, but that was a part of the story he conveniently preferred to forget. He also preferred to forget that he hadn't wanted to confess to his crime, but at least the confession had only meant community service and not another stretch inside.

Behind him a door opened and then closed again. Voices out in the hall suggested that the new senior partner, Hector Campling, was about to make an entrance. Spivey shivered. He wished it was still Henry. He was used to Henry.

Henry Campling was a bent solicitor of the old school. Devious, dishonest, crafty, operating just on the right side of the law himself, but aiding and abetting his clients to operate just on the wrong side. But it was all business with Henry, not personal, at least the stuff Spivey knew about. Henry had flats to rent, properties that he developed, and Spivey ran his errands. He liked that sort of thing, checking on the empty flats and making sure they were in good order, collecting the post, and so on. Henry might push the boundaries a bit by charging a saucy rent for a run-down flat, or stepping outside the planning regulations by converting a dining room into an undeclared third bedroom, but no unpleasantness. No dealing with people.

Spivey was uncomfortable dealing with people, at least

in the way Hector Campling wanted him to. Hector wanted him to collect the rents for the sizeable portfolio of rental properties that his father had built up over the years. Or to be more precise, Hector wanted him to collect the rent arrears.

Behind him the door re-opened and Hector Campling breezed into the room. He dropped into the leather chair behind his father's desk, leaned his elbows on the polished mahogany and steepled his fingers. He regarded Spivey with a forced smile. 'Well, Michael, I trust you have some good news for me this morning?'

Spivey licked his lips and cleared his throat. 'I went up the flats last night like you asked, Mr Campling.' He licked his lips again. 'There weren't no-one in.'

Hector Campling's eyes narrowed. 'There *wasn't anyone* in?' he corrected. 'And how do you know there wasn't anyone in, Michael? Did you knock loudly enough?'

A little croak came out of Spivey's mouth. 'I fink so.'

'You *think* so?' Campling took a deep breath through his nose and blew it gently out through pursed lips. 'Tell me from the beginning. I'm hoping the story starts with "I went to flat 2d at Bellevue Mansions"'.

Spivey nodded. 'I went to flat 2d at Bellevue Mansions, like you asked. I knocked on the door, but no-one answered. I knocked free or four times straight, Mr Campling, but no one came to the door.'

'What time was this?'

Beads of perspiration began to appear on Spivey's brow. 'I fink it was about nine o'clock, I can't ... quite ... exactly ... remember.' He thought for a moment, then said 'I knocked and knocked, because the lights was on, and I fought the bloke might be in the bath or somefing.'

'Could you hear any sounds? The television, perhaps, or music playing? Or someone moving around in the flat?'

'I fought the TV was on, but it could have been the flat next door, see? The walls are so fin you can't tell where the noises are coming from.'

'So what you are telling me, in a nutshell, is that you went to flat 2d to collect the rent arrears, there may have been someone in the flat who could have paid you, but you just knocked meekly on the door and went away when they didn't answer?' He leaned back in his chair and his eyes narrowed. 'Did you try to force the door?'

Force the door? Not likely. But he couldn't tell Hector Campling that he wasn't prepared to go that far. 'There were too many folk at home in the other flats, Mr Campling, it being Sunday night and that. Someone would have heard me.' He watched Hector Campling's face for any sign of acceptance, but didn't see it.

'So you didn't collect anything yesterday evening at all? Nothing at all in respect of the rent arrears?' Campling looked away out of the window, shaking his head, and then turned back to Spivey. 'Have you seen the news this morning, Michael?'

'The news? No Mr Campling, I don't watch the telly in the morning.' He shrugged, unable to see what this had to do with last night's proceedings.

'Well that's a pity. Because if you *had* seen - or even heard - the news this morning, you would know that the contracted tenant of flat 2d Bellevue Mansions is *dead*.'

The colour drained from Spivey's face and he began to tremble. 'Dead? He can't be dead. The lights was on, the telly was on, I heard him moving about ...'

'Oh, so you *did* hear someone in there while you were faffing about on the doorstep?' Campling gave an exasperated sigh and when he spoke again his voice was low. 'Did you have anything to do with this, Michael? With the boy's death?'

'Me?' Spivey's voice became a squeal. 'No! I ain't done nuffing to the lad. I never saw him, honest to God Mr Campling. I never saw him, and I never touched him.'

4

George Mulligan had arranged to meet Rose Bennett in the ENB's staff restaurant, and he rose to his feet as she approached his table. 'Well, you're a happy coincidence and no mistake.' His pleasure at seeing her again was genuine, and he grasped at her hand and shook it warmly. 'How are you, Rose? Has Clive Barden got you running his errands again?'

She returned his smile. 'I'm very well, thank you, all things considered. And you already know that Clive's got me running around.' Her tone was teasing. She slipped off her coat and draped it over a chair back, and dropped her briefcase to the floor, then sank into the chair next to him. There was morning edition of a local paper lying on the table and she pointed to it. 'May I?' She pulled it towards her and ran her eyes over the front page.

A grainy black and white photograph showed Andy Miller in a restaurant, enjoying an evening out with friends. He was holding a pint glass up to the camera and smiling straight into the lens, self-assured, confident, maybe overconfident. The poor picture quality failed to enhance any of his good points, but somehow seemed to heighten his small, brown eyes and his uneven, rodent-like teeth. Rose closed her eyes for a moment and remembered her first meeting with him. He'd shaken her hand a little too firmly, and his smile had been forced, his face creasing with the effort so that his eyes retreated into slits above his cheeks. He hadn't been pleased to see her.

She opened her eyes and looked back at the newspaper.

The report speculated that Andy's death was far from an accident, although there was little evidence to support a motive for murder. She turned to Mulligan with a questioning gaze. 'Is that report true? That he was run over by his own car?'

He shrugged. 'It's looking that way. It's a bad business, Rose. We don't believe it was an accident.' He thought for a moment, then said 'Clive tells me that you're investigating the team that worked for him.'

'I think it would be more accurate to say I'm investigating something that may have been *done* by one of the team that worked for him, if not by Andy himself. Two weeks ago, the Customer Services team here in Scarborough took a call from a guy called Laurence Donovan. He was calling to complain about the way his brother had been spoken to on the phone by an employee of the ENB. It turns out that his brother, Robert Donovan, lost his wife in the summer and is suffering a nervous breakdown. Because of his grief Robert has let things slide and his financial affairs are in a mess. He hasn't been opening his mail, paying his bills, that sort of thing. Laurence claimed that an employee of the ENB called his brother and spoke to him in a threatening fashion about the state of his credit card account. The account is seriously in arrears.'

'In what way threatening?'

'Using bad language. Accusing him of borrowing money he had no intention of paying back. Making inappropriate comments about his late wife.'

'All against regulations, I would guess?'

'Well it hardly constitutes treating the customer fairly. I've checked the state of his ENB accounts, and they were in a mess. His current account was way over his overdraft limit, and his credit card was over the limit and three months in arrears. He has significant deposits in savings accounts with the ENB which would way more than cover his overdraft and credit card balances, so there is no financial reason for his affairs not to be in order.'

'Has the bank apologised for distressing him?'

Rose frowned. 'It's not as simple as that. Customer Services couldn't discuss the matter with Laurence Donovan. He's not the account holder, and they couldn't breach Robert Donovan's privacy by discussing his accounts with a third party without written permission from Robert. The colleague who took the call told Laurence this and he lost his temper with her. He told her that Robert was receiving threatening calls from the bank, and that if she wouldn't do something about it he would go straight to the top.'

'And did he?'

'He certainly did. He wrote directly to the bank's CEO, Alex MacArthur. Alex doesn't get his hands dirty, so he passed the complaint to Clive. The ENB has already been fined in the past for not treating customers fairly if they are experiencing financial difficulties. Alex doesn't want to see it happen again.' She paused, then said 'Clive knows this has to be investigated, because it's not the only case. There have been other instances lately of customers complaining that they've been bullied over the phone. So far the ENB has managed to fend off these complaints with a goodwill gesture of a cash payment, around a £100 per complaint. Usually if a customer is in financial difficulties they are so grateful for a cash hand-out they go away quietly and don't mention it again.

'This customer is different. Robert Donovan is unwell, not in financial difficulty. A cash sweetener isn't going to make the problem go away, especially as his brother is on the case. Laurence Donovan has threatened to go to the media and tell them how the ENB has treated his grieving brother. That's the last thing the ENB needs.'

'So Clive called you in to investigate?'

She nodded. 'I'm here to look into the Recovery Team's behaviours. Do they take too strong a line when speaking to customers in difficulties, do they understand what's required of them, and most importantly is Laurence Donovan telling the truth, and did someone in that team threaten his brother? The call was made by a man, so that narrows the field a bit.'

'Are you making any progress?'

She screwed up her nose. 'Only slowly. I've interviewed each member of the team. They're not giving much away. But I didn't expect them to. They're hardly likely to admit it if they've been coming on a bit strong.'

'What about Andy Miller? Did he strike you as the sort to bully a customer on the telephone?'

'It's possible, I suppose. He wasn't lacking in confidence, and he seemed to be enjoying the power his role as team leader gave him. And he genuinely seemed to feel that his mission at this point in life was to recover money for the ENB. He understood what his role was, and he gave every appearance of a man who was intent on fulfilling that role.'

'Would he be encouraged to step outside the boundaries, do you think? If it meant recovering more money for the bank?'

Rose frowned. 'Encouraged by the bank? I haven't seen any evidence of that. Individuals and teams are targeted on what they recover, of course. Each team member has a target to achieve each week, and they have a team target for the month. It was Andy's responsibility to ensure those targets were met. Of course, the real evidence that will help with that point is the recordings of calls they make.'

'So the calls are recorded?'

'They should be. When they are making recovery calls, each team member uses a specific phone to make the calls. Those phones are linked up to a system which records both the details of the customer being contacted and the call itself. I've put in a request for the recordings of all calls made on the day Laurence Donovan claims that his brother was threatened, as well as sample calls made by each team member in the last couple of months, so that I can assess their approach to customers.'

'When do you expect to get the recordings?'

'I'm hoping some of them will arrive today. They haven't been able to retrieve them for me yet because of the way the system works. We can't get copies until the calls have been archived at month-end. As it's now the first of December we should be able to get access to November's calls.'

Mulligan thought for a moment, then blew out a sigh. 'I know this may sound a little crazy, but is there any way that either Laurence Donovan or his brother could have identified Andy Miller as the person who made that call?'

She tilted her head back and gave him a playful, quizzical smile. 'Goodness, are you *that* stumped for clues?' She laughed. 'No, I can't see it. We don't even know if it was Andy who made the call. In any case, Robert Donovan is an affluent, retired accountant and his brother Laurence is the senior partner in a large dental practice. Could you really see either of those carrying out a deliberate hit and run killing just because of a threatening phone call?'

Jodie Pearce sat perfectly still at her desk, her face fixed on the screen in front of her. Her headset balanced precariously over a spiky top-knot of bleached hair, and her hands hovered over her keyboard. To the untrained eye she might have been making or taking a customer call, but she wasn't doing either. Anyone looking closely would have seen that although her face was fixed on the screen, her eyes were looking upwards over the top of it, through the glass wall of a meeting room just some nine or ten feet away from her desk.

In the room a tall, well-built man in his forties was deep in conversation with a pretty, doe-eyed girl some twenty years his junior. The girl had long, chestnut hair and she had twisted a strand of it around the index finger of her left hand, and was winding it backwards and forwards as she spoke. She'd been crying profusely and her cheeks were blotchy with raw emotion and melting mascara, but despite the tears there was a coquettishness about her behaviour that was hard to miss.

Jodie's eyes narrowed as she watched the unfolding scene through the glass and a slow, visceral hatred began to burn in the depths of her gut. She'd watched Annabel Halmshaw flirt before, just as she was flirting with the detective now, watched her wind the strand of hair around her finger as she'd leaned against Andy Miller's desk back in the summer, worming her way into his affections with her coy looks and her fluttering eyelashes. She had watched helplessly as Andy had fallen prey to Annabel Halmshaw's doe eyes and lustrous, long chestnut locks without so much as a backward glance at his girlfriend. Without as much as a backward glance at her.

Bitch.

She dragged her eyes away from the meeting room and glanced over her right shoulder to where Chris Kemp was hunched over his own desk, pretending to read through his schedule of calls for the day. He looked tired, his blue eyes rheumy from lack of sleep, his pudgy face still unshaven from the day before so that yesterday's stubble had begun to develop into an untidy auburn beard.

She was still smarting from his neglect. How could he have known about Andy's death last night and not called to tell her? How could he have left her to hear the news on the radio this morning? It wasn't down to jealousy, she knew that. He'd never been jealous that she used to be Andy's girlfriend. There wasn't anything to be jealous of, was there? Andy didn't want her any more, not since the day Annabel had sashayed over to his desk and wound his heart around her fingers.

Chris was her boyfriend, but he didn't want to speak to her. He didn't want to speak to anyone. He'd only come to work, he said, to take his mind off things, to forget about last night. It was what Andy himself would have wanted, for the team to keep their eye on the ball, to forget about him and keep working towards their targets. But she knew Chris was hurting almost as much as she was. Even if he didn't love her, he had loved Andy. They had both loved Andy. She wanted to comfort him, to share her grief with him, and he had turned away from her.

Bastard.

She swallowed back a tear and turned back towards her screen. How were they supposed to work today? It wasn't just that Andy was missing from work, Andy was dead. He wasn't just their team leader, he was a part of their life. He was a flatmate and friend to Chris, he'd been a lover to Jodie once, and to Annabel.

Jodie turned her gaze back to the glass wall just as the door of the meeting room opened and a weeping Annabel emerged under the tender care of DS Scott. The policeman looked around anxiously, hoping perhaps for a sympathetic volunteer to take the grieving girl off his hands, but volunteers proved unnecessary. Chris Kemp rose to his feet and she flew at him, wrapping her arms around him and burying her head into his shoulder. There was no resistance. The two of them stood silently beside his desk, embracing in their mutual grief, as DS Scott melted thankfully back into the private office.

Jodie watched them for a moment, barely able to comprehend their spontaneous display of tenderness, and then turned her head away. The girl was whimpering into Chris Kemp's ear as he enveloped her protectively in his arms, stroking her hair and whispering words of comfort, cutting Jodie to the quick. He'd never spoken to her with such endearing tenderness, never held her tightly to take away her pain.

And he probably never would.

5

George Mulligan had wanted to interview Andy Miller's colleagues without any distractions, and Rose hadn't begrudged him the favour when he'd asked her to stay away from the Recovery Team for a few hours. How could she? Investigating a rogue phone call was hardly as important as investigating a murder. Anyway, she liked Mr Mulligan. Her Aunt Lu, who years ago had been closer to the policeman than she would readily admit, had warned her to look beyond his avuncular appearance, and declared him to be as sharp as a drawer full of knives. She smiled to herself. He wasn't looking too sharp this morning.

A late morning mail delivery from the bank's IT department had at least brought something to occupy her time. Recognising Stan Wilkins' hand-writing on the small padded envelope she had booked herself into a small private meeting room and settled in there with her laptop, headphones and a large latte. The envelope contained a CD case and a hand-written note in Stan's spidery scrawl. *Sample calls from Credit Card Recovery Team, October recordings. Recording of Laurence Donovan's call to Customer Services November 19th. Still trying to pinpoint the November 18th call to Robert Donovan. Heard about Andy Miller, think you are jinxed. Speak soon. Stan.* She took the disc from its case and clicked it into her laptop.

Stan had named the sound files by team member and by the date the call was made. She pushed the small headphones into her ears, clicked on a file called "Reggie Croft, 15th Oct", and listened carefully to Reggie's flat northern tones as he tried to recover some cash for the bank. Reggie had been with the Recovery Team for years and according to Andy Miller he always missed his targets. It wasn't long before Rose understood why.

'Mr. Sedgewick? My name is Reggie, and I'm calling you today from the East and Northern Bank, to discuss your credit card account.'

Silence.

'As things stand, Mr Sedgewick, your account is in arrears, and the balance exceeds the credit limit we agreed with you.'

More silence.

'The purpose of my call today, Mr Sedgwick, is to see what I can do to help you resolve the problems you're having with this account. Can I just establish, before we go any further, that you understand that the account balance is now three thousand, three hundred and sixty two pounds, that you are three hundred and sixty two pounds over the agreed credit limit, and that you haven't made any payments to the account for three months?'

Deafening silence.

She heard Reggie sigh. 'I am trying to help you today, Mr Sedgewick. I'd like to discuss how we can get your account back on track, by making what we call "an arrangement to pay". Under the arrangement, you would pay us an agreed amount less than the contractual monthly payment, but more than the account's fees and interests charged on a monthly basis. This would gradually bring the account back under the credit limit. At that point, the contractual terms would be re-applied, and you would be asked to resume monthly payments at the contractual rate.'

At the other end of the line the customer broke his silence with a sniff. 'Can't you just up the credit limit?'

'Excuse me?' Reggie was momentarily thrown off script.

'The credit limit? Can't you just up it by a grand? Then it wouldn't be over the limit, and there'd be another six hundred quid for me to borrow. It's Christmas coming up soon. How do you expect me to get the kids Christmas presents if I haven't got any credit?'

'Mr Sedgewick, I …'

'Have you got kids, Reggie?' The customer sniffed again. 'Expensive business, kids. I should know, I've got five of the buggers. Well,' he paused, 'three of mine, one of her ex's, and one she swears is mine but looks like him.' He clicked his teeth. 'That's five lots of Christmas presents, and something for the missus. And me road tax is due at the end of November. No chance of keeping me van on the road if I can't tax it. And if I can't tax me van, I can't work.' He chuckled. 'And if I can't work, Reggie, then I can't earn the money to pay any of it back, can I?'

Rose heard Reggie sigh again, then he said 'is there no way you can make a small payment on account, Mr Sedgewick? I can't increase your credit limit, that's not in my give. But if you can make a payment, I might be able to get some of the charges waived this month?'

Sedgewick sucked air in through his teeth. 'Wish I could, Reggie, wish I could.' He puffed the air back out again. 'You wouldn't want to be responsible for the bairns not getting any presents, would you?'

There was a long pause, and then Reggie capitulated. 'I'll tell you what I'll do, Mr Sedgewick. If you can promise to make a payment in November, I'll flag the account not to expect a payment this month to give you a bit of breathing space.'

'I knew you were a decent chap, Reggie. Very decent.'

'So if we can agree a payment in November of fifty pounds towards the account …'

There was an audible click as Sedgewick hung up, then another click and a sigh as Reggie terminated the call from his end.

Rose closed her eyes and contemplated. Reggie's tone on the call was far from bullying, but he wasn't doing anyone any favours by being so lenient. The customer was going to incur another month's worth of interest and charges, and Reggie had failed to collect any arrears for the bank. He was an experienced agent, he should have known better.

She opened her eyes and clicked on the next file, "Chris Kemp, 20th Oct". To her surprise, the call was to the same customer. She laughed inwardly. Just like Stan to throw her a curved ball. She leaned an elbow on the table and rested her head on her hand. After Reggie's call the customer's account should have been diarised not to receive another call until November. What sort of a game was this, then?

Sedgewick sounded annoyed. 'I've already spoken to the bank this month. Your mate Reggie said it was alright not to make a payment.'

Chris Kemp's tone was level, his voice firm in its response. 'I'm aware that you spoke to my colleague, Mr Sedgewick, but I'm afraid there has been an error on our part. I'm going to credit your account with a goodwill payment of thirty pounds to compensate you for any inconvenience caused.'

The man's tone changed to an irritating whine. 'Well that's very decent of you, Chris. Thanks very much, thirty quid will come in handy.' He didn't seem to follow that the thirty pounds would simply disappear into the pot of charges already accruing on the account.

Chris Kemp responded in a brisk but friendly tone. 'That's no problem, Mr Sedgewick. That's all done for you now.' Rose heard the click of fingers on a keyboard as Chris raised the request for a credit to Sedgewick's account. 'Now that's done, I'm afraid I'm going to have to ask you for a payment today towards your arrears.'

Sedgewick fell silent. Chris Kemp waited for a moment, then said 'your account is now three hundred and eighty seven pounds over your credit limit. I will need you to make a payment of at least one hundred and fifty pounds this month, and the same again in November and December. Your account will be frozen until those payments have been made, although charges and interest will still be applied. If those payments are made on time, and in line with what we have agreed today, we may be able to offer you continued credit facilities, although I must remind you that the account may still be in arrears due to continuing charges and interest ...'

'Now wait a minute ... I haven't agreed to anything. Who do you think ...'

Chris Kemp didn't let him finish. 'If those payments are not received, then with regret we will have to terminate your account.' He paused, and then added 'and of course that will register a default on your credit file, and may affect your ability to obtain credit elsewhere.'

'But your colleague said ... '

'I've already explained that my colleague made a mistake, and apologised for that mistake with a goodwill payment to your account. Now that you've accepted that payment ...'

'But I ...'

'Now that you've accepted that payment and I have resolved any complaint on your part, I am entitled to request payments against the arrears. Can you please confirm your understanding of this conversation, Mr Sedgewick, and also advise by what means you intend to make the first payment?'

After a brief torrent of abuse, Sedgewick grunted. 'I'll pay it on my debit card.'

The payment secured, Chris Kemp thanked the customer for his time, and after a further spew of invective from Sedgewick there was a click as the call ended.

Rose took off her headphones for a moment, and sat back in her seat. Chris Kemp was efficient, alright. Direct, to the point, just the right side of intimidating to make the customer think twice about their actions and get a result without compromising the bank's adherence to regulation. There was nothing inaccurate in his advice to the customer. But there was nothing sympathetic in it either. It was all cold, hard statements of fact. You are over your credit limit. You have arrears that need to be cleared. If they are cleared, we can keep lending you money. If they are not, we reserve the right to close the account and damage your credit file.

Could this be called intimidating? She thought about Laurence Donovan's claims, that his brother had been threatened and abused. It didn't seem possible that Reggie could have made the call to Robert Donovan, but it might have been Chris. She herself wouldn't call his tone abusive or threatening, but she guessed the definition of both could be pretty subjective, and it was a short step from being firm to crossing the line.

The Feathers public house was busier than usual for a Monday lunchtime, but not busy enough for Michael Spivey to completely lose himself from anyone who might be looking for him. Benny Bradman leaned an elbow on the bar and stared into his oily face. 'Where the hell have you been all mornin'?'

Spivey, perched precariously on a high bar stool, paused with his pint halfway to his lips. His scrawny neck shrank involuntarily into the collar of his shirt, and he looked up at Benny with a feigned innocence. 'I had an errand to do for Mr Campling, boss. I told you I'd be in at lunchtime.'

'Mr *Camplin*?' Benny snorted a derisive laugh. 'I thought you'd have learned your lesson last time, messin' about with Henry's affairs. That nearly landed you back inside, or have you forgotten?' He pursed his lips and shook his head. 'I don't know why I bother with you.' He jabbed a stubby finger on the bar dangerously close to Spivey's elbow. 'Get that pint finished and get yourself back into the shop, pronto.' He turned on his heel and blustered through the bar in the direction of the door.

Spivey relaxed and watched his retreating back with a

smirk. Benny was going soft in his old age. He put his pint glass up to his lips in a mock toast. 'To you, boss.'

He'd been working for Benny Bradman for three years now, as a sort of odd job man-cum gofer, first for the extensive chain of turf accountants that Benny had run in Essex, and lately in the more soporific surroundings of a single outlet in Market Melbourne. And if Benny couldn't remember why he bothered with him, Spivey himself wasn't going to forget any time soon.

Landed two years ago with a false charge of receiving stolen goods after a so-called mate hid seven crates of stolen whisky in the lock up that he used for his car, Michael Spivey had applied for legal aid and found himself represented by *Mrs* Benny Bradman. She was a lady, Catriona Bradman, and no mistake. A real lady. She hadn't just defended his innocence, picked up her cheque and walked. She'd talked to him, tried to understand him, almost befriended him. His cheeks reddened at the presumption. Well, not befriended him, then. Looked out for him.

She'd decided all he needed to stay straight was a hand to get on in life, and she leaned on her old man to give him a job running errands. Benny had resisted, of course, throwing up every objection he could think of. And she'd countered every objection with a kind word in Spivey's defence. Benny couldn't resist her. Nobody could resist her.

His face softened as he thought about her. Life had been sweet then. She was the first woman to really take an interest in him. Well the only woman, really, if he discounted his mother and his Auntie Jen. Mrs Bradman had popped into the shop every so often to see how he was getting on, and on one occasion had given Benny an earful in front of a shop full of punters for not being more interested in his welfare. He chuckled at the memory.

Of course, nothing that good in life endures. Not for the likes of him, anyway. A freak water-skiing accident last year had taken care of that. His face darkened. It nearly broke Benny, and their boy, losing her like that. And it nearly broke him. Except that no-one noticed his grief. He stared deeply into the murky amber liquid in his glass. Why would anyone notice *his* grief? He wasn't the husband, or the son, or even permitted to call himself her friend. He was nobody.

'Are you alright there, Michael? Can I get you another?'

He started at the question, and blushed, and turned surprised eyes left to look at the barmaid. 'Alright, Vienna?'

'Not bad, thanks.' Vienna leaned a tattooed arm on the bar and bent a head full of tousled black curls towards him. 'You're looking a bit peaky today. Is Benny working you too hard?' Her voice was soft and surprisingly well-spoken, and there was a flicker of genuine concern in the grey eyes that scanned his face.

He felt his cheeks start to burn and his pulse quicken. She was so pretty, Vienna. He'd always thought she was pretty. And here she was being nice to him. He wasn't quite sure what to say to her, but he knew he couldn't let the opportunity pass. 'Benny? Nah, he's alright. He's got the hump cos I'm doing a few errands for the Camplings.' He smiled at her, not too broadly, conscious of his nicotine-stained teeth, and not wanting to scare her off. 'Join me in a drink?' He tossed the question out carelessly, longing for her to say yes, but not wanting to sound like it mattered to him. If it sounded like it didn't matter, he reasoned, it might not hurt too much when she said no.

She glanced around the bar. 'Well, we're pretty quiet today. Why not? I'll have a G and T, if that's alright with you?'

Dumbfounded by her answer he could only nod in agreement. He pushed a hand into his trouser pocket and scrabbled around for some change, then dropped enough coins onto the bar to pay for her drink. 'How's things with you, then?' There was a tremor in his voice now that he was struggling to control.

She screwed up her nose. 'Oh, you know. Too many shifts, not enough fun, too many bills, not enough money.' She pointed in the direction of Benny's exit. 'Didn't I just hear him say that he wanted you back in the shop?'

Spivey smiled, his lips carefully folded over his teeth to keep them hidden. 'Benny's alright. He won't mind if I stay and have a chat with you. He's always telling me that I need to be more sociable. He won't mind if I tell him it was you I was talking to.' There was bravado in his voice, but he felt a guilty nerve twitch in the back of his neck.

Truth be told, Benny *was* alright. It just somehow pained him to admit it.

6

Annabel Halmshaw perched on the edge of a plastic chair. Her right leg was wrapped tightly around her left, one lithe limb snaked around the other, and her shoulders hunched over her knees, her arms folded over her lap. She clasped a sodden cotton handkerchief in one hand, and her mobile phone in the other.

Rose took a moment to look at the girl properly. She was pretty, with plump clear skin and long gleaming chestnut hair. Her soft dark eyes were swollen with tears but somehow that just made her look more appealing, that mark of vulnerability that made men want to cosset her. The girl was distressed alright, but Rose couldn't shake an inexplicable suspicion that the tears weren't just for Andy.

She brushed it to the back of her mind and opened her notebook. 'Can I get you something Annabel? A drink of water, or a coffee, before we start?' Rose wasn't good at sympathy but she did her best.

The girl shook her head. 'No, thank you. I'll be fine.' The words were a whisper.

'I know things must be really difficult for you today. We don't have to do this if you'd rather not.'

Annabel fixed her with tearful eyes. 'I'm OK, really. I know everyone thinks I should go home, but I don't want to be alone. I'd rather be at work. It's taking my mind off …' Her words trailed away and she tried again. 'I'd like to help, Rose. I'd like to keep busy.'

'Of course.' Rose swept her eyes over the scribbled notes in front of her. 'I just need to ask you a few questions about a specific call you took in Customer Services. The call was made by someone called Laurence Donovan, and he called to discuss his brother's accounts.' She looked up from the notebook into Annabel's face. 'Do you remember that call? It was the middle of November. I believe he was pretty angry when he called.'

Annabel's grieving eyes registered a sudden flash of shrewd comprehension, and she blinked it quickly away to leave only a hint of vague understanding. 'Yes, I remember. Mr Donovan claimed that someone from the ENB had made a threatening phone call to his brother. About arrears on a credit card account. He was angry because I couldn't discuss it with him. But you know, Rose, that I had to say that?'

'Of course.' Rose gave a nod of reassurance and looked back at her notes. 'Mr Donovan raised his concerns with Alex MacArthur the same day. And Alex passed the complaint to Clive Barden.' She looked up again and watched the girl's face as she phrased her next question. 'Did you tell anyone about this call, Annabel?'

Annabel's face remained impassive. 'Of course. I told my team leader. I hadn't been able to answer Mr Donovan's concerns, and he did make it clear that he was going to escalate his complaint. I made a note on the system that I had tried to explain to him that I couldn't discuss the account without the account holder's permission, and that he had hung up on me. And then I flagged up to my team leader that I'd had a difficult call.' She braved a half-smile. 'I work in Customer Services, Rose. Angry callers are part of our daily routine. And nearly every other customer threatens to escalate their complaint to the CEO. It's usually an empty threat but my team leader likes to know if she's likely to get a call from Alex or Clive, it helps if she is prepared.'

'I'm sure it does.' Rose returned her smile. 'Did you tell

anyone else, Annabel?'

The girl frowned. 'No, I don't think so.'

'You didn't mention it to Andy, or to anyone else in his team?'

The doe eyes widened almost imperceptibly and Annabel blinked once, twice, three times before answering. 'No, why would I mention it to him? We tried not to talk about work when we were out of the office.'

'I just wondered. You know, with Andy working in the Recovery Team. It's possible that the call to Robert Donovan could have been made by one of Andy's team.' The suggestion that it could also have been made by Andy himself hung unspoken in the air.

Now the pale, translucent skin flushed a very pale shade of pink. Annabel blinked again, then said 'Customer calls are confidential, Rose. It wouldn't have been right for me to mention it to Andy, even if he was my boyfriend.' The last word was barely audible, as if she was afraid to say it.

'I know they are, Annabel. But we are all human. And I know that a good Customer Services representative doesn't like to leave a customer unhappy. If I had taken that call I would have wanted to know whether the claim was true, whether someone at the ENB *had* made a threatening call to Robert Donovan. And I would have wanted to put that right for him. I wouldn't blame you if you had tried to find out who made that call. There's nothing wrong with feeling a degree of responsibility to the customer.'

The girl stared at Rose with unseeing eyes and said nothing.

Rose, for her part, stared back at Annabel and tried to read her. On the surface she was deeply upset but there was an underlying coolness, a self-control that Rose could only admire. If she had mentioned the call to Andy Miller, she seemed pretty determined not to admit the fact. Was that because she was trying to protect him?

Or was there someone else she was trying to protect?

A muted bleep from his smartphone alerted Stan Wilkins to the arrival of the email he'd been waiting for. The audio files for the Recovery Team's November calls were available to view. He put down his newspaper and began clicking proficiently at his keyboard, drilling down the file structure until he reached the date he was looking for, Tuesday 18th November.

He consulted a note stuck to the bottom of his computer screen and read Robert Donovan's phone number out loud. Zero one three two six, eight eight five, eight nine one. He opened a file bearing the title "Extension 926", Andy Miller's phone, and searched for the number in the "Outbound Calls" column.

No match.

There were six telephone extensions for that team, and he tried each file in turn, looking for Donovan's number. Each search drew a blank.

He slumped back in his chair and stared at the note. He was definitely looking for the right number.

He opened the file for Extension 926 again and repeated his search, in case he had mistyped the number the first time. Still no match. *OK, Stanley, so let's try something else.* He swept the cursor to the top of the screen and clicked on the top cell of a column called "Call Time". The first call from this number had been made at 7.52 am. Someone had started early. He rolled the screen up until he reached the approximate time the call was supposedly made to Donovan. Rose had said somewhere between 4pm and 5pm. He scrolled up one call at a time, checking each outbound number in turn. None of them matched Donovan's number.

He sighed and moved on to the file for Extension 927. Repeating the check proved fruitless, as did a close eyeball check of the files for the remaining four extensions. He could see only three possible explanations for this turn of events. One – Rose had given him the wrong number for Robert Donovan. He smiled to himself, remembering the last time he'd suggested Rose had made a mistake. Nope, he wasn't going to get his ear chewed off by Rose Bennett again. Two – maybe no call was ever made to Robert Donovan, at least not by the ENB. That was a possibility, but then why would the customer lie about it?

The third explanation was going to cost him a lot more work, and he'd have to cast his net a lot wider than the extensions used by Andy Miller's team. But that was no reason not to consider it. As far as he could see, the only plausible explanation was that the call was made by someone from the ENB alright, but from a phone which wasn't used by the Recovery Team.

'So what do you make of it so far, George?' DS Scott folded his arms and leaned back in his seat with a cynical grin. 'Are we looking at a car thief, or a crime of passion?'

Mulligan shrugged his reply and embellished it with a raised eyebrow. 'Truthfully, Scottie? It could be either at this stage.' They were sitting in the small glass meeting room opposite the desk used by Jodie Pearce. Jodie was deep in telephone conversation with a customer, and the headset perched over her topknot bobbed and quivered as she first nodded her agreement over something being said, and then shook her head at some point of contention. He nodded in her direction. 'What do you make of that one?' They had interviewed her together earlier in the day, DS Scott asking the questions and DI Mulligan listening to the answers.

'She's simmering over something.' DS Scott narrowed his eyes and peered at her through the glass. 'She didn't like being questioned. And she doesn't like Annabel Halmshaw. She wasn't too impressed when Annabel threw her arms around Chris Kemp this morning. Maybe she doesn't like the competition.'

'Which of them would you choose, Scottie, if you were in Chris Kemp's position? The feisty Miss Pearce, or the delicate Miss Halmshaw?'

DS Scott gave the question serious consideration. 'Curiously, George, I'd go for the feisty Miss Pearce. She's a bit rough around the edges for me, but I think I'd always know where I stood. There's something unfathomable, almost otherworldly about that Halmshaw girl. I can't pin it down. She's … what's that word? Feign?'

'I think you mean fey. But feign is an interesting slip of the tongue.' He tilted his head towards his colleague. 'You don't like your women enigmatic, then?'

'At the risk of sounding bitter, if my ex-wife had been a bit less enigmatic we might still be together.'

'There's nothing bitter about the truth. It's a shame there isn't a bit more truth flying about out there.' Mulligan fixed his eyes back on Jodie Pearce. There was something undeniably ugly about jealous anger, and yet he couldn't help feeling sorry for her. 'She was straight enough to tell us that she had been Andy Miller's girlfriend, and that he'd thrown her over for Annabel Halmshaw. From where she's sitting it probably looks as though Chris Kemp is going to do the same.' He put his hand up to his face and rubbed at his temple. 'Do you think she could have killed Andy Miller?'

'What, in revenge, you mean? No, I can't see that. They split up in the summer, why would she have waited this long? I can see her being angry at the start, but she soon took up with Chris Kemp by all accounts.'

'She had the opportunity. The time of death has been narrowed down to somewhere between eight and nine thirty. She left the pub around nine, she could have gone up to Bellevue Mansions, argued with Andy Miller, run him over, and then made her way home as if nothing had happened.'

'How did she get the car keys?'

'She's a regular visitor to the flat. If those keys are a spare set, she could have taken them the last time she was there. Chris Kemp wouldn't disturb her, she knew he was in The Half Moon. She probably knew that Annabel Halmshaw was away for the weekend.' He turned back to DS Scott. 'How about this? She wanted Andy Miller back. His girlfriend was away, and his flatmate was out drinking, so the way was clear for her to try a bit of seduction. She went up to the flat and offered herself up on a plate. He turned her down, and she killed him.' His face crumpled with concentration. 'In fact, if my theory is right it doesn't matter whether those keys are a spare set or his regular keys. She could have just lifted them from the flat on Sunday night. Maybe he saw her do it. Maybe he followed her downstairs, saw her get into his car, tried to stop her from driving off and she ran over him?'

'So why is she angry now? If your theory is right, and she wanted Andy Miller, then she has no feelings for Chris Kemp. So it wouldn't matter to her if he moved on to Annabel Halmshaw.'

A wry smile played at the edge of Mulligan's lips. 'Ah well now, Scottie, that's where an understanding of enigmatic women comes in handy. She didn't kill Andy Miller because *she* couldn't have him. She killed him so that Annabel couldn't have him.'

DS Scott began to laugh. 'You've lost me now, George. This is all getting a bit deep for me.'

'No, just think about it. What if she killed him so that Annabel Halmshaw would feel the pain of loss. The same pain Jodie felt when she lost Andy Miller. If Annabel falls straight into the arms of Chris Kemp, then maybe she isn't feeling the pain of loss after all. And that's why Jodie is angry. Because she hasn't managed to inflict the pain she wanted Annabel to feel.'

'OK, then. If we're going for theories, how about this theory of mine? Jodie does care about Chris Kemp, and she's angry because she thinks she's about to lose another boyfriend to Annabel Halmshaw. It's as simple as that.

'And what about the murder?'

'Chris Kemp. He'd already got bored with Jodie. Maybe he realised she still had feelings for Andy Miller, and felt cuckolded. Or maybe he just liked the look of Annabel, and fancied his chances. So he murdered Andy Miller to get him out of the way. All the grief on his part is just a cover up, so that no one suspects him. And his plans are working out nicely because Annabel is already crying on his shoulder.'

'And his alibi? He was in the pub all evening.'

DS Scott thought for a moment, and then smiled. 'Alibis can be broken, George. If we have to have a theory at this stage, then I think mine is as good as yours. Unless you can prove otherwise.'

7

Chris Kemp looked furtively around as he opened the outer door to Bellevue Mansions. It was unlikely that anyone would be watching him, but you never knew. He pulled the morning's newspaper out of his rucksack and jammed it, folded in two, underneath the door to wedge it open. If he wedged it open, he thought, she wouldn't have to stand out here in the freezing cold waiting for him to come down and open the door.

He sprinted up the stairs and let himself into the flat, switching on all the lights as he went from room to room. The central heating hadn't kicked in yet and the flat felt cold. He switched on a small fan heater in the lounge and shivered involuntarily. It would take the chill off the room, but they would have to stay in here until the rest of the flat had warmed through. He glanced around. The place was a bit untidy but she wouldn't expect miracles, given what had happened.

He closed his eyes. *Calm down, for God's sake.*

He glanced at his watch. It was ten past six, and he was expecting her at six thirty. Was that enough time for a shower? He didn't think so. She might be early.

In the bedroom he pulled off his work clothes, sprayed his armpits with cheap deodorant, and pulled on his best brown cords and the smartest shirt he possessed. He looked around. *Hell, what a mess.* He opened the wardrobe door and then gathered up all the shoes littered across the floor, throwing them one at a time into the bottom of the wardrobe. He sniffed at the air. A faint aroma of foot odour mingled with the vapours of the cheap aftershave he had applied this morning. Nothing he could do about that right now.

Back out in the hall he pulled a bottle of cheap Chianti from his rucksack and took it into the kitchen. He knew she preferred white, but there was no time to chill a bottle of white. And anyway, if food came into the equation he was planning to heat up a pepperoni pizza that already lurked in the fridge. Chianti would be spot on with that.

He was just about to check the label on the pizza box when the doorbell rang. He glanced again at his watch. It was six fifteen. Good job he hadn't jumped into the shower. He closed his eyes and steadied himself, then walked to the front door and opened it.

'I've come on behalf of Mr Hector Campling, to see Mr Miller.' A greasy looking man with tobacco-stained teeth grinned at him and thrust out a grubby-looking business card.

Thrown by this deviation from his plans, Chris took the card from him and looked at it. The words "Henry and Hector Campling, Property Agents" were printed on it, and scrawled underneath in untidy hand-writing someone had added the words "Michael Spivey – Recovery Agent". He looked back at the man. 'Mr Miller is ... well, Mr Miller is dead. Haven't you seen the news?'

The man grinned again, a sardonic smile which made him look comical rather than threatening. 'Oh yes, I've seen the news.' He slammed an awkward foot into the doorframe, wedging the front door open before speaking again. 'Mr Campling's compliments, and he would be grateful for a payment against the overdue rent.'

Chris Kemp's heart started to beat a little faster. 'Overdue rent? Our rent isn't overdue.' Bewildered, he cast his mind back to the end of last week. He'd given Andy his share of the rent money. This must be a mistake. He put out a hand to push the visitor away from the door, and found himself being forced back into the hallway of the flat and pushed against the wall. The door slammed behind them both.

'Mr Campling's compliments, and he's not interested in excuses. The rent is free months in arrears now and somefing needs to be paid on account. Otherwise we might have to help ourselves to various items within the property to compensate for our losses.'

The audacity of the suggestion jolted Chris Kemp out of his confusion and he laughed. 'You can't just come in here and start taking things. You're not a bailiff.'

For a moment the man looked unsure, and then he tightened his grip on Chris's shoulder and leered into his face. 'This property is rented to Mr Andy Miller, without permission to sub-let. And as you're not Mr Andy Miller, well … I'll have to ask who the bloody hell you are, won't I?'

Chris felt a spike of pain as the man dug his fingers into the flesh of his shoulder, and he gave an involuntary squeal. He struggled to break free, but the grip was vice-like. 'I'm Chris, Chris Kemp. I live here with Andy.'

The man let go of his shoulder and stepped back. 'Well, Mr Kemp. As Mr Miller isn't here, I'm afraid I'll have to ask you to pay the rent arrears.' He smirked. 'So if you'll just let me have the two fousand one hundred …'

'*How* much? You've got to be kidding me?'

'Two fousand, one hundred pounds in rent arrears - that's free months at seven hundred quid a month - I'll be out of your hair in no time.' He leaned forward and leered into Chris's face. 'I can take a cheque.'

'You have no proof that the money's owing. Our rent's up to date.'

The man shook his head. 'Sorry, *Sir*, but your rent is overdue. If you have a look at your statement, you'll see that it's overdue. Mr Miller is meant to make a payment by standing order into Mr Campling's account on the first of every month. And he ain't done that for free months now.'

'But I've been giving him my share regularly, every

month …'

'Well, now that's a shame, ain't it? It sounds to me like Mr Miller ain't exactly been straight with you.' The man seemed to soften a little. 'I'll tell you what I'll do. I can see you're in a fix, with Mr Miller … passing on, and all that … so I suggest you have a look around and see if you can find the letters what Mr Campling sent to Mr Miller about the overdue rent. I'll come back tomorrow evening, and then we can resume our little chat.' He stepped forward and Chris bent his head back to avoid the reek of stale tobacco. 'How does that sound?'

It sounded like he had no choice, and he nodded silently. He wasn't sure exactly what the hell was going on here, but he knew he'd given Andy his share of the rent money. If he could get this muppet off his back he could go through Andy's things and look for the letters, or even his bank statements. It must be a misunderstanding. He was sure to be able to sort it out.

The only thing he wasn't sure of was what the hell he was going to do if it was true.

It hadn't been a productive day for Rose. Irritated by her lack of progress, she had decamped back to Lu's cottage and mixed herself a large gin and tonic. She settled down at Lu's desk to wrap up her day's work, but first she flicked through the unread texts on her mobile phone. Seven from Mike, mostly outlining his plans for Christmas, and one from Lu asking if Rose could stay on at the cottage for a few more days. Rose smiled to herself. At least one of them was lucky in love.

It delighted her to see Lu so happy. As a young woman Lu Aylesbury had been too wrapped up in her journalistic career to consider marriage, preferring affairs to commitment. But this latest affair was beginning to look serious. Lu had been swept off to Hamburg for a weekend concert by her latest conquest, a travel-hungry retired stockbroker with a taste for the finer things in life. Now it seemed he wanted to travel on to Konstanz for the Christmas market. Lu, of course, was wallowing in the glorious unpredictability of it all.

Rose picked up her drink. 'Here's to you, Lucinda. Love every minute of it.' She sipped a toast, and then turned her attention away from the joyous spontaneity of Lu's life to the tedious, if unexpected, unpredictability of her own. The unforeseen prospect of Mike's kids taking over her home for Christmas. Her investigation hijacked by George Mulligan. Her most likely suspect murdered. She sipped again on the gin. Hopefully things would settle down a bit tomorrow.

Until then there was one more sample call she wanted to listen to before she called it a day to curl up with the dog and a good book. She powered up her laptop and plugged in her earpiece, brought up the list of files on the CD Stan had sent to her, and selected one entitled "Andy Miller, 22nd October".

She leaned her elbows on the desk and rested her chin on her hands, and listened as Andy Miller's voice ran through the first part of his script. He gave his name, verified that the right person was on the end of the line, and gave the purpose of his call. The customer was called Florence Fielding, and by the sound of her voice Rose judged she was in her mid-thirties.

Andy's tone of voice wasn't unfriendly, but it was firm. 'Mrs Fielding, your account is nearly seven hundred pounds over your credit limit, and two months in arrears. I am going to have to ask you for a payment today against the outstanding balance.'

Rose heard the woman take in a deep steadying breath before she spoke, and then couldn't help but smile as she listened to the response. 'It's Miss Fielding, not Mrs Fielding. And I'm well aware that my account is in arrears, Andy. Are you aware that the East & Northern Bank owes me several thousand pounds?' Her accent was provincial like Andy's, the vowels flat, but her tone was calm and reasoned.

If the question was intended to throw Andy Miller off his stride it didn't work. 'I'm not aware of any such thing, Miss Fielding. But I *am* aware that your credit card account is six hundred and ninety two pounds over the limit, with an outstanding payment due today of nine hundred and seventeen pounds, twenty seven pence. That's the amount over the credit limit, plus the outstanding minimum payments due for the last two months.'

'And I would estimate, Andy, that the East and Northern Bank owes me something in the region of three and a half thousand pounds. Seven years ago, the bank sold me a Payment Protection Insurance product that wasn't suitable for my needs. I lodged a formal complaint to this effect eight months ago, and I'm still waiting for a final response. By my calculation the bank owes me roughly eleven hundred pounds worth of insurance premiums paid on this account, plus contractual interest on those premiums, plus simple interest on any credit balances, calculated up to today's date.'

'Miss Fielding, PPI complaints are nothing to do with my department …'

'Your employer sold me the product without assessing whether or not it was suitable for my needs. The application form I completed had a printed pre-ticked box, which means the bank applied the insurance to my account whether I wanted it or not. It's a clear case of mis-selling.'

'As I've tried to explain to you, Miss Fielding, PPI complaints are nothing to do with my department …'

'Then I suggest that your department should talk to whichever department *does* deal with PPI complaints, and sort it out between you. There's no way I'm paying you any more money towards this account until you've admitted my claim for mis-selling and compensated me for my losses. When I receive the money from the ENB, I'll use it to settle the outstanding balance on the card. Now if you're not able to help with that, I have nothing more to say to you.' There was an audible click as Florence Fielding ended the call.

Rose stifled a laugh and closed the audio file. Andy Miller was business-like on this call, nothing more. There was nothing remotely threatening in his tone of voice or his choice of words. But then even if there had been, she very much doubted that Miss Florence Fielding would have been too troubled by it.

8

It didn't take Chris Kemp long after Michael Spivey's departure to find the box of documents buried at the bottom of Andy Miller's wardrobe. Now he sat trembling on the edge of Andy's bed, a selection of letters and statements spread out in front of him.

Seven letters from Hector Campling confirmed Spivey's claim that Andy had stopped paying the rent over three months ago. The letters had started with a reminder that a payment was overdue and ramped up in tone until, inevitably, legal action to recover the debt was threatened. The outstanding balance according to the latest letter was two thousand, one hundred pounds, plus late charges and disbursements. Just reading the letter made him feel sick.

He turned his attention to a credit card statement in Andy's name showing an outstanding balance of almost thirteen thousand pounds, just a few hundred to go before it would be over its credit limit. On the bed beside it a store card statement showed a balance of just over twelve hundred pounds, eight hundred of which had been run up in just one spend on a jacket and a pair of shoes. A bank statement confirmed an overdraft of almost three thousand pounds. Two more credit card statements showed a joint total of nearly twenty three thousand pounds. Judging by the outgoings on the bank statements there must be paperwork somewhere for the finance on the BMW.

A total debt, he reckoned, of over forty thousand pounds, and that didn't include the car or the rent arrears.

Still shaking, he got up and went through into the kitchen, took a corkscrew from a drawer, and opened the bottle of cheap Chianti. He poured himself a large glass and drank it down almost in one gulp, then topped up the glass again and carried it back through to the bedroom, setting it down on top of the chest of drawers.

Emotions were coming in waves now, unbidden and unwanted. Anger, then hurt, then guilt, then more anger. He thought he knew Andy Miller, thought he was a friend, a mate, someone he could trust. He looked up to him, believed in him, wanted to be like him.

You fucking idiot. He muttered the words under his breath. *You tosser, you complete fucking arsehole.* He wasn't sure if he was talking to Andy or talking to himself. He formed fists with his hands, and dug his nails into the soft tissue of his palms until the pain brought tears to his eyes. *He saw you coming, alright.* He realised now that he was talking to himself.

The mobile phone in the back pocket of his trousers vibrated with a text message and he pulled it out to look at it. It was a message from Annabel. She was running late but she was on her way. Hell, he'd forgotten about Annabel, forgotten in the wake of Michael Spivey's visit that he'd promised to keep her company tonight.

He took in a deep breath. She might as well come. He was probably going to lose the flat now anyway, why not make use of it for one more night? He didn't have the money to settle the rent arrears, and truth be told he knew he wasn't liable for them whatever Spivey or Hector Campling claimed. And even if he could have cleared the arrears, he wouldn't be able to afford the monthly rent on his own. He would have to move back in with his family. There wouldn't be much scope to entertain Annabel there.

Andy had told him that living there was no problem, that the lease permitted him to take in a lodger. *Fucking liar.* He'd taken the rent money and … done what with it? Paid bills, spent it on stuff he couldn't afford? For fuck's sake, he made his living trying to get people to pay back what they'd borrowed on their credit cards. How could he do this? How could he run up this amount of debt himself?

How could he steal from a mate?

Any sorrow he'd felt at Andy's death, any feelings of guilt about wanting Annabel for himself, had melted away with the realisation that Andy Miller had stolen his rent money and squandered it on crap. He deserved a better mate than Andy Miller, and Annabel deserved a better boyfriend than a liar and a cheat. She deserved someone who would take care of her, make her happy, someone like him. The thought cheered him up. It made him pull himself together.

He crossed the room and pulled the wardrobe door open for a second time. The trousers would be too long for him, Andy was a good four inches taller than he was. But the shirts and jackets were another matter. Andy owed him the rent money, and now it was payback time. After a moment's contemplation, he selected a grey cotton shirt with double cuffs, and a black three-quarter length leather coat. Andy's cufflinks were in the top drawer of the left hand bedside table, and he helped himself to a silver pair shaped like rugby balls, tucking them temporarily into his rear trouser pocket. He lifted his glass of wine from the chest of drawers and turned to leave the room, then paused and set it back down again. *Why not?*

He opened the top drawer of the chest of drawers and peered into it, then pulled out a bottle of Gaultier cologne and sniffed at it.

Of course there was something to be salvaged out of this mess. Something worth a lot more than the rent money, or the flat, or a mate to look up to.

There was Annabel.

9

Michael Spivey shuffled his feet like a nervous schoolboy. The cheap rubber soles of his shoes chafed as he shuffled, emitting an almost inaudible squeak-squeak-squeak. Without looking up from his desk, Hector Campling picked up his pen and tapped it loudly and rhythmically on the leather blotter to his right. Spivey's feet froze and his back stiffened, chastised into stillness and silence. Only the ticking of an antique wall clock made a sound now.

After several minutes Hector Campling took off his spectacles, laid them down on his desk, and fixed his eyes on Spivey's oily face. 'I understand you have something to tell me about flat 2d at Bellevue Mansions, Michael?'

Spivey's eyes widened and he turned them on the solicitor. 'Yes, Mr Campling.' The words came out as a harsh whisper, and he coughed to clear his throat. 'I went round to the flat again, like you asked, and I *insisted* on speaking to the tenant.' He watched Campling's face for a reaction, but seeing none he continued his tale. 'Well, there was a bloke there who told me the contracted tenant was dead …'

Campling closed his eyes, and held up a hand to stop the flow. 'Yes, yes, just get to the point. Did you collect any money?'

Flecks of perspiration appeared on Spivey's brow, and his mouth became suddenly dry. 'I asked for all the rent arrears like you said, Mr Campling, but the bloke said he wasn't the contracted tenant. He reckoned he'd paid his share of the rent to Andy Miller, and he didn't know anyfing about any arrears.'

'Did you collect any money?'

Spivey's mouth was so parched now, he could barely speak. 'I freatened to take goods away, Mr Campling, in lieu of payment like, but he said I couldn't do that cos I'm not a bailiff.' He saw the clouds gather on Campling's face and added 'he knows his rights, Mr Campling, straight up, more than I do.'

Campling let out a sigh. 'So you didn't take possession of any goods from the flat?'

'No.'

'Did you collect any money?'

'No.' Spivey's voice was a hoarse whisper. 'But I told him letters had been sent to say the rent was owing, and I'd be back tonight for the money. Straight up, Mr Campling, I'm going back at six o'clock tonight as soon as he gets back from work. And I ain't going to settle for less than five hundred against the arrears.'

Hector Campling took in a deep breath through his nose and blew it out again through pursed lips. 'And what makes you think he will be there when you go back this evening? This person is not the contracted tenant. He has no right to be in the property, and he appears to have been living there against the terms of the tenancy agreement. He can move out today, without leaving any forwarding address, and we cannot recover a penny from him. He will have lived in that apartment rent free for months, without paying us a penny.' He folded his arms across his chest. 'Did you get his name?'

'Yes, Mr Campling. It was Chris Kemp.' He cleared his throat, and then ventured a question. 'Scuse me asking, Mr Hector, but if he ain't the contracted tenant, shouldn't he be moving out anyway?'

Momentarily thrown by the childish innocence of the question, especially from the weasel in front of him, the solicitor permitted himself a smile. He muttered under his breath, and then said 'that is the crucial point, Michael.

This Chris Kemp is not the contracted tenant. Had he been simply staying with Andy Miller as a guest, then he would not have been liable for any payment of rent. But he admitted to you, I believe, that he had been living there and paying money in lieu of rent to Mr Miller, money which Mr Miller chose not to pass on to us. In my book, that gives us the moral right to pursue him for the outstanding rent.'

Unconvinced, and still frowning, Spivey nodded his head. 'Yes, Mr Hector. Fank you, sir.'

Campling's eyes narrowed and he turned his head to look out of the window. Regrettably the moral right was of no significance in this situation. This Chris Kemp, whoever he was, was not the contracted tenant, nor was he liable for any rent arrears. The arrears could only be claimed from the estate of the late Andy Miller. And Campling had a hunch that if Andy Miller had been pocketing Kemp's money rather than using it to pay the rent, then Andy Miller's estate was likely to consist only of debt. In which case, there would be no hope of recovering the arrears. No, they would have to strike while Kemp still had the keys to the property. Assuming he hadn't cleared out already.

The solicitor folded his face into an insincere smile and motioned for Spivey to sit down in the leather client's chair facing him. 'Please take a seat Michael, and I will explain what I would like you to do this evening.'

Spivey started at this unexpected kindness, and followed his instructions, perching uncomfortably on the edge of the chair. He licked his lips and leaned towards the solicitor with an expectant gaze.

'Firstly,' Hector Campling began, 'we are going to ensure that we curtail our losses on flat 2d at Bellevue Mansions.' He leaned his elbows on the desk and steepled his fingers. 'I will prepare a letter this afternoon offering Mr Kemp the opportunity to take over the tenancy of the flat. You will deliver that letter this evening. At the same time you will collect any monies which Mr Kemp is prepared to pay you in respect of the arrears. You will convey my compliments to Mr Kemp, along with a message that we will give him twenty four hours to decide whether he wishes to take on the property, after which time we would ask him to contact us with his decision. If he chooses to leave then you, Michael, will return to the flat and collect all the tenant's keys to the property, along with sundry items of Mr Miller's to cover our losses. I will prepare for you a list of items to look out for.' He smiled to himself and intoned 'we do not wish to be considered unreasonable.' He fixed Spivey with a direct gaze. 'But you have my full permission, Michael, to *be* unreasonable if you consider Mr Kemp does not fully understand the offer being made to him.'

Spivey nodded, although as things went he didn't fully understand what Hector Campling was asking of him, never mind the offer he was supposed to make. He repeated key words to himself silently, flat 2d, collect the money, collect the keys, a letter to deliver, be unreasonable. He could do that. He could do all of that. He nodded again.

Campling unsteepled his fingers and reached out to an in-tray with his right hand, pulling the top document off the pile and placing it down in front of him. He looked directly at Spivey. 'So we understand what is to be done at Bellevue Mansions, Michael?'

'Absolutely, Mr Hector.'

The solicitor nodded. 'Now when you have dealt with the client at Bellevue Mansions, I have another collections job for you. I imagine this one will be far simpler, and well within your capabilities.' He tapped the document in front of him with a finger. 'This is another rent arrears, on a property on the Barnfield estate.'

Spivey nodded. He knew the Barnfield estate, a sad affair of neglected seventies ex-council housing, a vast landscape of concrete harling, unmown lawns and sticky kids. His Auntie Jen used to live there, and rumour had it that these days every house was occupied by an unmarried mother. If this collections job was going to be an unmarried mother it would be a doddle, even for him. He nodded again. 'I know where that is.'

'Good.' Hector Campling picked up the document and handed it to Spivey. 'This is a list of the rent arrears for the property. The tenant has been paying a nominal sum each month, but the current position is that the rent is technically three months in arrears. I cannot let this continue, we are a business and not a charity.' He waited until Spivey had cast his eyes over the document. 'I would like you to visit the property this evening after you have dealt with Bellevue Mansions and extend my compliments to the tenant, with a request for a payment of three hundred pounds to reduce the arrears on her account.'

'Free hundred pounds.' Spivey muttered the amount under his breath, and nodded to himself. 'Free hundred pounds. In rent arrears.'

'That's right, Michael. The tenant has not run up arrears with us before and clearly understands her obligations. I cannot imagine that collecting something from her will present any difficulties.' He stretched out a hand to point at the document. 'Her name is on the account sheet, here next to the address.' He tapped on the paper and Spivey's eyes followed his fingers down the page until they rested on the name of Florence Fielding.

Rose gave an involuntary shiver and pulled her cardigan tight around her shoulders. The atmosphere in the office was tense this morning, almost hostile. She had settled herself at a spare desk close to the Recovery Team and they had barely acknowledged her with a glance. And why should they? Their team leader was dead, the police were breathing down their necks, and a new team leader had already been appointed to replace Andy Miller and keep them hard at work. She was the least of their problems. At least, that's how it would look to them.

A couple of desks away Chris Kemp was deep in conversation with a smartly-dressed man in his forties. The man was observing Chris with sharp, intelligent eyes and looked disconcertingly at ease sitting at the late Andy Miller's desk. By contrast Chris Kemp's discomfort was palpable, his head bent down and slightly away from the man as he spoke, avoiding any risk of eye-contact.

Rose knew the smartly-dressed man to be Graham Clarke, one of the ENB's longest-serving employees, a kind of "manager without portfolio" that Clive Barden trusted to smooth troubled waters and keep a sharp grip on anything that threatened the bank's reputation. She cast a glance in the direction of Jodie Pearce. The girl was muttering into the mouthpiece of her headset, making an early-morning call to an unsuspecting customer. Exhaustion showed in dark circles under her eyes, and sorrow in the downward curl of her lips. Rose couldn't help thinking that Graham Clarke was going to have his work cut out today.

She turned her gaze back to the look again at the two men. Chris was frowning, his cheeks pink, his head shaking slowly as he disagreed with something being said to him. He looked different today, smarter somehow, clean-shaven, his close-cropped hair glistening with some sort of oil or gel. His ill-fitting trousers still trailed over the heel of his boots, but his black and grey shirt was crisp and stylish, the collar sharp against his neck. He put up a hand to rub at his ear, and something small and silver glinted at his wrist, perhaps a cufflink. From what she knew of him so far, Chris Kemp and cufflinks didn't seem a likely combination.

She was considering whether this change of image was his way of dealing with the grief, or perhaps the anxiety of dealing with the police, when her mobile phone danced into action, skittering across the desk with a loud vibration.

She scooped it up and noted the familiar incoming number, then pressed the answer key. 'Morning, Stanley. How's the world looking in Kirkby? Got much snow down there?'

At the other end of the line Stan Wilkins grunted. 'I've no idea what the outside world looks like, I've been in the office all night chasing non-existent phone calls for some consultant called Rose something or other.'

'As *if.*' She smiled into the phone. 'So nothing's turned up?'

'Nothing's turned up from the desk phones you asked me to check. But if you speak very nicely to me, I might have details of a call that might interest you.'

'I always speak nicely to you. Cut to the chase.'

'I've found the call you were looking for, to Robert Donovan's number. But it wasn't made from any of the phones used by Andy Miller's team. And the phone used wasn't linked up to the team's logging system.'

'It wasn't recorded, then?'

'I don't know that yet. But I can tell you where it was made from. I tracked it to a landline on desk number B24 on the same floor. Looking at my floor map, that desk should be in the area adjacent to Andy Miller's desk. The desks were cleared a couple of months ago, when the project team that used to be there were relocated to the third floor of the building. All the phones used by that team should have been disabled when they moved, but it looks like this one has been missed.'

Rose reached for her notebook and pen. 'What's the number?'

'It's extension 887. It should be written on the phone. And there should be a label on the back of the desk with the number B24 on it.'

'Thanks Stan, I owe you.'

'*Again.*' His tone was teasing.

She laughed. 'I know. And I'll owe you even more if you can do me another favour.'

'Depends what it is.'

'Could you get me a list of all calls made from that number since the project team moved out? I want to see if it's been used to make other calls to customers.'

'You mean, you want me to get a list of calls made from that number … and then you'll be asking me another favour, like what's the name and address of each customer, and …'

'OK, dinner on me when the investigation is complete.'

'Bar meal at The Jug and Ferret?'

'If you can get me the account numbers as well as the names and addresses, I'll make it a full banquet at The Spice Garden.'

'With wine?'

'Don't push your luck.'

10

'Something … some*one* … brought Andy Miller down into that car park last night. Whoever was driving his car had a set of keys. Now that Chris Kemp has identified them as a spare set that narrows the field to people who had access to the flat.' Mulligan leaned an arm on the door sill of Ian Scott's Audi and stared out of the window into a cloud of swirling snow. 'I think someone rang the intercom, Andy went down to let them in, and while he was going downstairs they used the keys to get into the car. By the time he'd opened the door, the driver was already in the car with the engine running.'

DS Scott gently braked up to a junction then turned the car left towards Scarborough. 'So the question is, who had access to the spare keys?'

Mulligan grunted. 'That's the problem, isn't it? Jodie Pearce, Chris Kemp and Annabel Halmshaw all had access to the flat. They probably all knew about those keys. They were kept in a drawer in the hall weren't they? It could have been any of them.' He put his thumb up to his lips and chewed on his thumbnail. 'My money's still on Jodie Pearce. She left The Half Moon round about nine o'clock, it's a twenty minute walk up to Bellevue Mansions, she would have got there before nine thirty. And she had a motive.'

'Do you really think she was jealous enough to kill, George?'

'She's a feisty piece. I wouldn't want to be on the wrong side of her.' Mulligan squinted out of the window at the passing buildings, seeing only indistinct shapes behind the eddying snow, mirrors of his nebulous theories.

'And what about Chris Kemp? Could he have been jealous enough of Andy's relationship with Annabel Halmshaw to kill?'

'Chris Kemp's got an alibi. He was in The Half Moon all evening. The landlord has confirmed that.'

'Alibis can be broken. We can't reasonably expect that the landlord was watching him every minute, can we? He must have been serving other customers. Did he see Kemp go to the gents? Use the fruit machine? Pop out for a smoke?'

'Does he smoke?'

'I've no idea, George. I'm just trying to break his alibi.'

Mulligan shook his head. 'The time of death's been narrowed to sometime between eight thirty and nine thirty. Chris Kemp was in the pub with Jodie Pearce until nine, and then he was with the landlord until we picked him up.' He thought back to the previous evening, and the expression of numb bewilderment on the lad's face at the news of his flatmate's death. He'd seen that look too many times before in his career, but never on the face of a killer. 'What about the girlfriend? She was a regular visitor to the flat. Her alibi isn't up to much. On her way back from Cambridge, in her own car, travelling alone?'

'She didn't get home from Cambridge until after eleven. She told me she sent Andy a text to let him know she was home safely. She showed me the text on her phone when I interviewed her yesterday.'

'Didn't she worry when he didn't reply?'

'No. She reckoned she just thought he'd turned in for an early night.'

'She lives alone, so there's no-one to corroborate what time she got back. She could have arrived back much earlier, and just waited until after eleven to send the text. And she had access to the keys.'

DS Scott puffed out a sigh. 'You saw her yesterday,

George. She was distraught about Andy Miller's death.'

'Too distraught?'

'All for our benefit, you mean?'

'You told me yourself that she fell into Chris Kemp's arms after you interviewed her yesterday. Did it look like she made a habit of it?'

'You mean they both wanted rid of him?'

'Did you see any texts to Chris Kemp on her phone?'

'No, but I'll admit I wasn't looking for them at the time. Anyway, what motive would she have? If she didn't like him, she just had to end the relationship. There was no need to do away with him.'

'True.' The motive was still troubling Mulligan. Beyond the churning snow the outline of Bellevue Mansions came and went as the car glided along the main road in the direction of the ENB's offices.

They travelled the next mile and a quarter in silence until DS Scott turned the Audi into the car park and backed into a reserved parking space. He turned off the engine. 'Are we going to start with Annabel's alibi, then?'

'No, we'll leave that until this afternoon. Let's start with Jodie Pearce. I want to see if we can find any holes in her version of events.'

Chris Kemp closed the door to the small meeting room opposite Jodie's desk and sat down on a faded chair at the far side of the table. Through the glass wall he could see his desk, his colleagues, the snooper Rose Bennett, and that smug bastard Graham Clarke. He glanced down at his watch. He was ten minutes early for the meeting.

He supposed he could have made another customer call in that ten minutes, but he was almost at the stage now of not caring. The strands of his life were beginning to weave in a way that was out of his control, as if life was leading him rather than the other way around. Through the glass wall of that small office he could see those strands in the way an impartial observer might see them, past choices closing in on him, chickens coming home to roost.

Forty eight hours ago everything in his life was sweet. Good job, good bonuses, good flat, good girlfriend, good mate. Just forty eight hours ago. He closed his eyes and rubbed at his creased forehead with stubby fingers.

It all hinged on his good mate. Except Andy wasn't a good mate, was he? He was a thief, and a liar, and a cheat.

And anyway, he was gone.

He opened his eyes and stared out through the glass wall. How could he have thought it would be so easy to step into Andy's empty shoes? How could he be dumb enough to think he could just walk in this morning and drop his rucksack onto Andy's desk and claim it for his own? To think that claiming the desk would open the way to claiming Andy's role of team leader? Now Andy's desk wasn't even there any more.

Well it was there, of course, physically. There was still a desk and a chair, and they were the desk and chair that Andy had used. But every last vestige of Andy's presence had already gone. His books, his calendar, his clock, the handwritten checklists pinned to his noticeboard, all gone. And in his seat, deep in contemplation, a printed copy of the team's targets and performance for the month spread out across the desk, sat Graham Clarke.

Graham *fucking* Clarke. Using Andy's desk, Graham fucking Clarke, sitting there like he owned the place, like he owned the team.

Which, of course, it turned out that he did.

Chris leaned his elbows on the table and rested his chin onto his hands. His good job had depended on Andy. Not being able to assume Andy's role was one thing, but the position he had gained within the team, the "first among equals" authority that he'd always adopted with the rest of them up until today, that had been down to Andy too. To being Andy's mate, his trusted lieutenant.

He stared out through the glass and saw Reggie's head

nodding up and down as he chatted into his headset. He was probably letting some low life off with paying their arrears, sympathising with them, making things easier for them rather than trying to recover money for the bank and reach his collection target. If it hadn't been for Andy the team would never have hit their targets, would never have made their bonuses. So with Andy gone he could wave goodbye to his good bonuses as well as his position in the team.

And as for the good flat … He puffed out a sigh and buried his face in his hands. That had gone west with Andy, too. He'd locked up as normal this morning and tried not to think about the rent arrears, or the fact that he shouldn't have been living there in the first place. He couldn't afford the rent on his own, and if the tenancy agreement didn't permit sub-letting then he wouldn't be able to take a lodger in to help towards the cost.

He lifted his head out of his hands and saw Rose Bennett get up from her chair and gather up her notebook and pen and mobile phone. *Nosy bitch*. He couldn't blame her for what had happened to Andy, but he was sure she was on to them. If Andy hadn't been killed, they might still have lost their good jobs and good bonuses. He'd met her sort before, all smiles on the outside and hard as nails on the inside. She would have shafted them alright, got to the bottom of their scheme, put a stop to it, put a stop to them meeting their targets. His eyes narrowed as he watched her push her chair under the desk and turn to navigate the narrow gap between Reggie's chair and Jodie's.

Jodie had just finished a call to a customer and she slipped off her headset to speak to Rose as she passed. Her bleached hair was dull today, the usually spiky top-knot hanging lank and lifeless, and she hadn't bothered to apply any makeup. She looked as if she had been crying. A lot. He wondered what he had seen in her but it didn't take him long to remember. She was Andy's girlfriend. And when Andy had finished with her, like most things that Andy had finished with, she was passed on to Chris.

But things had changed now. Andy was gone and although the good job, the good bonuses and the good flat might have gone with him, there was still the question of the good girlfriend. Jodie wasn't the good girlfriend any more. And he didn't have to wait until Andy cast his latest girlfriend aside. He'd helped himself to some of Andy's clothes last night, to compensate for his losses, and found it surprisingly easy. Why stop at the clothes?

Jodie was looking very much like a cast off today. Jodie would have to go. Because he didn't have to make do with Andy's cast offs any more. Andy was gone, and Annabel was his for the taking.

11

Hector Campling slipped the spare key into the lock and turned it quietly. The door was well-oiled and it slid open without a noise. He stepped into the hall and let it close gently behind him. A glance at his watch reassured him that the tenant would be out at work.

Not that it mattered too much, of course, if Chris Kemp had found him snooping around the flat. After all, Chris Kemp had no right to be there, and Campling was the owner and landlord of the property, with a landlord's right to enter the premises. But still, to be discovered there wouldn't be at all useful, given the purpose of his visit.

The hallway of flat 2d was dark, without windows to give it natural light, and he felt his way down the hall, running his hand along the wall for guidance. He pushed open the first door he came to and found himself in the lounge. Natural light flooded in through a south-facing sash window, and he nodded to himself with a smile. The old man knew what he was doing when he took on these flats for the firm. This was a nice property, well-proportioned and with a good aspect. Pity it had been wasted so far on a couple of beer-swilling louts. He would have to think about sprucing the place up, and finding an ambitious couple who could afford a higher rent.

He took off his gloves, took his mobile phone from his pocket and tapped it into camera mode. No need for a pen and paper these days, thanks to digital technologies. He held the phone up and framed a shot of the impressive sixty-inch TV, then the stereo system. Yes, they would be worth a bit. He looked around the room, frowned, and backed out into the hall.

He traced his way with the back of his un-gloved hand along the hall to the kitchen, the phone still in his other hand. He pushed the door open with his foot and glanced around. The impressive larder fridge would have been worth removing, but there was no way Spivey could manage that by himself. That would have to stay. But all was not lost, and he lifted the phone to snap the Italian coffee machine and a high-tech juicer.

It occurred to him that if Andy Miller had been so fond of the latest technologies, then somewhere in the flat there must be other less domestic gadgets. A laptop, perhaps, or an X-Box. He hadn't seen anything of that sort in the lounge, nor had he seen any drawers or cupboards where such items might be stored. The bedroom, then? Did Andy Miller distrust his flatmate so much that he hid his toys and gadgets away where they couldn't be found?

He let the kitchen door swing quietly closed behind him and walked further down the hall to what appeared to be a bedroom door, slightly ajar. He pushed on the door gently with the back of his hand and recoiled as the aroma of foot odour and cheap aftershave hit his nostrils. He couldn't imagine this was Andy Miller's room. He turned on his heel to look at another door immediately opposite. This one, then?

He pressed down gently on the door handle with his elbow and let himself into Andy Miller's bedroom. Everything was tidied away into cupboards and drawers. He slipped the phone back into his pocket and put on his gloves, then walked over to a chest of drawers and pulled open each drawer in turn. He noted designer briefs, socks, and t-shirts in the first three drawers with an appreciative nod of the head. There was no residual value in them of course, but he couldn't deny that if Andy Miller had developed a debt habit then at least he had displayed a modicum of good taste in the items he had wasted someone else's money on.

The bottom drawer was more rewarding. He put out a gloved hand to lift a laptop out of the drawer, and then thought better of it. It was unlikely that the goods in the flat were inventoried in any way, but there was a risk that items may be missed by the family. Best then to let Michael Spivey do the taking.

There was no need to photograph these items. He would remember the laptop and the iPad, bottom drawer, chest of drawers. He nodded to himself, pushed the drawer closed, and turned to examine the rest of the room. A quick glance in the drawers of the bedside cabinets yielded personal items which may have been gifts, and possibly too risky to take, and he was about to declare his innings at the items he'd already found when his eye landed on the wardrobe, and more precisely on the fact that the wardrobe door was slightly ajar.

It intrigued him that the door should be open, given that the room's occupant was now deceased, and he skirted the bed and pulled it open with a gloved finger. At eye level, designer clothes were crammed into the wardrobe's narrow confines. He looked up at the shelf above the hanging rail to see jumpers neatly folded on the left and a selection of leather bags on the right. He smiled to himself, young enough to know that young men now carried shoulder bags, yet too old to understand why they did.

He lowered his eyes to the door handle, preparing to shove the door closed again, but his gaze ran lower than the handle and caught sight of a cardboard box nestling underneath the hanging clothes. He paused and licked his lips and held his breath for a moment, assuring himself of the silence in the flat, assuring himself that he was completely alone.

He bent down and pulled the box out of the wardrobe and lifted it up onto the bed. The box appeared to be full of documents and his eyes quickly scanned the uppermost piece of paper, a credit card statement showing an overdue balance and a healthy chunk of arrears.

His pulse quickening, Hector Campling took off his right hand glove and slipped his hand back into his pocket, pulled out his mobile phone, and once again tapped it into camera mode.

'So the workflow system is always followed? If a customer has been allocated to a recovery agent, it's always that agent who contacts the customer for continuity, and always in line with the workflow diary?' Rose could see that Chris Kemp was uncomfortable, but she wasn't sure it was her line of questioning that was causing the discomfort. He was grieving today, of course, still reeling from the shock of Andy Miller's death. And there was an obvious discord between him and Jodie Pearce, even though they were supposed to be an item.

Across the table he was looking down at his hands, rubbing the thumbnail of his left hand with the thumb of his right, a nervous habit he'd developed in childhood. The tension in his hands was unmistakable, his anxiety showing in the rigidity of his fingers, and a small vein had started to pulse at the side of his thick neck. 'I don't really understand the question, Rose. The workflow is there to be followed.'

She thought for a moment. Perhaps it wasn't discomfort. Perhaps he was just impatient at having to answer her mundane questions about the debt recovery process. 'I know the workflow is there to be followed. What I'm asking is whether there have been times that the team haven't followed it. For instance, has anyone called someone else's customer to chase them for a payment? Could Andy have called one of Jodie's customers before the next call was due, to persuade that customer to make a further payment against their account?'

He didn't answer, but kept his eyes downcast.

'OK, let me try asking another way.' She closed her notebook and folded her hands on top of it. 'Might you have called one of Reggie's customers before the next call was due, to persuade that customer to make a further payment against his account?'

There was no scope for misunderstanding this time. Anger, as well as blood, flushed into Chris Kemp's stubbled cheeks. 'Of course not. That's against process.'

'Yes, it's against process.' Rose kept her tone calm and steady. 'But I know you've done it, Chris. I've heard the recordings.' She waited for her words to sink in and then added 'you know, all the calls are recorded. Not just the ones that are automatically dialled by the workflow system. Just because you dialled the number manually doesn't mean that you circumvented the call logging system. We have details of every phone call made from those phones.' She pointed out through the glass wall of the meeting room. 'Every phone call, including those dialled manually and made outside of the workflow.'

The angry colour fled his cheeks as quickly as it had arrived, leaving his face pallid, and some of his belligerence seemed to drain away with the colour. 'So why ask me, if you already knew?'

Why indeed? Rose gave a sigh and sat back in her seat. 'Because I wanted to give you the opportunity to cough it up and tell me why. Because I wanted to give you chance to explain yourself. You know, a bit of honesty can go a long way.'

He lifted his head now and regarded her with resentful eyes. 'What difference would it have made? You've made your mind up anyway. You've heard the recordings.'

'Well, perhaps you might have been able to explain to me *why* you were doing it. And perhaps you might have felt that reason was justified.' She paused for a moment, and then asked 'was this just something you did, because you felt Reggie wasn't tough enough with customers? Or was it something the whole team did on a regular basis?'

He blinked, but didn't answer.

She tried again. 'Was it your idea to do it? Or was it something Andy dreamed up?'

At the mention of Andy's name, Chris Kemp's expression changed. He flinched as if stung, and then looked momentarily surprised, as if realising some fact that had previously eluded him. Rose watched these changes of expression with equal surprise, and figured that it had just dawned on him that if Andy Miller was dead, then Andy Miller might make a convenient scapegoat. So much for the grief.

'It was Andy.' Chris nodded to himself, justifying his choice. 'Andy will ... would ... do anything to make sure we made our targets as a team.' He relaxed a little into his seat and his expression softened. 'Reggie is the weak link for us. He's always way below his target but Andy thought we ought to help him. That if we helped him, then we'd be helping the team as a whole. So we made some extra calls to Reggie's customers to try to bring in some extra cash.' He frowned. 'We didn't do anything wrong, Rose. Apart from make some extra calls. We didn't threaten anybody, or breach regulations.'

Rose smiled at him. 'No one said you'd breached regulations, Chris. And it's only internal process, you know, to stick to the scheduled workflow calls.' She reached out and put a hand on his arm. 'For what it's worth, I was pretty impressed with your approach on the call I listened to. You were firm enough without being threatening, and you stuck rigidly to the facts. I think the ENB would be pleased to know how you dealt with that customer.' She leaned forward lowered her voice to a conspiratorial whisper. 'The call I listened to was the one you made to a Mr Sedgewick. It sounded like you really caught him on the hop.'

Across the table Chris Kemp relaxed a little further. 'We get a few like that. Quick enough to borrow the money, but don't give a toss about paying it back. I mean

…' He frowned, wondering if he had said too much. 'I mean, there are some customers we know have the means to repay their debts, but we know they are choosing not to. We're just trying to move things along a bit.'

'It's OK Chris, I get it. Your job is to recover money for the bank, and you and Andy just got a little bit creative in your methods. I'm sure you believed you were doing it for the right reasons.' She tilted her head to one side and regarded him with a sympathetic gaze. 'And I know it must have been tough for you, this last day or two. You and Andy were close, weren't you?'

'Yes, we were.' He looked away, sheepish now in the wake of his betrayal.

Rose for her part kept her eyes fixed on Chris Kemp's face. Yes you were, she thought, as close as any friends could be. But I don't think you are any more. And I don't think it's just because he's gone.

12

Reggie Croft pushed his plate away and folded his arms onto the table. He turned his head to look at Jodie, who was sullenly picking at the remains of a half-eaten jacket potato. They had never lunched together in the eighteen months they had been work colleagues, and they wouldn't be lunching together today if Andy Miller had still been alive and Chris Kemp hadn't been avoiding her. Reggie had hoped that one of the other girls in the team, Joanna or Carol, would take her in hand but both had found convenient reasons to be out of the office over the lunchtime break. He'd been reluctant to invite her to lunch, but fearful to leave her alone in the office. He'd seen the astonishment on her face earlier that morning when DI Mulligan had asked to speak to her a second time, and the resentment in her eyes when the police interview was over. He couldn't shake off the feeling that she was a storm waiting to break.

Around them the staff restaurant was beginning to fill up and the noise level was rising. It was unlikely that any conversation between them would be overheard. He offered an uncertain smile. 'Were they kind to you, then, the police?' The question was well meant, an awkward attempt to start a conversation, but it sounded nosy and he knew it.

Jodie frowned and gave the potato one final prod, then threw her fork onto the plate and pushed it away. She turned red-rimmed eyes towards Reggie. 'They wanted to know what I did after I left the pub on Sunday night. They wanted to know where I went, was I with anybody and, most importantly, did I go up to the flat to see Andy?' Her voice was flat, unemotional.

They were looking for an alibi, then. He put a gentle hand on the girl's arm. 'They have to ask you that, Jodie love. They're only doing their job. It doesn't mean …'

'It doesn't mean that they think I had anything to do with it?' Jodie pursed her lips and nodded to herself, her eyes still fixed on Reggie. 'Is that what everybody's thinking? That I had something to do with what happened to Andy? What, because he dumped me for that snivelling little cow from Customer Services?'

'No, of course not. Don't be daft. Nobody thinks that. All I'm trying to say is that they have to ask everyone the same question.'

'Have they asked you?'

Reggie winced. 'No, not me. But then I wasn't near the flat on Sunday night, was I? They did ask me yesterday where I was on Sunday night and I told them I was at home with my family. They asked me if I'd spoken to Andy at all over the weekend, and I told them I wasn't friendly with him outside work, he was just somebody I worked with.'

Tears were beginning to well up in Jodie's eyes now. 'But he wasn't just somebody that *I* worked with, was he? He was my ex-boyfriend. And he shared a flat with my current boyfriend. And I've been to the flat.'

'Did you tell them? That you used to go out with Andy?'

'Of course I did. I told them that yesterday. And that I'm going out with Chris now.'

'What does Chris make of it all?'

'I don't know.' A single tear escaped from Jodie's left eye and made its way down her pale cheek. 'He isn't speaking to me.'

Reggie sighed. He didn't like Chris Kemp any more than he had liked Andy Miller, but this wasn't the time or place to share his true feelings. 'It's probably just the shock. He was very close to Andy, wasn't he? Maybe you just need to give him a bit of space to process it all. He'll come round in a day or two.'

Jodie's eyes narrowed. 'Annabel doesn't need to give him space, does she?' The words came out quietly, a low, menacing whisper. 'Didn't you see her yesterday? She was all over him.'

'She's grieving, Jodie love. She's lost her boyfriend.'

'And so have I.' Jodie folded her arms and sank back into her chair. Her voice was becoming firmer now, her reluctance to speak receding. 'I called him fifteen times last night, Reggie. Fifteen times. I've texted him, I've left voice messages for him, and nothing. He hasn't called me back. He hasn't texted me. He came in this morning and ignored me.' Truculence was creeping into every word.

Reggie felt his cheeks redden at this sudden outpouring of anguish. Up until this point in their working relationship their conversations had been limited to work matters and minor pleasantries, and he wasn't sure how to reply. He didn't want to be in her confidence. And anyway, he'd seen all too clearly how Chris Kemp had embraced Annabel Halmshaw yesterday, and who could blame him? The girl was enchanting. He felt his heart start to beat faster and the colour in his cheeks deepen, and he cleared his throat to cough away his thoughts. 'I don't think he was ignoring you. He was busy with Graham.'

Jodie blinked and a cascade of tears overflowed and streamed down her face. 'It doesn't take a second to send someone a text.' She put out a hand and picked up her mobile phone, and gazed at the display. The phone responded to the attention and gave a loud serendipitous bleep. She stared for a moment, and then gave a quiet laugh. 'It's a text from Chris.' Her face softened a little and she flicked at the phone with eager fingers, opening the message. 'The *shit*.' She spat the words out. 'The devious, lying little shit.' Louder this time, loud enough for the occupants of the table next to them to turn round and stare. She slammed the phone down on the table and turned bitter eyes to Reggie. 'He's dumped me, Reggie. The little shit has dumped me. By text.' She reached out and pushed the phone towards him, and it came to rest against his arm.

He looked down at the display and read Chris Kemp's clumsy words quietly to himself. 'It's not working. We're finished. Don't text me back. It's best that way. Sorry.' He looked across at Jodie with raised eyebrows and opened his mouth to speak, but Jodie was already on her feet. She grabbed the mobile phone and shoved it into her pocket, then barged away from the table, pushing past the steady stream of colleagues flowing into the restaurant.

Behind her, Reggie was slow to follow. 'Jodie, wait for me. Don't do anything stupid. You can't tackle him at work. You'll get yourself into trouble.'

'I don't give a shit about getting into trouble. And it's not *him* that I'm going to tackle.' She was out of the restaurant before Reggie could reach her, turning left and making for a staircase. She was still speaking, but quietly now, her words just mumblings of reassurance to herself. 'It's not him that I'm going to tackle,' she repeated. 'I'm going to find that snivelling little bitch Annabel Halmshaw, and deal with her for once and for all.'

Chris Kemp let himself into the flat, letting the door slam shut behind him, and switched on the hall light. Something on the floor caught his eye and he bent down to pick it up. It was a piece of writing paper, neatly folded in half. His name had been written across the front in an unsure hand, and he opened it up to read what was written on the other side. It was a note from Michael Spivey, reminding him about the overdue rent.

He moved into the kitchen, screwing up the note as he went, and tossed it into the bin. While the kettle was on he searched in the fridge for something to eat and settled on a ready-made lasagne, piercing the lid and throwing it into the microwave without much thought. He didn't make a habit of going home in his lunch hour but today it was necessary, not because he wanted to be there, but because he needed to avoid Jodie.

He knew Jodie would have received his text by now, and he knew he had to stay out of the way for as long as he could while her temper flared and then cooled again. He knew his clumsy disassociation wouldn't have hurt her. He'd never been under any illusion that she cared for him in the way she had cared for Andy. In the way he knew she still did care for Andy.

But he also knew that she would cut up rough about him being the one to end their affair. She was an expert in the dog-in-a-manger grudge, and she would play the card of wronged girlfriend if it meant that she could spoil things for him and Annabel. He couldn't understand women like that. *I don't want you, but even though I don't want you I'm going to make sure that no one else can have you.* What's that all about then? Why do women have to be so complicated?

The microwave pinged and he pulled the plastic tray out onto a plate and peeled off the cellophane lid. A burst of garlicky steam stung his eyes and he turned away and blinked. If he did go home to stay with his family at least he wouldn't have to eat this sort of crap any more.

He climbed onto a bar stool next to the kitchen counter and ate his lunch while considering his future. He was on borrowed time in this flat now. He still had the keys, and the landlord hadn't asked him to leave yet. He wondered whether the landlord was waiting to see if he would pay up the overdue rent, and then wondered whether the landlord even knew that he was there. Michael Spivey didn't seem that sharp, but there was a possibility that he might try to keep the presence of an unauthorised tenant to himself so that he could collect the rent arrears and pocket them without the landlord's knowledge.

He was going to have to come up with a plan, and soon. Work wasn't a problem, he could see that now. It might be uncomfortable for a while, but his interview with Rose Bennett had shown him that he could blame Andy for any wrong-doing about the phone calls, and he was sure they couldn't sack him without good reason. All he had to do there was keep his head down. Jodie was dealt with, bar all the shouting. It was going to be shitty working with her, but he could tough it out. And as for Reggie and the team targets, well … screw the team targets. He wasn't going to put himself out for Graham fucking Clarke to take all the glory.

That just left somewhere to live, and Annabel. He allowed himself a moment's fantasy to meld the two together, where Annabel invited him to move into her flat. He knew she had a flat, knew she lived alone, it would be sweet, the two of them cosied up together. But it was too early. She let him kiss her last night, but only on the cheek. At least it was a kiss. No, they couldn't go public this soon, given what had happened to Andy.

He scraped the last remnants of the lasagne out of the plastic tray and licked them off the fork, then pursed his lips in contemplation. He'd try to brazen it out one more night in the flat. He was meeting Annabel tonight, so he could avoid that weasel Spivey. All he had to do was be out for the evening, and come back late enough that he could be sure Spivey wouldn't return. Then late tonight he could pack his bags, and take them into work with him tomorrow.

That could be tricky. He leaned across the counter and switched the kettle back on to re-boil it. Did he have enough bags to take all his stuff in one go? He knew the answer was no. He slid off the bar stool, lifted a mug from the draining board and made himself a coffee, hoping a caffeine hit would provide inspiration. Maybe he could take a bag into work with him this afternoon and store it in his locker. If he took a bag today he could take another couple tomorrow morning, the rest at lunchtime, and then maybe, just maybe, he could get his dad to drive over tomorrow and ferry both him and the contents of his locker back home.

Yes, that's what he'd do. He'd start packing now, and make sure he took the most important stuff first. He'd left his rucksack at work, but he had a hold-all which would take his laptop, and his radio, and other small precious stuff. He carried his coffee through to the bedroom and paused outside the door, then turned and looked across the hall to Andy's bedroom. The door was ajar, and he pushed it open. Everything inside looked just the same as he'd left it, neat, tidy, no evidence that he had helped himself to various items of clothing.

He walked over to the bedside table where Andy kept his most personal belongings and pulled open the drawer. He cast his eyes over the contents, a small digital radio, a couple of good quality watches, a fountain pen given as a gift by his grandparents, a chunky black leather box with Andy's initials on it. He knew what was in the box, and he knew that Andy had bought it for himself just a few weeks ago. After scouring Andy's credit card bills he also knew that Andy had paid for it using a credit card that he probably had no intention of paying off.

Chris figured that the contents of that box were another of Andy's dirty little secrets, and that nobody much knew about it other than Andy, and himself. He took the box out of the drawer and carried it through to his bedroom. He'd already helped himself to enough of Andy's belongings to cover his losses on the rent, this was just a little something extra to make up for the lies and the deceit and the misery of having his life turned upside down, something that no one knew about and that no one would miss.

And in any case, he reasoned, given an opportunity like this, who wouldn't want to have a Patek Philippe watch?

13

'Thanks for giving us your time Rose, you know we appreciate it.' George Mulligan ushered Rose into the small meeting room and closed the door. 'Have a seat.' He pointed to an empty chair opposite DS Scott.

Rose paused before sitting, and held out a hand to DS Scott. 'We haven't met yet.'

Scott took her hand and shook it with a wry smile. 'And yet I still know all about you.' He cast a sideways glance at his superior officer. 'DI Mulligan thinks you might be the key to solving our puzzle.'

'No pressure, then?' She sank into her seat with a laugh. 'I take it things aren't going too well?'

Mulligan shrugged. 'We have officers questioning Andy Miller's neighbours while we concentrate on his bank colleagues, but nothing's turned up so far. No one saw anything, no one heard anything.' He didn't want to share his frustration, but there was little he could do to hide it. 'As far as the bank is concerned, we've interviewed all of his key colleagues, and none of them can offer anything material that would help us.' He exchanged glances with DS Scott and then asked 'I don't suppose you've seen or heard anything useful on the grapevine yet?'

Rose thought for a moment. 'Yes, I possibly have.'

'Feel like sharing?' Scott's tone was teasing.

Mulligan turned to look at him, and gave an inward smile. He knew Scottie was ambitious, but surely he wasn't that ambitious? Rose Bennett? He might have to rethink his opinion of the lad. He leaned an elbow on the table and rested his chin on his hand. 'Come on then, Rose. Make my day, if you can.'

'Well, I can't solve your case for you, I'm afraid. I have no idea who killed Andy Miller or why. But I can tell you one or two things I've turned up that might fit into your jigsaw puzzle.' She smiled at Mulligan and then at Scott. 'The call to Robert Donovan that I've been investigating, that was definitely made from a phone here at the ENB. It wasn't made from any of the phones used by Andy Miller's team, but it was made from a landline phone very close by.'

The senior officer nodded. 'So someone here has definitely been harassing customers.'

'It would appear so. But at this stage I'm afraid I still can't tell you who, or why.' She paused, and then said 'Do you remember me telling you that the team didn't just make their monthly targets, but that it exceeded them? It seems that that Andy Miller and Chris Kemp have been making follow up calls to customers over and above those scheduled by the workflow system.'

DS Scott frowned. 'Which means?'

'Customers in financial difficulty will usually receive one call a month from the ENB to discuss their account, and whether or not their financial situation has changed. If it's improved, the bank will ask for an additional payment to reduce any arrears outstanding. If it's worsened, a new arrangement to pay a smaller amount each month might be put in place. If it's worsened significantly, then the customer may be advised to seek independent advice about their debts. But whatever the situation, the ENB has a policy of only calling such customers once a month, to ensure they are not accused of applying undue pressure.'

'But Andy Miller and Chris Kemp have been making more than one call a month?'

'Yes. Of course, that's not a breach of regulation, just a breach of bank policy. According to Chris Kemp they have been doing it to make sure the team reach their recovery targets.'

'So this is why the call was made to Robert Donovan?'

Rose shook her head. 'I don't think so. I've heard the recordings of some of the unscheduled calls made by Andy and Chris. They were made from the phones on their own desks. Their tone was firm but I wouldn't call them threatening. Of course we only have Laurence Donovan's word for it that the call made to his brother was abusive. I'm still waiting to hear if the call was recorded so that we can be sure of the facts. All I'm saying at this stage is that Andy and Chris were stepping outside the process in the pursuit of cold, hard cash.'

It was Mulligan's turn to ask a question. 'Did they cook this up between them?'

'Not according to Chris Kemp. He says it was Andy's idea and he just followed orders. Of course it's easy for him to say that now that Andy is out of the way.'

'I can't see any way that would have blown up into a fight between Andy and Chris?'

'Neither can I. I'm just sharing the facts, like you asked.' Rose paused and then said 'but there *is* something I can't quite put my finger on. With Chris Kemp. You know, when I first spoke with him last week he came across as utterly loyal to Andy Miller. I couldn't have imagined him laying the blame for these calls at Andy's door. They would have closed ranks and cooked up some story between them. And yesterday … well, it was obvious that he was grieving deeply.' She frowned and looked away. 'A loyal friend is a loyal friend, even in death. If you really cared for a friend you would care about their reputation if they weren't there to defend themselves, wouldn't you? But *he* didn't. Chris Kemp, I mean. I saw it in his face when I interviewed him this morning. When I challenged him about whose idea it was to make those extra calls, he didn't care about Andy's reputation, In fact he looked almost pleased to have Andy as a neatly trussed scapegoat.' She turned back to George Mulligan. 'I think something has happened. Something to change Chris Kemp's opinion of Andy Miller. Because let's face it, loyalty doesn't just die overnight for no reason, does it?'

Annabel Halmshaw had only ventured down to the first floor of the building because she'd heard that Jodie Pearce was looking for her. It hadn't been a shrewd move.

'Why is she doing this to me?' She shrank back against the wall, her doe eyes full of fear as they swept wildly from left to right and back again, pleading for an answer that no one could provide. 'I don't understand. What have I done?' She was shaking now, her body hot and clammy with the sweat of fear, her voice an imploring, tremulous whisper. 'Please, somebody help me.'

Her words were barely audible but Jodie repeated them in a mocking, wheedling voice. 'Why is she doing this to me?' She pushed her again and sank the heels of her hands into the terrified girl's shoulders, pinning her to the wall. 'As if you didn't know.'

Around them the day to day cacophony of office noise fell silent as colleagues in every nearby team stopped what they were doing and turned to stare at the unfolding drama. Graham Clarke got to his feet. 'Jodie, what the hell do you think you're doing? Let her go.'

Jodie shook her head without looking at him, her narrowed eyes still focused on her prey. 'I'm not done with her yet.'

'Oh yes you are.' He was beside them now, close enough to touch. 'Whatever's going on here stops now.'

His voice was strong and steady, sure in its authority, and for a moment Jodie took her hands away from Annabel's shoulders as if considering his words. She took a small step backwards and Annabel relaxed, her body slumping against the wall, and as she did so Jodie let fly with her right hand and struck the girl hard across the cheek. 'You lying, snivelling, conniving little *bitch*.' She spat the words into Annabel's face and then grabbed at her lustrous chestnut hair, winding a hank of it tight around her hand and pulling hard.

Annabel screamed in pain. 'Oh God, please help me. Please make her stop.'

Graham Clarke turned to Reggie. 'Call Security.'

Reggie, dismayed at the unfolding events, put out a hand to pick up the phone but an aging security guard was already limping towards the warring girls. The guard turned an anxious face towards Graham, who just shook his head in disgust. 'Break them up, Walter, for God's sake, and get *her* off the office floor.' He pointed a furious finger at Jodie, who was still hanging on to Annabel's hair, pulling the helpless girl's head backwards towards the floor.

Walter, more accustomed to spending his time tackling the Daily Mail crossword in the safety of his cubby hole than to splitting up cat fights, stretched out a gentle hand towards Jodie. 'Come on, love. You don't want to do this.' His voice was soothing, avuncular. 'Whatever it is, let it go. She's not worth losing your job over.'

Something in his quiet sense seemed to touch her and she turned to look at him, her eyes full of angry tears, and slowly she released her grip on Annabel's hair. Somewhere beyond Walter she could see her team mates Joanna and Carol, their eyes wide with astonishment, Graham Clarke, and Reggie, and then the bigger picture, desk after desk of silent colleagues, all agog at the spectacle she had created.

She was confused now, awake from her rage and aware that something was dreadfully wrong, but still not quite comprehending what it was. Walter took hold of her arm and began to steer her gently towards the nearest staircase. 'That's it love, you come with me down to Reception. We'll pop into my cubby hole downstairs and have a little chat. A cup of tea will sort you out.' He turned towards Graham Clarke and nodded. 'We'll be alright now for a little while, Mr Clarke. Pop down and see us when you're ready. You know where I live.'

Graham waited until Jodie was out of earshot and then turned to look at Annabel. She was leaning against the wall breathing heavily, her face a mess of tears and snot, a black bruise already beginning to form on her cheek where Jodie had struck her. He put a hand on her shoulder. 'I think you and I need to have a little chat.' His tone wasn't sympathetic.

Annabel didn't respond immediately. She closed her eyes, her head bent forward, silent and still. And then with a deep breath in she lifted her head and looked at him, the doe eyes wide and innocent and curiously adoring. 'Oh Graham, I can't thank you enough for saving me.' She fell forward onto his chest and wrapped her arms around his neck, and buried her face into the collar of his shirt, tickling the flesh of his neck with fluttering eyelashes and smearing his skin with melting mascara.

Graham shrank away under her touch. He lifted his hands and took hold of her arms at the wrist, gently freeing himself from her grip. 'Reggie?' He called over his shoulder, unable to move, the weeping girl now dangling by her wrists from his hands. 'Could you come over here and take care of Annabel for a moment while I call her manager? I think she needs to go somewhere quiet to calm down, she seems to be a little ...' He paused and peered down at her through condescending eyes. 'She seems to be *more* than a little overwrought.'

'Vienna? It's her day off.' The barmaid put Spivey's pint down on the counter and held out her hand. 'That'll be three pounds twenty, love.'

He handed her a ten pound note and tried to hide his disappointment. 'I'll have a Scotch as well. Take it out of that.' He'd called in to The Feathers hoping for a kind word from Vienna to bolster his confidence, a bit of encouragement to get out of his comfort zone before he tackled his evening calls. He'd begged Benny for an early finish, trading his Friday afternoon off for the privilege, and she wasn't even at work.

He shot a furtive glance around the bar to make sure that Benny wasn't spying on him. It would be like Benny to tail him, to poke his nose into his affairs. He was just in the mood for it today, as well. The girls in the shop had been gossiping about Benny, and some story that he'd been asking about a woman called Rose Bennett. Rose Bennett, the girls said, was the woman who helped to find Pandora Mitchell in the summer, to find his son's missing girlfriend. The rumour was that Rose Bennett was back in Market Melbourne, staying at her aunt's cottage, and that Benny was made up at the idea of seeing her again.

They'd asked Michael Spivey if he knew anything about it but he'd kept his counsel. He knew all about Rose Bennett alright. About her finding Pandora, about her working with George Mulligan, about her role in exposing Hector Campling's father as a money-launderer. But he didn't want to talk about it. She was a bad omen, Rose Bennett. Good job the errands he was doing now for Hector were nothing to do with the bank.

Thinking of Hector Campling reminded him of the task ahead, and he pulled a piece of paper from his jacket pocket and unfolded it onto the bar, to remind himself where Florence Fielding lived. It was 23rd Avenue. He knew it well, just around the corner from his Auntie Jen's old house. Good job his Auntie Jen didn't live there now, or he'd never hear the end of it.

A wistful thought came unbidden into his mind, and he tried to chase it back out with a swig of whisky. Auntie Jen had been the only thing he'd known as family for years, before she passed on. A gutsy old girl who'd emigrated to Yorkshire when she married a northerner, he remembered his one and only holiday with her as boy, when his mother brought him up to Scarborough during the school holidays. They'd come without his dad, and while Auntie

Jen's husband Frank was away at sea, and spent the days on the beach building sandcastles, and the nights sitting on the sea wall eating fish and chips out of newspaper. Sandcastles every day, fish and chips every night, and just his mum and Auntie Jen. It was the nearest thing to heaven.

But Auntie Jen was gone now, like his mum. And there were no siblings, no cousins, to remind him. He gulped down the rest of the Scotch. Jesus, he was getting as soft as Benny. He refolded the paper and put it back in his pocket, and turned his attention to the pint. It was no substitute for Vienna's smile, but it was all he was going to get today so he might as well enjoy it.

14

Rose sat down at Jodie's desk, powered up her laptop, and sent an email to Stan Wilkins. 'Have found extension 887 on desk B24, and yes it's still connected. All the other phones are dead. Any progress on whether the calls were recorded? Sorry to chase, but Clive is breathing down my neck'. She stopped to think for a moment. The desks in that area were dusty, neglected by cleaning staff who rarely bothered with abandoned spaces. Each desk showed small marks in the dust, made perhaps when someone tried each phone in turn to see if it was live. Desk B24 showed signs of more attention, possibly scratches and scrapes in the dust indicative of a repeat visitor.

She plugged her headphones into her laptop and opened up the file of calls she'd listened to earlier. The call to Florence Fielding interested her. She liked a customer who fought back. She listened to it again, and then sent Stan another email asking him to search for any calls made to or received from Florence's number. His reply was succinct. 'It'll cost you the wine to go with dinner.'

She was about to listen again to Reggie's call to Sedgewick when her mobile phone began to ring. She peered at the display. It was Clive Barden.

'Rose? I know we said four, but I've just heard about Jodie Pearce. What the hell is going on up there?'

'I really can't say, Clive. I heard there was a squabble between her and Annabel Halmshaw, but I was taking a late lunch and I missed all the action.'

'Lunch? I'm not paying you to take lunch.'

'I know. But you're not paying me to hand-hold the police investigation either. I met with George Mulligan in my lunch break. If you're going to make me choose between eating and keeping the police off your back, I might have to rethink my options.'

He coughed to clear his throat. 'Yes, well ... of course your willingness to assist in all aspects of our work is always appreciated.'

Rose smiled to herself. Clive wasn't good at apologies, but at least he was trying. 'Why don't we start again? I can't really tell you what's going on with Jodie Pearce. I'm sitting at her desk now. All I know is that there was a cat-fight in the Recovery Team, and Graham has taken her off the office floor for the rest of the day. To be honest, I think Jodie Pearce is the least of your problems this afternoon. Stan has confirmed for me that the call to Robert Donovan was definitely made from a phone at the ENB, here in Scarborough. And I've tracked the phone down. I can see it now, from where I'm sitting.'

'Oh, dear God.' It was the news he was dreading, his dismay evident in his voice. 'Do we know yet who made it?'

'No, Stan is following up for me today. I'll send you an email later with all the details, but whoever made the call used a rogue phone that should have been disconnected. Stan's trying to find out if the call was recorded, but we think not.'

'Then we can't know for certain who made that call.'

'Maybe, maybe not. I have an idea how we can find out, although it's not fool-proof and I need to give it a bit more thought. In the meantime I've asked Stan for a list of all calls made from that phone since the last legitimate occupant of the desk moved out. I'm hoping he'll have that for me by close of business today, or at least first thing tomorrow morning. As soon as I have more I'll let you know.'

'Thank you, Rose.' His tone was conciliatory now. 'And Jodie Pearce. Can we talk now about that? Did you know that personal relationships in the team were so … what shall we say? So volatile? I have a conference call set up for six o'clock to cover this off with the Head of Recoveries. Anything you can share with me now would be most useful.'

'Well, there's certainly a disturbed balance of energies in the team, but it all seems to be personal, not professional. Jodie Pearce used to be in a relationship with Andy Miller, but I understand he ended things to move on to Annabel Halmshaw from Customer Services. At that point, Jodie took up with his friend Chris Kemp. Now Chris Kemp has thrown her over, and he's making sheep's eyes at Annabel Halmshaw.' She felt a laugh rising in her stomach and fought hard to keep it down. She didn't have to see Clive to know that his face would be contorting with disdain.

They were both silent for a moment, then Clive asked 'have you imparted this information to DI Mulligan?'

'I didn't need to, I think Mr Mulligan managed to work it out for himself. I'm sure he'll let us know if he thinks it's material to his investigation.'

'Perhaps.' Clive didn't sound convinced. 'Oh well, I suppose we did agree to assist in any way that we could.' He sniffed his disapproval. 'Rose, my initial thoughts are to suggest that we suspend Jodie Pearce pending disciplinary action, and put Chris Kemp on gardening leave until the police investigation into Andy Miller's death is complete. Perhaps you will pass that on to the Inspector on my behalf.'

'Of course, if you wish.' Rose frowned. 'What about Annabel Halmshaw?'

'Ah yes, the victim. She's in Customer Services, isn't she? Yes, I'd better have her line manager on the six o'clock call, too. Thank you for the suggestion.'

'Clive, don't be too quick to think of Annabel Halmshaw as a victim.'

'The young woman has been assaulted by a colleague. What else should I think of her?'

'I don't know. I just think … well, I think she is good at taking people in.'

'The assault was physical, not verbal. Are you trying to imply that she in some way provoked the attack?'

'I suppose it depends on your definition of provocation. She's deprived Jodie Pearce of two boyfriends in the last six months.'

He thought for a moment, and when he spoke again an inflection in his voice suggested that he too was beginning to see unwelcome connections. 'I am aware that with each passing day it appears more likely that Andy Miller's death was murder, not an accident. And however much I don't like it, I am going to have to face up to the possibility and to the repercussions it would have for us at the ENB. Would it be asking too much to ask you if you think … well, I can't quite believe I'm asking this, but is it possible that an ENB employee may be named as a suspect in DI Mulligan's investigation?'

There was something in his voice that she couldn't quite place, perhaps an uncharacteristic melancholy. He was probably thinking back to the summer, to his ex-wife's incarceration, the pain still raw, the fear of more scandal for the bank ever-present in his mind. Despite all his pomposity and affectation he was still human, then. She tried to sound kind. 'Truly, Clive, I don't know. But I think you would be wise to be prepared. I can't see a link between the call to Donovan, Andy Miller's death and Jodie Pearce taking a swipe at Annabel Halmshaw. But that doesn't mean there isn't one. I'll ask Mr Mulligan this evening what his thoughts are so far, and I'll let you know if he has his eye on anyone.'

'Thank you Rose, I would appreciate that.'

'No problem.' She leaned back in her seat and looked

around her. Jodie, Graham and Chris were all missing from their desks. Carol and Joanna, their day disrupted by the antics of their colleagues, had given up trying to work through their calls and were sitting at Carol's desk chatting quietly over a coffee. Only Reggie was still working, chatting to a customer through his headset, nodding in agreement at something being said. 'Clive, before you go … I know it's not my remit to comment, but if you suspend two members of staff from this team you might want to think about the backlog. You've already lost Andy Miller, and from what I've seen so far Andy and Chris were putting in extra effort to compensate for weaknesses elsewhere in the team.' She lowered her voice. 'I'm sure Joanna and Carol are pulling their weight, but I've listened to some of Reggie Croft's calls, and I think he can be a pretty soft touch. Chris Kemp reckons he always misses his targets.'

Clive clicked his teeth. 'Yes, it's unfortunate about Reggie, isn't it? I understand there is an awareness of his poor performance, but under the circumstances … well, I don't want to say too much Rose, and it was a long time ago, but it is a shame when we have to clip the wings of a star performer.'

A star performer? Rose turned to look again at Reggie. He was almost slumped over his desk now, his eyes right up to his computer screen, nodding away benignly as he listened to a customer. 'Reggie was a star performer?'

'Oh yes, indeed. I'm going back some years, of course, but Reggie Croft was one of the most efficient and productive recovery agents this bank has ever produced.' He clicked his teeth again. 'Things change, Rose. Sometimes life throws us things we don't expect, they turn our world upside down, and we have to live with the consequences. I, of all people, should know that, I suppose.' His tone was unexpectedly humble now. 'But we make the best of it, don't we? Reggie was only doing his best on behalf of the bank. We could hardly hang him out to dry for that, could we?'

Chris Kemp was beginning to feel tired. He had been sitting with Annabel in the empty staff restaurant for what seemed like hours, drinking unpalatable instant coffee and sharing an assortment of chocolate bars from a nearby vending machine. It was almost six o'clock, well past the end of the working day, and the ENB's housekeeping staff were beginning to hustle and bustle around them, preparing for the evening shift.

He took hold of Annabel's hand. 'Do you feel well enough for me to take you home now?' He desperately wanted her to say yes. Taking her home would mean that he could try to put the day behind him. He could forget about Graham Clarke, and Rose Bennett, and the phone calls he shouldn't have made. And of course it would bring him an added bonus. Taking her home would give him a bona fide reason not to go back to Bellevue Mansions, and the inevitable confrontation with Michael Spivey.

She didn't answer him straight away. She pouted and put her free hand up to her cheek. 'Is the bruising very bad? Has it started to spread?'

He tilted his head back and stared at her face. There was a deep violet contusion across the peak of her left cheek where Jodie's hand had struck hard, pressing the soft flesh of her face against the hard bone. Around the eye of the bruise a discoloured swelling had started to form. He shook his head with a duplicitous smile. 'It's fine. You were lucky.'

She frowned. 'I still don't understand why, Chris? Why would Jodie attack me like that?'

He had a pretty good idea but he'd been avoiding the truth. Now he was beginning to realise that they weren't going to move on past this conversation until he told her everything. 'I think it's my fault. I think it's because I dumped her at lunchtime.' His voice was low, guilty.

Annabel looked puzzled. 'Dumped her? You mean you broke up with her? I'm so sorry. Why didn't you tell me?' Her surprise seemed genuine. 'I can understand her being upset by that.' Her frown deepened. 'But what has it got to do with me?'

Did she really not know? Was he really going to have to spell it out? 'Because she knows I care about you.'

Annabel blushed. 'You're so kind, Chris.' Her face began to crumple and her eyes filled with tears. There was an underlying message in his words and she seemed to be skirting the subject. 'You've been so good to me, but Jodie has no reason to be jealous. I miss Andy so much. Why did he have to be taken like that?'

Chris wasn't sure how to answer her. He didn't want to hear about how much she missed Andy. He thought for a moment about the box of papers in the bottom of Andy's wardrobe, about Andy's debts, about his lies, and whether or not she knew just what kind of a man Andy was. She couldn't have. This sweet, precious creature wouldn't have wanted a liar and a cheat for a boyfriend. Perhaps he should tell her one simple truth, tell her about Andy's debts, that would put paid to her hero-worship.

Andy didn't deserve hero-worship.

She was gazing into the distance now. 'I can still remember the day I met him for the first time. He was so helpful, so kind.'

'I remember that too.' And he could, all too clearly. He could remember looking up from his desk to see her leaning over Andy, see her cool clear skin and her long chestnut hair, just as he could see Andy's face leering up at her with its familiar predatory grin.

'His death must have hurt you dreadfully, Chris. You were so close, you'd known him for so long. You know you can talk to me about it, if it helps.'

'Of course it hurt.' He tried to look melancholy. It didn't hurt any more, of course, but he couldn't tell her that. Not that it mattered. He could play the long game now, there was no way he could lose out to a corpse. He squeezed her hand. 'I didn't realise how tough it would be, Annabel. In fact, I don't think I can go on staying in the flat. Too many memories. I'm going to contact the landlord tomorrow and tell him I'm moving out. I'm going to look for another place to stay.'

'I suppose everything must remind you of him.' She nodded in understanding. 'Look at the pair of us, both sitting here pining, both on our own again.' She fluttered long eye lashes at him. 'We'll have to look after one another until we both find someone else.'

It wasn't the response he was looking for. He pulled his hand gently out of hers and put it up to her face, brushing his fingers tenderly across the bruised flesh of her cheek. 'Come on, let me take you home.'

'I'm not ready to go home yet.' She shrank back, away from his to touch, all the time her eyes watching his face. 'You look so sad, Chris. Why don't we go out and grab something to eat? I know my face must look a mess, but I can try to patch it up with some make up. We could go into town, find a restaurant where no one knows us. I just … don't want to sit in the flat and mope.'

She wasn't giving him much choice. At least the option of a restaurant would still keep him away from the flat until the coast was clear. He smiled and nodded. 'There's a new Italian restaurant just behind the sea front, we could go for a pizza?'

She echoed his words with a smile. 'We could go for a pizza.' She took hold of the hand that had brushed her cheek, and twisted it gently so that she could see the cuff of his shirt. 'Those are pretty cufflinks.' Her face clouded. 'I can understand why you want to move out of the flat, Chris. How can we forget Andy when there are so many reminders?' She swallowed down a tear. 'I gave Andy a pair of cufflinks just like those when we first started dating.'

15

The Boar was familiar to Rose. A traditional country pub somewhere between Market Melbourne and Scarborough, hidden down a network of lanes just off the main road, she had first travelled there at the age of seventeen, crammed into the back of Danny Mitchell's Vauxhall Astra Mk II, tagging along as an unwelcomed chaperone on his dates with her best friend Janis Porter.

It wasn't the first time she had used the place to rendezvous with George Mulligan, either. Back in the summer, when Janis had been instrumental in the disappearance of Pandora Mitchell, the policeman had invited her to The Boar to meet Pandora's boyfriend Craig Bradman. And now here she was again, meeting up with Mr Mulligan because her work at the bank was once more threatening to overlap with a police investigation.

He was already there when she arrived, sitting at a corner table with DS Scott. Scott waved to her as she came through the door and got to his feet as she approached. 'What can I get you, Rose?'

'I'll have a tonic with ice and lemon, please.' She smiled at Mulligan as she sat down and nodded towards his drink of choice. 'Coffee to keep you awake?'

'Something like that.' He didn't look happy. He picked up his mug and swirled the dregs around, and swigged them down with a scowl. 'It's not hitting the spot yet.' He turned his head towards the bar and motioned to Scott to bring him another, then turned back to Rose. 'I'll be honest with you, Rose. This one is tying me in knots.'

'Still no progress, then?'

'No, not much. In fact,' he leaned back in his seat and blew out a puff of frustrated breath, 'strictly between you and me we have no real leads at all. The only witness to Andy Miller's murder is his car, and unfortunately for us technology hasn't advanced far enough yet to produce a model of BMW that can remember what it's seen and provide the details in a police statement.' He looked away, troubled by another thought. 'I'll have to speak to the family again tomorrow. They're in bits. If we had a lead it might be different. But right now I've got nothing to offer them.'

'You re-interviewed Jodie Pearce this morning, didn't you?'

'We did, for all the good it did us. We thought it might be possible she went to see Andy Miller after leaving the pub on Sunday evening, and Chris Kemp might not have known about it. At the very least, she might have passed Bellevue Mansions on her way home, and seen something relevant. Of course, she denies it.' He glowered into his empty cup. 'We asked her about her working relationship with Andy Miller, and she said it was fine. But when I asked her how she felt about him dating Annabel Halmshaw, she just clammed up and refused to speak.' He looked up. 'What's she hiding, Rose?'

Rose smiled at him. 'She's a young woman, Mr Mulligan. She was probably just hiding her embarrassment. Possibly even a degree of shame. Young women at that age, they feel it very deeply when their feelings are hurt.'

The policeman raised an eyebrow. 'Well, I'll have to concede you'd know more about that than me, Rose, having been a young woman yourself.' He turned to glance at DS Scott, who had returned from the bar and was placing fresh drinks down on the table. 'I think we should interview her again, but Scottie here doesn't agree.'

Scott smiled affably at Rose as he sat down. 'The old man just has a suspicious nature, Rose. He thinks everyone is guilty until he lands his man. Me, I try to think the best of people but keep my options open. Mind, I will allow she comes across as a pretty angry young woman. It might be worth talking to her again.'

Rose picked up her tonic and sipped on it. 'Well if you do, it will have to be at home. The ENB have decided to suspend her first thing tomorrow morning, pending a disciplinary hearing. For assaulting Annabel Halmshaw on bank premises.'

Mulligan paused, his coffee halfway to his lips, and turned to Scott with an almost triumphant grin. 'I knew that girl was trouble.' He whistled through his teeth and turned back to Rose. 'Is Annabel alright?'

'I haven't seen her, but I believe so. I heard it was only a healthy slap across the face. A few days for the bruises to heal and I'm sure she'll be fine.'

'And Chris Kemp, what does he make of his girlfriend being suspended?'

'Ah yes, that's the other thing I have to tell you.' Rose took another sip of tonic. 'I can't tell you what he makes of it, because I haven't seen him since it happened. He volunteered to take Annabel home. And I won't be able to ask him tomorrow, because he is also being suspended until the investigation into Andy's death is complete.'

DS Scott's laugh was spontaneous. 'I hate to admit it, but the way things stand that could be a hell of a long suspension.'

'I think Clive knows that. He hinted it was because of the dynamic between him and the two girls, but I don't know. Looked at in another light you could say Clive has made a pretty shrewd move. This afternoon's events have given him the opportunity to move the two people who interest the police most safely off site.'

Mulligan's face had momentarily brightened at the prospect of fresh information. Now it clouded again. 'You mean he's distancing the ENB from the investigation? Does *he* think one of them could have been involved in

Andy Miller's death?'

'He hasn't said as much. I think it is more likely that he is just trying to protect the ENB from the risk of it being one of them.' Rose offered Mulligan a disarming smile. 'Clive wants me to ask you about your suspects. Whether *you* suspect an ENB employee of being responsible for Andy's death.'

Mulligan thought for a moment then said 'I'm sorry Rose, I can't answer that question as directly as Clive would probably like. But I can tell you that with murder, the most likely suspects are close to the victim. In the absence of any new information we are going to have to start paying more attention to those people close to Andy. To be more precise, someone close enough to access the spare keys to his car. The spare keys to the vehicle were still in the ignition when we took the car away. We need to consider who Andy trusted enough to give those keys to. And we need to consider who had access to the flat, knew where those keys were kept, and could just take them. And that certainly narrows the field.'

Michael Spivey parked his car on Broadway and walked around the corner to 23rd Avenue. Some wag back in the seventies had decided to name the streets of the Barnfield Estate after the streets of New York. He'd heard it said that some bloke called Julie-Arnie had cleaned up New York so that it was barely recognisable. Shame they couldn't have persuaded him to come and do the same to the Barnfield.

It was a bitterly cold night and Spivey sank his ungloved hands deep into the pockets of his cheap overcoat. In his right hand pocket the key to flat 2d Bellevue Mansions was burning a hole. Hector had given him the key to let himself in, in case Chris Kemp had done a bunk. No one had come to the door when he'd knocked, but he still didn't want to let himself in. No, he reckoned that Chris Kemp was just hiding out until later. He preferred to deploy his own plan, drop Hector's letter about the tenancy through the letterbox for Chris Kemp to find, do the Florence Fielding job, and then go back much later and try to catch Chris Kemp on the hop.

Anyway, this Florence Fielding job was going to be a doddle. 23rd Avenue was well lit, and he walked along briskly looking for the house, counting the house numbers as he went, noting peeling paint, dirty curtains, and rotting garden after rotting garden. Number 16 had an abandoned mattress lying in the middle of its unmown lawn, 18 had lost its gate, and 20 had a rusting VW Golf hanging out onto the pavement where the fence should have been. He tutted to himself. These used to be good houses when his Auntie Jen lived here. These people didn't deserve a decent place to live.

Still, he reasoned, if Florence Fielding turned out to be a slattern he wouldn't feel so bad leaning on her for the rent. He counted more doors along, 22, 24, 26, and came to number 28.

His heart sank. A sharply mown lawn filled most of the space in front of the house, and neatly clipped shrubs lined a clean gravel path from the front gate to the front door. A pair of small standard holly trees flanked the door, each under-planted with a burst of seasonal colour to complement their smart blue ceramic pots, and the door itself bore a matching brass door-knocker, letterbox and door knob, all highly polished.

This was a tidy property. He would expect that from Mr Campling, no rubbish where Mr Campling was involved, but this was more. This property had been looked after. This Florence Fielding woman, she'd looked after the place, made it look nice, a proper home. Butterflies started to dance, unbidden, in the pit of his stomach.

He took in a deep breath. Come on now, Mikey, he thought to himself, you don't have to be heavy with this one. Just send Mr Campling's compliments and say you need something extra for the rent. It doesn't have to be three hundred if she can't run to it. She might be an old dear, like Auntie Jen. A bit extra would do, wouldn't it?

He took another deep breath in, and then blew it out, in, out, in, out, until his nerves had steadied. How hard could it be? He opened the gate and walked slowly down the path, then lifted his hand to knock on the door, and paused. From inside the house he could hear a little girl laughing, giggling as if someone was tickling her.

Kids.

He never thought about kids. Mikey, you idiot. She's not an old dear, she's an unmarried mother. She must be, if she's on the Barnfield. And if she's an unmarried mother, then there must be kids. Or at least *a* kid. A boy's voice joined the laughter. Two kids then. His chest deflated and he shrank into his overcoat, nervous now.

He muttered under his breath. What is *wrong* with you? You're not doing anything wrong. This woman owes the rent, all you're doing is trying to get it back. He closed his eyes. Down in his gut the two pints of bitter and three Scotches that he'd sunk in The Feathers were mingling with the greasy kebab that he'd downed in the car after leaving Bellevue Mansions, and he was starting to feel nauseous. Jesus, if he flunked this call as well as Bellevue Mansions, then Hector would go apeshit.

That thought was all the motivation he needed. He lifted his hand and rapped sharply on the front door. For a moment everything went quiet, the children's laughter halted by the knock on the door, and then a woman's shape became visible through the front door's frosted glass window. He saw her put up a hand to open the door, smelled the aroma of a roast chicken supper as the door swung back on its hinge, and he lifted his head to look up into her face.

Her face. Oh Jesus Christ, her face. *That* face.

He stood rigid for a moment, then the two pints, the

kebab and the three Scotches all conspired against him, and he turned his face away from her towards one of the smart blue ceramic pots that flanked the front door, and threw up over a totally unsuspecting winter-flowering cyclamen.

16

You might at least try to sound pleased.

It was the third text Rose had received from Mike since George Mulligan had left The Boar, leaving her alone with DS Scott. She stared at it for a moment and then deleted it with a flick of her thumb. The girls were coming to stay for ten whole days over Christmas while their mother took a skiing holiday with her latest toy-boy. Rose didn't see much to be pleased about.

She turned and looked over her shoulder towards the bar, where DS Scott was waiting patiently to order more drinks, and smiled to herself. She'd quite enjoyed the amused look on Mr Mulligan's face when she'd accepted Scott's invitation to stay on at The Boar for a bite to eat. Mulligan had given her a wink and a knowing look as he'd left their table to travel home alone. And Rose had given him an equally knowing look in return, and thrown him a coquettish smile for good measure.

Of course, Rose being Rose she had reasons of her own for accepting the invitation to supper, and they bore no resemblance to those of George Mulligan's imaginings. She glanced over her shoulder again to make sure Scott was still occupied at the bar, and then tapped a text to

Mike into her phone. Within a few seconds she had received a response. *Who the hell is Detective Sergeant Scott?*

She smiled to herself. It would do Mike good to think there was a bit of competition on the horizon. It might even wake him up to the realisation that she would like a bit more in their lives that didn't revolve around his ex-wife and kids. She switched off her phone and dropped it into her bag just as Scott returned to the table with their drinks.

'The food order will be about twenty minutes.' He took off his jacket and hung it over the back of his chair before sitting down, then loosened his tie and undid the top button of his shirt. He looked tired. 'Thanks for agreeing to stay out this evening, Rose. I could do with an hour to switch off.' He'd ordered a pint of lager and he took a long drink from it, his eyes closed, relishing the simple pleasure of a relaxing drink after a hard day's work. Then he opened his eyes and lifted his glass to her. 'I can't tell you how good that tastes. I'm usually the one with the car keys. It's a rare luxury for me to be getting a lift home.'

'It's my pleasure. I'm glad you suggested it. You're not the only one who needs a bit of down time.' She leaned an elbow on the table and rested her chin on her upturned hand. 'There's no Mrs Scott to dash home to, then?'

He grinned. 'There's an ex-Mrs Scott. I won't be dashing home in that direction again anytime soon.' He regarded her with warm, brown eyes. 'And what about you, Rose? Is there a Mr Bennett waiting at home for you?'

'No, there's no Mr Bennett.' She caught a glimpse of interest in his eyes and then watched it fade slightly as she told him about Mike. 'We've been together about eighteen months, we met at a friend's birthday party. He's an architect, a very different line of work from me, so at least we don't get to bore each other to death over supper every evening.' She felt his eyes probing her face for the truth and gave a self-deprecating laugh. 'OK, it's a fair cop. He's about as interested in my investigations as I am in whether or not he can manage to fit a basement cinema into his plans for a client's house.'

'Is he a keeper?'

It was an intrusive question for such a short acquaintance, but his tone was so mischievous that Rose could only laugh. 'Probably not. But don't let my aunt hear you say that, or I'll never hear the end of it.'

'She doesn't like him, then?'

'She doesn't think he's right for me.' In spite of herself, Rose was beginning to relax. Ian Scott was unnervingly easy to talk to.

'Do you? Think he's right for you?'

'I don't know.' The words were out before she could stop them. *Shit, I didn't mean to say that.* She blew out a sigh. 'Well, I guess you caught me out with that one.'

The warm, brown eyes smiled at her across the table. 'I wasn't trying to catch you out, Rose. But it might be that your aunt knows you better than you think.' He stared down into his glass. 'We've all been there, trying to push that square peg into a round hole so that we don't have to be alone.' He thought for a moment and then said teasingly 'I'm interested. In your investigation, of course.'

'Oh, of course.' She folded her arms onto the table with a playful shrug. 'What would you like to know?'

'Do you think Andy Miller made the threatening phone call that you're investigating?'

'Do I think he did? Yes, I think I do. Can I prove it? No, I can't. I have evidence that the phone call was definitely made from the ENB's office, but the call wasn't recorded so I have no evidence of who made it.'

'Andy Miller and Chris Kemp were working together to improve the team's performance, weren't they? To collect more money for the ENB. Was that driven by a desire for bigger bonuses?'

'Possibly. But not totally. I met Andy Miller. He was ambitious. I don't think he just wanted the money, I think he wanted the kudos. He wanted credit for his team's good performance. That's not something to be ashamed of, but debt recovery is a sensitive area. There's something distasteful about chasing people for money if they genuinely can't afford to pay it back.'

'I suppose it must take a certain sort of brass neck to cold call people who owe money. I wouldn't like to do it.'

Rose nodded with a smile. 'I can see why you would think that. These days it actually should take a certainly sort of diplomacy. In the bad old days the banks could just harass people over their debts, regardless of their circumstances. These days it's not politically correct to talk about people being in debt. We dress it up and say they are in "financial difficulties", and we have to nurse them back to "financial health", not bully them into making payments they can't afford. Banks are struggling with that.'

'Why?'

'Well, for years they've been training staff to pile on the pressure, recover money in any way they can, and see the customer as some sort of criminal who's deliberately avoiding payment. Now the regulators are saying that's not acceptable, that you have to display some understanding of people's individual situations. The trouble is, the bullying culture is deeply embedded in some places and introducing a culture of understanding isn't easy.' Rose grinned. 'Especially when the bank itself is sending mixed messages by telling recovery agents to be understanding, and then saying they'll be rewarded not for showing that understanding, but for the amount of cold hard cash they actually recover.'

Scott was frowning, slow to catch on. 'So these bonuses, they are paid out depending on how much money has been recovered by the team?' He scowled at the thought. 'What's your view on that, then, Rose?'

'My view is that it's horses for courses. Some people don't pay their debts because they can't. Some people don't pay them because they don't want to. If you're really on the ball, you'll employ kid gloves for those in genuine difficulty and a tougher crew for those who can afford to pay it back but just don't want to. And if you're really, really on the ball you'll make sure that you assign the right approach to the right accounts.

'Meaning?'

'If you assign kid gloves to a deliberate non-payer, you won't recover much. If you assign someone less understanding to collect from a customer with true financial difficulties then you run the risk of pushing that customer deeper into debt. With a genuine financial difficulty case you want someone like Reggie Croft, someone who will try to understand why the payments aren't being made, not just try to bully their way to a payment.'

Scott was interested now. 'So what category did Robert Donovan fall into?'

'The kid glove category. He wasn't in financial difficulty, but he was bereaved. Reggie Croft was assigned to his case, and Reggie kept rolling the case forward due to his bereavement. Unfortunately, someone at the ENB didn't care about the bereavement and decided to push the point.'

'And you think that person was Andy?

'It's my best guess.'

'Can't you just take a recording of Andy Miller's voice to Robert Donovan and ask if he can identify it?'

'I'd love to. But Clive has forbidden it. He doesn't want the investigation to run that deep. He was convinced there would be no record of the call at the ENB. Now that I've identified the phone used to make the call, he wants to pull back on the investigation.'

'But I thought he brought you in to get at the truth?'

'Hell, no.' Rose answered him with a laugh. 'Most of the time Clive just brings me in so that he can say he's brought in an independent investigator. It makes it look as though the bank is taking a complaint seriously. He much prefers it if I *don't* find anything. Then he can just waffle on about how the bank tried, but there's nothing they can do.'

'But you foil his plans now and again by going the extra mile and finding something he doesn't want you to find?'

'That's about it. He's proposing to tell the Donovans that the bank has done everything it can to identify the caller but that the call wasn't recorded. He'll promise that staff will be retrained so that it doesn't happen again, and offer a substantial donation to a charity of their choice.'

Across the table Ian Scott pouted his disapproval. 'Come on Rose, that's no good. The last thing we need is an end to your investigation. We need you in the middle of that team to keep an eye on things for us. And in any case,' he lifted his glass to his lips and smirked into it, 'I can't imagine you're in too much of a hurry to get back to your square peg.'

'If I'd known you were here Vienna, straight up, I would never have come.' Michael Spivey shook his head, miserable beyond belief. 'I came here to see some tart called Florence Fielding. The last fing I expected was for you to open the door.' He gazed at her with doleful eyes. 'I'm sorry about the … I'm sorry that I …' He wanted to say 'I'm sorry that I threw up on the doorstep' but he couldn't make the words come out.

Vienna perched on the edge of an armchair opposite him, her hands wrapped around a mug of coffee, her expression solicitous. 'That's alright, Michael, I'm sure it was an accident.' She looked confused. 'I still don't really understand what you're doing here? How do you know Florence?'

He squirmed in his seat, uneasy. 'Well, I don't actually *know* her, I more sort of know *of* her, if you get my drift.' He could see from her face that she didn't. 'I've been asked to come here, by Mr Campling. You know Mr Campling, Vienna, the gent what's a solicitor in Market

Melbourne? He comes in the pub sometimes.'

'Oh yes, I know him.' She pointed to the small coffee table in front of him. 'Aren't you going to drink your coffee?'

He licked his lips. Of course he wanted to drink the coffee. He was cold and nervous and in desperate need of comfort. But somehow he just felt he didn't deserve it, that he didn't deserve her kindness and consideration. He put out a hand to pick up the mug, and then drew it back again. He looked at her sheepishly. 'Mr Campling has a bit of outstanding business with Florence. He asked me to drop by, like, and just leave a message with her.'

Vienna glanced over at the kitchen clock. 'She won't be back for another couple of hours yet. She does a cleaning shift in the evenings, at the ENB's call centre. She usually gets back around ten.' The living room door was ajar and she pointed through the gap in the direction of the kitchen, where a boy and girl were perched on bar stools in front of a small portable television. 'That's what I'm doing here, baby-sitting the twins until she gets back.'

He nodded in comprehension, and more than a little relief. 'You're the baby-sitter then? You don't live here?'

'No, of course not. I'm in a flat-share in Market Melbourne, I thought you knew that?' Her smile was warm and friendly. 'No, I just do what I can to help Florence out. She hasn't had it easy since the summer.'

'Oh?' He tried to sound interested, but it was difficult when he suspected that whatever story she had to tell him was only going to make him feel worse than he already did.

'Yes, Steve - that's the twins' dad – he did a runner in the summer. He ran off with some girl he met in the pub while Florence was out at work.' She scrunched her face into a frown to show her disapproval. 'She's well rid, if you ask me. He was workshy, that one. He did a bit of seasonal work on the seafront in the summer, but mostly he sat in front of the telly watching the racing. She doesn't really miss him, except she misses his benefits. It's hard to keep a roof over your head, and keep three kids fed, when there's just you to go out to work.'

'Free kids?' He shook his head. He didn't really want to hear any more, but Vienna seemed to want to talk about it.

'Yes.' She sipped on her coffee. 'The twins are eight and they have a brother who's ten. He's out at football training tonight. They're all Steve's, and he never sends a penny back for them. Too busy spending it on himself.'

'It must be hard.' He cringed inwardly, embarrassed by the platitude but unsure what else he could say.

'It is. Very hard for her.' Vienna was thoughtful. 'You know, she's holding down three jobs at the moment. She does part time in Carvers, the bookies on the sea front, working as a cashier. And she works part time in the chippy next door. And then in the evenings, she's doing cleaning shifts at the ENB. Honest to God, Michael, I don't know how she does it.' She pouted and shook her head. 'The bastard even took their car with him, so she has to use the bus. If I didn't help out I don't know what she'd do.' She turned her clear, blue eyes directly on him. 'You won't believe this, but when you knocked at the door, I thought it was the rent collector.'

She was looking at him for some sort of reaction and he opened his mouth to speak, but the words wouldn't come. He reached out and picked up the coffee she had made for him, and drank it down, gulping at the sweet milky liquid. He cleared his throat. 'Good job it was just me, then, eh?'

She was still staring at him. 'She ran out of savings in August, and bust the limit on her credit card in September. Everything else is up to date. Well, everything except the rent, of course.'

'The rent?' His heart started to beat quickly deep inside his chest.

'The rent. The rent she owes to Hector Campling.' Vienna smiled, and her smile was still warm and friendly. 'I know she's behind with the rent, Michael. She tells me everything. I'm just glad it was you that came to talk to her about it, instead of some heavy-handed lowlife that would have tried to screw the money out of her.'

Spivey felt a wave of dismay flood over him. She knew. She knew why he'd come, and she knew what he was. The one person in his life that mattered to him, the one person who showed an interest, who spoke to him kindly, who gave him a reason to hope for the future … she knew what he was, and she was trying to shame him into admitting it. 'Vienna, I didn't know you'd be here, honest I didn't. I fought I was just collecting the overdue rent from some tart.'

'I know you didn't expect to see me here, Michael. But I still don't understand why you said you wouldn't have come here if you'd known.' Her smile began to fade. 'I hope you're going to explain it to me. And I hope that when you do, you might see your way to stop referring to my sister as a tart.'

17

George Mulligan was still smiling to himself as he pulled DS Scott's Audi onto the Market Melbourne bypass in the direction of Kirkby. The lad was punching well above his weight if he had designs on Rose Bennett, but he couldn't blame him. Rose didn't look anything like her aunt, but she had the same quick wit and free spirit that had tempted him to punch above his own weight and set his cap at Lu Aylesbury some twenty odd years ago. And much good it had done him.

He pondered momentarily how different his life might have been if the elegant and sophisticated Lu had chosen him over the chance to further her career overseas, and then decided that his day had been bad enough without remembering what he'd once had and then carelessly lost. He switched on the radio and searched for a classical station, turning the volume down low so that the music provided an unobtrusive backdrop to his thoughts.

He did some of his best thinking in the car, alone with the road and the music, no one to distract him. And thinking was all he had at the moment, because two days on there were still very few facts available about the death of Andy Miller. Forensics were still working on the BMW, and witness statements had proved fruitless. If there were no new facts, then there would have to be some conjecture, some artful speculation.

Clive Barden had wanted to know if the police suspected an ENB employee of involvement in Andy Miller's death. There were no direct grounds for any such suspicion, but Clive Barden's skill was in managing risk. If he was looking at Andy Miller's colleagues and seeing risk for the bank, then maybe he was coming to the same speculative conclusions as Mulligan.

Mulligan knew that Clive was planning to suspend Jodie Pearce and Chris Kemp so that he could distance the ENB from the police investigation, distance the bank from Andy's death, to mitigate the risk of bad publicity. He couldn't help wondering if Clive could smell risk in the way that he himself believed he could smell guilt.

Both Jodie and Chris had the opportunity to murder Andy Miller, working either together or alone. Both had access to the flat, and therefore to the BMW's spare keys. Either of them could have taken the keys before Sunday evening. A spare set was unlikely to be missed. Jodie had left the pub at nine o'clock on the evening of Andy's death, and didn't have an alibi from nine until she arrived home at just after ten. Chris had an alibi, but Scottie didn't think it was unbreakable. Mulligan himself didn't particularly agree, but he couldn't deny that it was a possibility.

And whichever way you looked at it, they both had a motive. Jodie wanted Andy, but Andy had stopped wanting her back. Chris wanted Annabel, but Andy was in the way. He muttered it to himself again, under his breath. *Chris wanted Annabel, but Andy was in the way.*

If Jodie wanted Andy, she was hardly likely to murder him. She would have murdered Annabel, wouldn't she? Didn't it make sense that she would get rid of the opposition and leave the way clear for a reconciliation with Andy? But what if she had decided not to bother getting rid of the opposition? What if she *had* gone to Bellevue Mansions on Sunday evening to offer herself up to Andy Miller on a plate while his girlfriend was out of town. What if he rejected her, laughed at her, maybe pushed her out of the flat? Mulligan had seen and heard enough of her anger today to believe she was capable of lashing out, of wanting to punish Andy for the rejection.

Was that theory more or less likely than the possibility of Chris Kemp murdering his flat mate so he could clear the path to the lovely Annabel's door?

They could have been in it together, of course. Chris Kemp stays safe in the pub, calls Andy Miller to ask him to open the outer door to the flats in advance of arriving home, while Jodie Pearce walks up to Bellevue Mansions, lets herself into the BMW with the spare key, and waits until Andy comes down into the car park. She revs the engine to make him think the car is being stolen, he dashes out to stop the thief, and she runs over him.

No, that's not it. There's no motive there. What possible joint motive could they have? Mulligan shook his head, dissatisfied with his own theories. Jodie wanted Andy and hated Annabel. Why would Jodie collude with Chris to murder the man she supposedly still loved? Even if she wasn't looking for a reconciliation, even if she wanted to murder Andy for revenge, she was hardly likely to take a course of action which would clear the path for Chris Kemp to make hay with Annabel. It didn't make sense.

No, there was only one possible scenario that made sense to George Mulligan, even if he hadn't yet worked out how it was done. Clive Barden was suspending Jodie Pearce and Chris Kemp because he could smell risk hanging over both of them. But Mulligan couldn't smell guilt in the same places. Mulligan could only smell guilt on one of them.

And if he trusted his gut and his sense of smell on this one, it had to be Chris Kemp acting alone.

The blow came from nowhere, totally unexpected.

It hit him on the back of the head with a dull thud and momentarily everything plunged into darkness, and then a million tiny pinpricks of light flashed behind his eyes. His body stiffened, a subconscious reflex against … what? He grasped at memories, trying to recall why it was so important to stay still, stay upright, stay on land.

Stay on land. That was it. He was next to the water, next to the Mill Beck, the stream that skirted the edge of the cemetery. What was he doing in the cemetery? Walking home. He'd been out with Annabel, and now he was walking home past the cemetery, home from the pub, going home to pack. If he was going home to pack, why was he in the cemetery? And why did his head hurt so much?

The blow had left him dazed, bewildered, confused. The fingers he'd used to touch the back of his head felt sticky and he pulled them away, and tried to focus on them in the moonlight. They looked dark and red and wet, but he didn't know why. What was that dark, red, wet stuff on his fingers?

He swayed slightly and started to turn his head. There was someone behind him, someone holding something. He tried to focus his eyes but everything was blurred. The something was waving at him, level with his chest, as if the someone holding it was trying to push him with it. Who was the someone? And why were they trying to push him?

He swallowed hard. His head hurt so much and his eyes were beginning to ache. They filled with tears, distorting even further the indistinct shapes in front of him. He put out a hand, the hand without the dark, red, wet stuff on it, and tried to speak. 'Who?' It came out like an exhalation of breath, a puffing of air, almost soundless. He blinked hard. Why wouldn't his voice work?

The shapes were moving to the other side of him now, and he turned his body to follow them. The stiffness in his limbs was starting to relax, and he could feel his knees starting to fold. He lunged at the someone and tried to grab the something, desperate for an anchor on dry land, but he misjudged the move and his hands grasped on empty air.

It was a costly mistake. The something hit him straight in the chest, another forceful blow that punched the air from his lungs and tipped his body backwards. And he was falling, falling into the freezing cold water of the Mill Beck, his arms flailing and thrashing as he frantically tried to keep his balance.

The icy water enveloped him in seconds, squeezing the remaining air from his chest, freezing his clothes to his skin. The stream was barely eighteen inches deep, but it was deep enough. He lay motionless in the water, his eyes open, watching the someone stand over him. He saw the someone toss the something into the stream and it landed beside him, rippling the water over his face. He opened his mouth to speak, to scream, to plead. To beg the someone to help him. But no sound came out.

He should have kept his mouth shut. Freezing cold water made its way into his open mouth, down his throat, into his stomach and his lungs. He coughed violently as his body tried to expel the water, and then collapsed back into the stream as it failed in its effort.

Somewhere above him the someone watched as he struggled to free himself from the Mill Beck's icy grip, waiting for him to surrender to his fate, staring coldly into the water, just waiting for Chris Kemp to die.

18

'There weren't no-one in, Mr Campling. Straight up.' Michael Spivey shuffled his feet and kept his eyes downcast towards them.' I went back to the flat at six o'clock like I'd agreed with him, but there weren't no-one in.'

Hector Campling fixed him with a resigned stare. 'There *wasn't anyone* in,' he corrected. He exhaled his disappointment with a deep audible sigh and leaned back in his leather chair, his eyes fixed on Spivey's face. 'Did you go back, Michael? Did you try again, later in the evening?'

Spivey's cheeks flushed. 'I meant to. But I was busy, like. On the other call.' He risked a glance at the solicitor's face, registered disappointment, and lowered his eyes back to his boots.

'So nothing again from Bellevue Mansions.' Campling clicked his teeth. 'Then I think we have waited long enough.' He reached down and opened a drawer in the right hand pillar of his desk, and pulled out a small set of keys. He leaned across the table and offered them to Michael Spivey. 'These are the keys to flat 2d, Michael. I would like you to go back there this morning and recover goods from Mr. Miller's estate to cover our losses.'

Spivey hesitated, then swallowed hard and took the keys from Campling's hand. His voice became a whisper. 'Yes, Mr Campling.'

Campling picked up his pen and tore a sheet from a notebook at the side of his desk. 'In Mr Miller's bedroom,' he lifted his eyes to look into Spivey's face, 'that is the room with a fur throw over the end of the bed,' he looked back at the piece of paper and began to write a list, 'you will find a large chest of drawers. In that chest of drawers you will find a laptop computer and an iPad. In the bedside table you will find a black leather box containing a watch, bring only the watch and leave the box behind. In the kitchen you will find a coffee-making machine, and in the lounge a stereo unit and a wide-screen TV. I would like you to recover these goods to offset our losses.'

Spivey listened in silence. He didn't want to know how the solicitor knew exactly where he could find Andy Miller's most valuable possessions, but he had a pretty good idea. He cleared his throat but his voice still rasped a hoarse whisper. 'Scuse me, Mr. Hector, but I am allowed to do that? I mean, I ain't a bailiff, am I?'

Campling gave a low incredulous laugh and shook his head. 'Your honesty is refreshing Michael, and it does you credit. You know,' he relaxed into his chair, 'sometimes the world simply doesn't work the way it is supposed to. Mr. Miller failed repeatedly to repay the rent he owed to us, even though he had the money to pay. Is that not a form of theft? He deprived us of the moneys rightfully due in return for the privilege of living in flat 2d. Mr Kemp also owes us money for the privilege of living in flat 2d, but seems equally disinclined to pay.' He paused to give Spivey time to catch up. 'Sometimes, Michael, when the law lets us down we might find it necessary to give it a helping hand by applying a more natural set of laws to the situation. Mr Miller sadly no longer needs his laptop, his iPad, watch, coffee maker, stereo or TV. I don't think anyone would begrudge us the opportunity to offset our losses with items which are no longer required.'

Spivey considered for a moment, his face twitching as he contemplated what was being asked of him, and then he whispered his reply. 'Yes, Mr Campling.'

'Good.' Satisfied momentarily, the solicitor turned his

attention to another matter. He picked up a second piece of paper from his desk, and glanced at it. 'So now shall we discuss your other errand? What progress did we make with Miss Fielding?'

Spivey shuffled his feet. 'I went to Miss Fielding's house, like you asked, Mr Hector.' He gave a sniff. 'She's a nice lady, Mr Hector, keeps the place real nice.'

Campling looked up from his desk and raised an eyebrow. 'I'm glad to hear it.'

Spivey swallowed hard. 'It's hard for her, like. Free kiddies and free jobs. And still a struggle to pay for everyfing.'

The solicitor's eyes narrowed. 'Thank you Michael, I wasn't looking for a lecture on the socio-economic challenges faced by single mothers on the Barnfield Estate.' He chuckled at his own facetiousness.

Spivey didn't share his amusement. Lost for a moment in the depth of his own thoughts, he found himself unexpectedly torn between honesty and deceit. It wasn't a choice unfamiliar to him, and he didn't usually have any difficulty pulling a hefty lie out of the bag when it was needed. But this felt different.

Hector Campling was expecting him to produce three hundred pounds in rent arrears, like three hundred rabbits out of a hat. Three hundred pounds from a young woman who was struggling to keep her head above water and her pride intact. And he couldn't do it. He couldn't do it, because she simply didn't have that sort of ready money. His hand strayed to the left hand pocket of his jacket and he fingered the fifty quid Vienna had given him last night, five crumpled ten pounds notes out of her own pay. Something on account, she'd said. Something on account, because she's my sister.

He frowned, thinking for a moment of flat 2d, and what was expected of him. What was going to happen when Hector found out that he hadn't collected the full rent arrears from Florence Fielding? Was he going to present him with another set of keys and send him back to the Barnfield to collect the microwave?

No, fifty quid just wasn't going to be enough, not when he'd failed to collect on flat 2d. Across the desk Hector Campling was watching him, an intense, almost questioning gaze, as if the solicitor was trying to penetrate his thought process. He forced a smile. 'Sorry Mr Hector, wrong pocket.' He pulled his hand out of his jacket pocket and slowly retrieved his wallet from the rear pocket of his trousers. 'I forgot I put it here for safe keeping.'

He pulled a small wad of twenties from the wallet and counted them out on the desk while the solicitor watched with incredulity. 'Two sixty, two eighty, free hundred, Mr Hector. Free hundred in rent arrears for Florence Fielding, just like you said.'

DS Scott hated the smell of hospitals, that pungent mix of disinfectant and surgical spirit that invaded your nostrils and refused to leave, lingering sometimes until long after you had left the building. The stench in this particular hospital was strong, almost overpowering, and coupled with lack of sleep was beginning to make him feel nauseous.

He swigged the dregs from his third plastic cup of machine coffee and screwed up his face in disgust. Even the coffee had an antiseptic flavour. If Chris Kemp didn't regain consciousness soon he would have to risk missing the moment and go in search of breakfast and a decent brew.

He leaned back against the wall in the small waiting room, resting his head against the cold painted surface. There was no door on the room and he could see out across the ward and into a glass cubicle where Chris Kemp was hooked up to various monitors and beeping boxes. There was no question that the lad had been lucky.

At least one of them had. Scott pursed his lips at the

thought of his ruined evening, his first taste of female company in months cut short by the discovery of Chris Kemp's body in the Mill Beck, and a call summoning him to the crime scene. It had been good of Rose to drive him back over to Scarborough so late at night. Maybe there would be an opportunity to make it up to her.

He was about to follow a train of thought that would lead to Rose, himself, and a decent restaurant somewhere in Kirkby, when his mobile phone began to vibrate in the depths of his pocket, and he fished it out with a frown, glancing at the display before answering. 'Thanks for getting back to me, George.'

Mulligan's voice crackled at the other end of the line. 'Any news?'

'Not much. I spoke to the doctor about an hour ago. They found a head wound to the back of the skull. It looks as though someone attacked him and left him in the water, hoping it would finish him off. The doc says it's almost a miracle he survived. He would have been concussed after the blow. The water wasn't deep enough for him to drown, but given the temperature he wouldn't have lasted long. She reckons given the loss of blood from the head wound, the shock of the blow and the effects of the icy water, he wouldn't have lasted beyond an hour.'

'So the attack was within an hour of him being found?'

'I guess so. He was found at around ten twenty, the ambulance responder reached him very quickly, maybe as soon as five minutes. His core body temperature had dropped, so they think he had been in the water about twenty to thirty minutes by that point.' Scott paused and thought about the timings. 'He must have been attacked sometime after nine thirty, more likely closer to ten o'clock.'

Mulligan growled at the other end of the line. 'I thought we had him, Scottie. He's involved in this Andy Miller business somehow, I just know he is.' He let out a heavy sigh. 'Have you spoken to him yet?'

'They won't let me. The doc says it could be a couple of hours yet. I've spoken to a nurse who was here when he was admitted. She said he had moments of consciousness but nothing he said made much sense. He kept asking for Annabel.'

'Annabel Halmshaw?'

'I suppose so.'

'Did he ask for Jodie Pearce at all?'

'Not that I've heard. There was something else, something about a bag. And a locker. But she reckons it was all very incoherent. Odd words and phrases.'

'A locker and a bag? A sports bag, maybe? A locker at the gym? If he'd had a bang on the head he wouldn't be thinking straight, he may just have been mumbling whatever came into his mind at the time. Do we know what he'd been doing earlier in the evening? Had he been to a gym?'

'I dunno, George. Who would we ask? He doesn't have a flatmate now, does he?'

'Try Annabel Halmshaw or Jodie Pearce. Either of them might know what he did after leaving work yesterday.' He thought for a moment. 'It's pointless you spending all day over there sitting around waiting for him to come round. Give it another hour, and see what you can get out of his parents. I'll arrange for someone to come up there and take over from you. After that get yourself over to the ENB's office and see what you can turn up. You can always go back to the hospital when Chris is ready to talk.'

'OK. Anything else?'

'I don't think so.' Mulligan thought for a moment, then said 'Chris Kemp wanted what Andy Miller had, Scottie. He had access to Andy Miller's car keys, and when Andy was murdered he had the flat to himself, and could safely cast off Andy Miller's ex and make a move on his current girlfriend. According to Rose he's even starting to dress like him. There's something unhealthy at the bottom of all this.'

'So you don't think the same person attacked both Andy Miller and Chris Kemp?'

'I don't know. The attack on Chris Kemp could have been pure coincidence. Someone looking for easy pickings, just targeting a young bloke who'd had a few on his way home from the pub. Make sure you check all of Kemp's belongings while you're there. Check for his wallet, phone and keys. If any of those are missing it could indicate a mugging.'

'OK. Anything else?'

'No. You stay on the Chris Kemp trail for now. I'm going to try to get access to that flat at Bellevue Mansions. There might be something useful in there.'

'How are you going to do that? One tenant is dead and the other is unconscious. And I can't see you getting a warrant just to have a sniff around.'

'Well, I'll just have to be a bit creative, won't I? Can we touch base again at lunchtime?'

'Sure.'

'How about the ENB's car park at twelve thirty? You could invite Rose Bennett along for an update. You probably owe her lunch after cutting short your date last night. I wouldn't want her to think that policemen are totally lacking in good manners.'

19

'I heard about Chris Kemp.' Stan Wilkins was not his usual jocular self. 'Seriously Rose, do you think someone's got it in for the ENB?'

Rose glanced around the staff restaurant. Every nearby table was occupied and she didn't want to be overheard. She tucked her mobile phone close to her ear and spoke into it quietly. 'I wouldn't worry too much. If it's a vendetta against the bank it's not likely to reach the IT department. Most people don't even know that you exist.'

'Good job for you that we do, though, eh?' He sounded tired. 'I've got you a list of calls made from that rogue extension. There's been about a sixty calls from that phone since the desk was vacated at the end of September, all of them made after core business hours.'

Rose gave a low whistle. 'So the call to Donovan wasn't a one-off.' She picked up a pen and started to scribble in her notebook. 'Is there any sort of pattern to the calls?'

'I should say so. They were all made in the late afternoon or early evening, say between five thirty and seven o'clock. And only on Mondays, Tuesdays and Thursdays.'

'Someone working late, then.'

'Mm. I did a bit of extra digging for you which might help. I had an idea where this was going.' He sounded thoughtful. 'When we leave a rogue phone line live in the office it's usually a magnet for personal calls. Someone finds out by accident that the phone is live, and tells everyone they can think of so they can make calls at the

ENB's expense without running up their mobile phone bills.'

'Lots of calls to Uncle Fred in New Zealand?'

'That sort of thing. Anyway, this phone is different. All the calls were made to numbers recorded on the ENB's systems. Every person called has a credit card account with the ENB, and that account is seriously in arrears.'

'So it's possible that the phone was being used just to harass customers?'

'Yes, it's possible. I'm going to send you the list of calls along with the names, addresses and account numbers of the people called. Some of the numbers have received multiple calls, although not all the calls were answered.'

'What about Robert Donovan?'

'He was called fourteen times over a two week period, but only that one call on November 18th was answered.'

'I'll have to feed this back to Clive.' Rose put down her pen. 'Stan, when you send the data over can you flag for me which calls were actually answered? We might have to cross check those numbers to Customer Service calls to see if there were any other complaints.'

'Sure.'

'Thanks. By the way, did you have any luck with the Florence Fielding calls?'

'Yes, I did. Two calls were made to her from this rogue number, one unanswered on November 14th and one answered on the 15th. Then on the 16th she made an inbound call to Customer Services which was answered by extension 334.'

'Can you get me the recording of that call? As soon as possible?'

'Leave it with me. Do you want to know which desk in Customer Services it's attached to?'

Rose licked a finger and used it to flick back through the pages of her notebook. 'No, it's fine thanks.' She stopped flicking and ran her finger down a page of contact numbers until it came to rest on a familiar name. 'I already know who uses that extension. It's Annabel Halmshaw.'

Chris Kemp opened his eyes slowly and tried to work out where he was.

He was lying on some sort of bed, under what felt like a starched white sheet and a coarse blanket. Or perhaps more than one coarse blanket, judging by the weight. He was lying partially on his left side and through blurry eyes he could see only a magnolia-painted wall and, right at the edge of his field of vision, a blue plastic chair with a woman's brown coat draped over it. The coat looked vaguely familiar, but he couldn't be sure.

He wanted to move his head, to look in the other direction to see if it would give him any clues to his whereabouts, but his head felt heavy, like he was wearing some sort of hat or helmet that was weighing him down. He thought about lifting a hand to touch his head but both hands felt leaden, as though they were encased in weighted mittens. He blinked for a few moments, trying to clear the blurring in his vision, and then with immense effort slowly tried to roll his head to the right without moving the rest of his body.

The effort made his head hurt like hell, all of it, throbbing with a dull, interminable ache. But it also rewarded him with a different view through what appeared to be a glass wall, and beyond it to a bench some twenty feet away, occupied by what might be a middle-aged couple. His vision was too hazy to make out their features, but instinct recognised the couple as his parents. He blinked again, more forcefully now, and the blurring began to clear. The couple appeared to be deep in conversation with a tall man in a navy suit. The shape of the man reminded him of that policeman. What was his name? Scott? DS Scott, talking to his parents? Shit.

He squeezed his eyes tight shut again. Shit, shit, shit.

What was this place? A hospital? Why would he be in a

hospital? He gently rolled his head back towards the magnolia wall and tried to remember. It was cold. So cold. Like ice. He remembered feeling cold, clammy, wet. He was in the water. How did he come to be in the water? Who put him there?

It hurt too much to think and he relaxed for a moment, letting nothingness flood into his mind. Then he tried again. He remembered Annabel. He was with Annabel in the office. Annabel had a bruise on her face, and her lip was split and bloody. Jodie did that. Jodie attacked Annabel. He winced at the thought.

Annabel had been attacked by Jodie, and he'd offered to take her out for a pizza to cheer her up. And she had said yes. So they'd gone for pizza. They'd gone for pizza, and somehow he'd ended up in the hospital?

No, there was a bit missing. He had to remember.

Something about Graham Clarke. Yes, that was it. Graham Clarke had stopped them as they were leaving the office. He needed to speak to Chris. Chris was to stay away from the office until Andy's killer had been found. Andy's killer? Christ, that was it. Andy was dead.

He took a deep breath in through his nose and pushed the air out through his mouth. Steady now, it's coming back. He was to stay away from work until Andy's killer had been found. Why were they trying to get rid of him? Did they think he had something to do with it? He would get full pay, Graham said, but they wanted him out of the office.

Was it something to do with Mulligan? He pondered the name. Who was Mulligan? His mind rummaged for the facts, trying to remember. Mulligan was a policeman too, and Mulligan suspected him. He couldn't shake off the feeling that Mulligan suspected him of hurting Andy. Why would he hurt Andy? Andy was a mate. A brother. He loved Andy like a brother. Used to love Andy like a brother.

Did Annabel love him like he used to love Andy? Like

a brother? She'd gone out with him for pizza, and then gone home. She didn't want him to kiss her. He wanted to so much, and she wouldn't let him. She didn't trust him. He knew she didn't trust him, he could see it in the way she looked at him, but he didn't know why.

His mouth felt dry now and he opened his eyes and tried to tilt his heavy head forward a little so that he could look around the cubicle. There must be something for him to drink. His eyes found a jug of water on a small trolley at the other end of the room, but he knew he couldn't reach it, and he wasn't ready yet to let them know that he was awake. He closed his eyes again to think.

The Half Moon. After the pizza he'd gone to The Half Moon for a couple of pints, gone to think about what happens next. What happens to the bag in his locker? He'd forgotten to mention to Graham Clarke that he had stuff in his locker at work. Graham Clarke had taken his pass away from him, so now he couldn't get into the building. He needed to get that bag out of his locker.

If he could get hold of Annabel, he could give her the key and she could bring the bag to him. Get it out of the office in case he lost his job. If he lost his job, they would give the locker to someone else. And if they were going to give it to someone else, they would have to open it and make sure it was empty. But it wasn't empty. Somewhere in the office there would be a spare key, and Graham fucking Clarke would take that key and open his locker, and see what was in it. He needed Annabel to open the locker for him, before that happened, and take the bag back to his flat.

His flat? No, not his flat. Not now. That's why he'd stayed out late. He was avoiding somebody. Who was he avoiding? Something about the rent. A man. A man trying to collect the rent, intimidating him, threatening him. That's why he'd stayed out late. He was avoiding the rent collector.

Campling? Was that the name? Michael Campling? No,

not Campling. It began with an S. Slimey? Spiky? Spivey?

Spivey. That was it. Michael Spivey, and something about Campling? He opened his eyes. That's why his parents were here. He was going home. He was going home because the flat wasn't his anymore. The flat had never been his. And it couldn't be his now because he couldn't pay the rent. Was that how he'd ended up in hospital?

Because he couldn't pay the rent?

'Of course I will be pleased to assist in any way that I can.' Hector Campling leaned his elbows on the desk, steepled his fingers, and peered over the top of his reading glasses to fix unfriendly eyes on DI Mulligan's face. 'I take it this is in connection with Mr Miller's death?'

Mulligan noted that the solicitor looked anything *but* pleased to assist, and responded with a cheerful nod. 'As he was your tenant I thought you must know something about him. I've come to ask for any information you might have which may be useful to our enquiry.'

Campling's eyes widened a little and he forced an insincere smile. 'There is regrettably little I can tell you. Mr Miller was a satisfactory tenant. He took the tenancy on earlier this year and gave little trouble. As far as I am aware he maintained the property in line with the terms of his tenancy agreement. Ours was a purely business relationship, I had very little contact with the young man myself. I met him once, I think, when he came to the office to sign the tenancy agreement, but after that his rent was paid by standing order direct to the firm's bank account.'

'And Mr Kemp?'

The solicitor thought for a moment. 'Mr Kemp is a guest of Mr Miller's. Mr Miller's tenancy agreement gave him full authority to accommodate guests in the apartment.'

'And when did Mr Kemp first arrive at the apartment?'

'I'm afraid I don't know, Inspector. There was no requirement under the terms of the lease for Mr Miller to inform us if he had a guest to stay.'

'But you're happy for him to stay there at the moment?'

The solicitor's brow creased in contemplation. 'It appears Mr Kemp has made himself quite at home as Mr Miller's guest, but of course that situation cannot continue indefinitely, given Mr Miller's untimely demise. However, I don't wish to appear unsympathetic, so I haven't pressed the point. I'm sure the young man is well aware of the need to make alternative arrangements. If he doesn't contact me after a week or so, I will make an enquiry as to his intentions.' He forced a smile. 'As a business man I need to ensure that the property is tenanted. However, I am aware that Mr Kemp will need to move on, and Mr Miller's family will need the opportunity to remove his belongings from the apartment.'

Mulligan nodded thoughtfully. 'That's very decent of you, Mr Campling.' He leaned back in his seat, his eyes still fixed on Hector Campling's face. 'Have you spoken to Mr Miller's family? Have they been in touch with you?'

The solicitor's face reddened almost imperceptibly, and he gave a slight shake of the head. 'I'm afraid I am at a disadvantage there, Inspector. I am not acquainted with Mr Miller's family. They have made no attempt to contact me so far, and I was rather hoping that Mr Kemp would point them in my direction when the time was right.'

'I see.' Mulligan paused, and then asked 'have you met Chris Kemp, Mr Campling?'

'No, I'm afraid not.'

'So you know nothing about the attack on him?'

What colour there was in Hector Campling's face drained away and he straightened in his seat. 'An attack? At the flat?'

The policeman shook his head. 'No, not at the flat. Mr Kemp was attacked on his way back to the flat yesterday evening, halfway between The Half Moon public house and Bellevue Mansions.'

'I'm sorry to hear that.' The news had rattled him. 'May I ask if you have a suspect for the attack?'

Mulligan shook his head again. 'We're not aware of any witnesses and at this stage Mr Kemp isn't well enough to be interviewed.' He cleared his throat. 'We had hoped to access the apartment today to pursue one of our lines of enquiry, but of course Mr Kemp won't be able to assist with that now. I wonder … as you've so kindly agreed to help in any way that you can, could you perhaps step into the breach and make that possible for us?'

The solicitor's face registered first incredulity and then something that looked very much like distrust. He thought for a moment, his eyes away from Mulligan now, staring out of the window as he considered his response. 'May I ask what it is you are looking for?'

The policeman gave a self-deprecating laugh. 'I wish I could answer that, Mr Campling. Perhaps we're just looking for inspiration.'

Campling's eyes narrowed. 'It is a rather irregular request. You would have needed Mr Miller's permission to enter the property, and even though Mr Kemp is … indisposed … as a tenant of the property he would have to give his consent.'

Mulligan smiled. 'But as you've just rightly pointed out, Mr Kemp isn't a tenant of the property, is he? He's a non-paying guest. Which means I have to ask you, as the landlord. And as you have no personal interest in the property, you don't live there yourself, I can't imagine there would be any reason for you to refuse a reasonable request for access?'

The solicitor turned his gaze fully on George Mulligan's face. 'May I ask if you have considered applying for a warrant to search the property?'

Mulligan nodded. 'A perfectly reasonable question.' And one which he had no intention of answering. 'May I ask if you have any reason to refuse me access to the property?'

Backed into a corner, Campling bowed his head with a smile. 'Of course not, Inspector.' He glanced at his watch. 'I have a busy morning today, I'm afraid. But I could perhaps arrange to take you to the property myself this afternoon. Would three o'clock suit?'

'Three o'clock would suit very well, sir, thank you.' Mulligan got to his feet. 'I'll see you there, then. Bellevue Mansions, three o'clock.'

Outside in the hallway of Campling's office Mulligan permitted himself a quiet self-satisfied smile. He was looking forward to his next meeting with Hector Campling, and not just because he would have voluntary access to flat 2d Bellevue Mansions.

20

'I'll try not to keep you too long, Reggie. I know you must be snowed under with work now that Jodie and Chris are off site.' Rose offered a reassuring smile. She opened her notebook and scribbled his name and the date at the top of a clean page, then looked up at him over the top of her reading glasses. 'How are things going with the backlog?'

Reggie Croft blinked at her with inexpressive grey eyes and the merest hint of a smile. 'As well as you would expect, given that we're all working a double work queue.' For a man supposedly carrying twice his normal workload, his demeanour was curiously relaxed. 'We'll miss this month's targets, of course, we're not miracle workers.' He glanced away out of the window. 'But we'll do our best.'

'I heard that you've picked up Andy's workload as well as your own. I thought perhaps Graham might deal with that himself?'

Reggie thought for a moment. 'That would have been one solution, yes. But Graham has his own way of working. He's created a seventh queue for himself and has pulled a number of calls from each queue into it, so that his time is evenly spread across all six. That way he helps all three of us in equal measure.'

'That seems a very fair solution.' Rose suppressed a smile. It also afforded Graham a subtle way to monitor the progress of every queue being worked.

'As team leaders go, Graham seems to be very fair in his methods.'

'Was Andy Miller unfair?'

'Everyone has their own measure of fairness, Rose. And everyone has their own methods.' The cool grey eyes were still unreadable. 'I believe you wanted to speak to me about a call to Robert Donovan?'

'Yes. I understand his case was assigned to your workflow?'

'It was.'

'And you knew that he was a special case? That he was fairly recently bereaved?'

'Yes, I knew that. He didn't answer any calls. The workflow required me to repeat my calls on a daily basis until he answered. I just kept rolling the case forward to the next day.'

Rose put down her pen and folded her arms onto the table, leaning forward towards him. 'The trouble is, Reggie, someone at the bank *didn't* care about the bereavement and decided to push the point.' She fixed her eyes firmly on his face, but it remained impassive. 'I've learned in the last twenty four hours that Andy Miller tried to call Robert Donovan from his own phone line, even though the case wasn't in his work queue. Do you know anything about that?'

'Andy told me that he had called Mr Donovan during business hours, but that the call wasn't answered.'

'So you knew that Andy was following up on your calls?'

This time he paused and thought for a moment. 'Yes, he made no secret of the fact that he called customers from my work queue.' He tilted his head to one side and regarded her with a quizzical gaze. 'Forgive me, Rose, I thought you were only interested in one specific call to Mr Donovan? The one which his brother claimed breached regulations on customer treatment?' His lip curled into a contemptuous smile. 'That *is* the real reason you're here, isn't it? To see if one of us made that call?'

'Do you think Andy Miller made that call?'

The placid grey eyes narrowed almost imperceptibly.

'Do you?'

'I have no view one way or the other, Reggie. Tell me,' Rose leaned back in her seat, 'were you aware that Chris Kemp had also been following up on your calls?'

'Yes.'

'And you didn't report it to anyone?'

'Why would I?' He looked puzzled, and then his expression registered a glimmer of comprehension. 'Ah, because the making of follow up calls outside of the queue is against bank policy?' He nodded to himself. 'Yes, I can see why you would ask that. Frankly,' he fixed the grey eyes back on her face, 'I didn't think it was my place to report it. The calls weren't made from my number, Rose. Or from the workflow system. So they wouldn't be tied back to me in any way. And it's not my job to police the actions of my colleagues.'

Rose arched an eyebrow. 'You don't think it's your responsibility to report wrong-doing amongst your colleagues?'

His face relaxed into an unexpectedly friendly smile. 'Come on, Rose, surely even an independent investigator like yourself understands that not everyone is happy with the idea of being a snitch? Not even an old-timer like myself.' The idea evidently amused him. 'My job is to recover monies owed to the bank in line with the processes I'm asked to follow. I do what is expected of me. That is, I do my job to the best of my ability, within the parameters set by the ENB.'

'And no more?'

'Look, when I started in recovery work nearly thirty years ago it was common practice to do whatever it took to recover money for the bank. We were told that it was OK to pursue debts in any which way we could. We used threatening letters on ENB-headed notepaper. When they didn't work, we invented a fictional debt-collection firm called "Edgar, Neville and Brown" and registered them under the back-door address of the Scarborough office.

Then we sent more threatening letters using headed notepaper with the fictional debt-collection firm's details on it. And when that didn't work, we searched for details of the customer's relatives and sent threatening letters to them. If I go back as far as 1989 I can remember sending a letter to a grandmother demanding that she repay her grandson's debt unless she wanted debt collectors calling at her home.'

'And that approach didn't fit with your own moral compass?'

Reggie shook his head. 'Whether I liked it or not didn't come into the equation, Rose. I was paid to do as I was told. In those days if you wanted to keep your job at the ENB you couldn't afford the luxury of a moral compass. But I don't have to do that now.' He took in a deep breath. 'I don't have to do anything that feels wrong. Because the regulation doesn't just protect the customer. It protects the employee. If we are not permitted to bully customers to repay what they owe, then that's fine by me, because it also means I don't have to act like a bully in order to earn my salary.'

'And what about other people bullying customers? Robert Donovan was in your work queue. He was your customer.'

'No Rose, he was the ENB's customer. I am a cog in the wheel.'

'So you don't care who made the harassing phone call to him, even though he was in your workflow? Your responsibility to look after? Your responsibility to ensure he got fair play?'

He closed his eyes and shook his head gently. 'It's not a question of whether I care, Rose. I'm not paid to care. I'm paid to go through the process.'

Rose picked up her pen and scribbled a cursory note in her notebook. She kept her eyes downcast, fixed on the page, so that Reggie couldn't see her face while she considered her next move. There was something about

Reggie that just didn't stack up. That comment of Clive's about clipping his wings, that didn't make sense. All through the conversation she had tried to visualise Reggie as a latter-day Andy Miller, ambitious, motivated, the rising star that Clive had referred to. But however hard she tried to look past the mild-mannered demeanour, past the middle-aged choice of sober shirt and tie, through the placid grey eyes into what made him tick, she just couldn't see it.

She smiled and lifted her head to look at him. 'Just one more question, Reggie, if you don't mind?'

'Of course.'

'Did you make that harassing phone call to Robert Donovan?'

The question hung between them for two, three, maybe four seconds, and then Reggie's eyes shrank into malevolent slits. 'I beg your pardon?' He asked the question so quietly Rose could hardly hear him.

She held her smile steady. 'The harassing phone call to Robert Donovan was made by a male caller, from a telephone on an empty desk maybe less than fifteen feet away from your own. Robert Donovan was listed on your work queue. Did you make that call?'

'No.' His voice was louder now, his tone firm, just the safe side of angry.

'Do you know who did?'

'No.'

'Clive speaks very highly of you, Reggie.'

Reggie stiffened. 'What the hell has that got to do with anything?' He was unsettled now, and the clear grey eyes were turning cloudy.

'Clive has told me that you were one of the best recovery agents this bank has ever produced.'

'And now I'm one of the worst? Is that the implication?'

Rose smiled. 'Not at all.' Her own tone of voice was still level, conciliatory. She put down her pen and closed her notebook. 'Thank you for your help.' It was an invitation to draw the conversation to a close.

An invitation he hadn't expected. For a few moments Reggie remained seated at the other side of the table and then he realised that she was dismissing him and he rose to his feet. 'I'll see you later then, Rose?' His tone had softened again, his face a little concerned now that he had shown too much of his true nature.

She looked up at him and smiled with an inscrutability that rivalled his own. 'Sure. Thanks again for your time.' She watched as he turned and walked away down the office, and then picked up her pen and re-opened her notebook. There were two questions she still didn't have answers to.

Question One: did Reggie mind that Andy and Chris were chasing his customers for payment? The obvious answer would be yes unless, of course, you didn't want to bully those customers yourself and were happy to let someone else do it for you.

And Question Two: if the answer to Question One was yes, Reggie did mind, because he was tired of being made a fool of by Andy and Chris, then did he mind enough to take it upon himself to do something to make them stop?

It was almost midday when Michael Spivey pulled his aging Vauxhall Vectra into the car park of The Feathers. He turned off the ignition and felt his own body relax as the car's engine stuttered to a halt. He leaned forward and rested his forehead on the steering wheel, exhausted by his morning's work.

It hadn't been tiring in a physical sense. Shifting a few bits and pieces in and out of his car, that was no big deal. He did that sort of thing all the time. No, it was the anxiety that got to him, that constant feeling that he was just a few seconds or a few inches away from being caught out.

He'd collected most of the items from flat 2d that

Hector Campling had requested. The laptop, the iPad and the coffee maker were all safely nestled in a cardboard box on the passenger seat beside him. The stereo unit and the widescreen TV had fitted neatly – just – into the Vauxhall's spacious boot.

But the watch?

He squeezed his eyes tight shut and retraced his search for the watch in his mind's eye. Mr Campling had said it would be in the drawer in the bedside cabinet. A black leather box, Mr Campling said, containing a watch. Bring only the watch, and leave the box behind. Those were his instructions.

Michael had found the right bedroom, the one with a fur throw on the bed, and found the laptop and the iPad without difficulty in the chest of drawers. But there was no black leather box in the bedside cabinet. No black leather box, and no watch.

He'd tried the other bedside cabinet, but found only two pairs of pyjamas and an unopened packet of condoms. He blushed at the thought. That was something else that the poor bloke didn't need any more.

A further search of Andy Miller's room had proved fruitless and, never one to give up too easily, Spivey had applied to the problem what bit of common sense he possessed, and searched the other bedroom, the one used by Chris Kemp. A search of the wardrobe, chest of drawers and bedside cabinets had proved equally unproductive. There was no sign of either the black leather box or the watch.

He could only think that Mr Campling had made a mistake.

He chuckled to himself at the thought and the laugh jolted his head, gently banging his forehead against the steering wheel into the bargain. He sat up and stared out through the windscreen, across the car park to the rear entrance of the pub. He was going to need a pint at least before breaking that news to Hector. And a smile from

Vienna. She was working this lunchtime. He could tell her he'd squared things with Hector, that Florence wouldn't be chased for the rent arrears for a while. She'd like that.

And so would he. He liked the idea of doing something good for her, it made him feel … well, important. He'd matter to her now. He was her knight in shining armour. Except it wasn't Vienna he was rescuing, it was her sister. He chuckled to himself again. He didn't have any shining armour, either, just a rusting Vauxhall.

What did it matter? He pulled the keys out of the ignition and put out his hand to open the car's door, and then remembered his mobile phone. He'd received a text while he was driving, he remembered the phone vibrating in his jacket pocket as he'd turned left at the traffic lights. He pulled the phone from his pocket and tapped at it. There was a text from Benny, and two missed calls to go with it.

Missed calls and texts from Benny were never good news. He opened up the text and read it, then switched off the phone and pushed it back into his pocket. That was another tricky one to add to his list for this afternoon, then. Conjure up three hundred quid out of fresh air to pay Benny's business account at the newsagents.

Somehow he didn't think Benny was going to agree that paying Florence's rent was more important than receiving his regular copies of the Racing Post.

21

The Riverside Café was a tidy little establishment tucked down the side of the ENB's Scarborough office, and nowhere near a river. Most of its trade came from bank workers who queued steadily from late morning to early afternoon to buy sandwiches, burgers, jacket potatoes and other unimaginative lunchtime offerings. When Mulligan and Scott arrived the queue for takeaway food was already snaking along the counter, out through the door, and along the front of the building.

Fortunately for them dine-in customers were a rarity and the proprietor, a hard-faced blonde with blood-red lips and nails to match, ushered them past the mayhem of the counter to the peace and quiet of a corner table before taking their order.

Mulligan slipped off his overcoat and threw it over an empty chair before sitting down. 'So the lovely Rose has blown us out then?' He grinned at DS Scott as he took his seat. 'Are you losing your touch?'

The sergeant laughed. 'Give me time, George, I'm still in first gear.' Divested of both his coat and his jacket he tugged up his shirt sleeves and leaned his elbows on the table. 'It doesn't do to rush these things, not if they're worth doing properly.' The blonde reappeared with two Italian coffees, which she placed down on the table without a word before retreating back behind the counter.

Scott scooped a spoonful of sugar into his cup and slowly stirred it round. 'Rose is up for meeting with us, but she's asked if we can do it after office hours. She thinks it makes more sense, then she can fill us in on everything she's turned up today.'

'Fair enough. Let's hope she has something for us.' Mulligan sipped on his coffee and savoured the caffeine hit. 'Did you get anywhere with Jodie Pearce?'

'I managed to get through to her on the phone. She was at home licking her wounds. She reckons Chris Kemp plays football with some of the lads from work, and he's a member of the local running club, but he doesn't have a gym membership. I asked if she'd ever heard him mention a locker, and she said that every member of staff at the ENB has a locker in the office. It's company policy for them to only keep business documents in their desks, so all their personal belongings go in a locker.'

'Do they, now? Maybe that's something Rose could follow up for us.' Mulligan looked thoughtful. 'Had she heard about Chris Kemp being attacked?'

'No. At least that's what she told me. I told her not to worry about him, that he was on the mend.' DS Scott shook his head with a wry smile. 'She told me she had no intention of worrying about him.'

'Well, I don't suppose I can blame her for that. Did you ask if she had any idea about his movements last night?'

'It was a touchy subject. She thought he was out with Annabel Halmshaw.'

'Did she, now? And does Annabel corroborate that?'

'I couldn't get hold of her. She's in the office today, but she wasn't at her desk when I went looking for her. She'd gone out for an early lunch. I got her mobile number from her team leader and tried calling but she's not answering. I'll try again this afternoon.' He nodded to himself. 'Did you get anywhere with access to Bellevue Mansions?'

Mulligan looked smug. 'I've persuaded Mr Hector Campling to give me a guided tour this afternoon.'

'Without a warrant? I'm impressed, George. I didn't think he'd be that helpful.'

'Neither did I, to be honest, considering I nabbed his

old man for money laundering. Maybe he decided it was a good idea to keep on the right side of me.' Mulligan sipped on his coffee. 'I asked him about Andy Miller. He reckons he only met him the once, and he's never met Chris Kemp. Chris Kemp was just staying at the flat as a guest.'

Scott's face lit up with a broad grin. 'A guest? And you fell for that?' He leaned forward across the table. 'He's had you there, George. I've been speaking to Chris Kemp's father at the hospital this morning. According to him, Chris had been planning to go home and live with the family again. There's been trouble over that flat. Chris had been paying a share of the rent to Andy Miller, but there was no right to sub-contract. Meanwhile Andy Miller hasn't been paying the rent at all. According to Mr Kemp the rent was three months in arrears and the landlord had been pressing for the money. He reckons Chris was threatened by a debt collector on Monday evening, pay up or else.'

Mulligan turned incredulous eyes on his partner. 'When the hell were you planning to tell me this?'

'I'm telling you now.' Scott laughed and wagged a finger at his senior officer. 'And don't be losing your rag with me because you fell for Mr Campling's patter.'

'The devious, lying …' Mulligan scowled and shook his head. 'How is Chris Kemp now? Any chance of being able to speak to him yet?'

'He's poorly, but he'll live. The doctor thinks I should be able to talk to him this afternoon so long as I keep it brief. I'm going back to the hospital after I've seen Annabel Halmshaw. Do you want to come with me?'

'And miss my appointment with Hector Campling? Not bloody likely.'

'It's very kind of you to let me share your table.' Annabel rolled her doe eyes towards Rose and threw in a mournful smile for good measure. She looked tired today, her face pale, her normally lustrous chestnut locks dull and lifeless. 'To be honest, I'm not really hungry but my team leader insisted I take a lunch break so I thought I should at least come up to the restaurant and take some time out and have a coffee.'

If Rose resented the intrusion she was too polite to say so. And anyway, the girl looked as though she needed a square meal and a good night's sleep. Rose didn't count compassion amongst her finer qualities, but she wasn't stone-hearted. 'Don't you think you should eat something?'

The doe eyes blinked back at her. 'I just don't seem to have an appetite today.' She wrapped her hands around her cup for comfort. 'You've heard about Chris?' She didn't wait for Rose to answer. 'Oh what am I saying? Of course you have. Everyone is talking about it.' She lowered her voice. 'The poor lamb. They're saying he might not make it through the day.' Her eyes widened. 'I was with him last night, Rose. I feel so awful. I left him to walk home on his own.' She bit her lip. 'He wanted me to stay and have another drink, but I was so tired after … well, after Jodie and everything. I just wanted to get home. And he wouldn't let me give him a lift back to the flat. He said he was just going to have another pint and then walk home.' Her eyes became suddenly moist. 'If I'd stayed a bit longer, he might have accepted a lift and then he wouldn't have been hurt.'

'You can't take responsibility for that, Annabel. It was probably a mugging. It's not anyone's fault.' Rose didn't actually believe her own explanation, but somehow she felt obliged to make the girl feel better. 'I'm sure he'll be OK.'

'Oh I do wish you were right, Rose, but that's not what people are saying. First Andy and now this.' She stared into her coffee. 'It all seems so unreal. Andy dead, and Chris dying, and here we are in the office chatting and drinking coffee as if nothing had happened.'

'Dying?' If Chris Kemp was dying it was news to Rose.

'Surely he's not that badly hurt?'

'It's what I've been told.' Annabel flicked the doe eyes up across the table. 'Rose?'

'Mm?'

'Do you think they will catch whoever killed Andy?'

Rose thought for a moment. 'Truthfully? I don't know. They don't seem to be making much progress so far.' She tried to look at Annabel through sympathetic eyes. The girl looked exhausted, lonely and lost. And yet the sympathy that she was trying to muster just wouldn't seem to come. She leaned a little closer to Annabel. 'What have the police got to say about it? Have they given you any indication that they are close to finding the killer?'

'Not really. They're just not including me in the investigation, to be honest. I was away over the weekend and on my way back from Cambridge when it happened. I'd been to visit my aunt and uncle.' She gave a shrug. 'Andy and I had been going out together for months, but I hadn't met his family. He didn't seem that close to them. But it's his mum and dad and his brother that are being kept in the loop, not me.' She swallowed back a tear. 'I've answered all DS Scott's questions, told him exactly where I was on Sunday night, but then after that it's like I don't count. Like I wasn't a part of Andy's life. We were going to move in together soon. Andy was going to ask Chris to move out, so that we could have the flat to ourselves. And I've never even met his family.'

Rose put out a hand and placed it gently on Annabel's arm. 'Well, it doesn't matter now, does it? Everyone here knows that you were a part of Andy's life. Chris knows. And Chris was close to him. Chris knows how important you were to Andy.'

At the mention of Chris Kemp's name Annabel's expression changed, the tearful sorrow morphing into a coy smile. 'Poor Chris. He was so kind to me yesterday. He was so kind to me, and yet …' Her face clouded, and the smile faded. 'I don't know if I should tell someone.' She fixed enquiring eyes on Rose's face, serious now. 'I know he was Andy's friend, they were almost inseparable.' She laughed. 'I should know, I spent enough evenings in the flat with the two of them, wishing Chris would give us some time to ourselves.' She paused, and then said 'but there was always something in the air. I can't explain it. It was like … Chris was jealous of him;'

'Jealous of Andy?'

'Yes.'

'Well, maybe he was. People can be friends and still be jealous.'

'Do you really think so? You know, I went out with Chris for a pizza last night. I just didn't want to be on my own. And … well … he didn't seem bothered that Andy was dead. He seemed … almost pleased. He kept talking about us, about me and him.' She shivered. 'I don't know where he got that idea from. I've always been friendly with him, but I've never led him to think … well … you know.'

Rose did know. And she'd seen and heard enough to believe that Annabel had done plenty to lead Chris Kemp into thinking that he had a chance. But if that was the game the girl wanted to play, she could afford to play along with it a bit further and see where it led. 'Perhaps he got the wrong end of the stick yesterday? After all, isn't that why Jodie attacked you?'

The question touched a nerve. Annabel's lower lip began to quiver and her eyes blinked back non-existent tears. 'I didn't know then that Chris had finished with her. It was only later that he told me he ended it because of me.' She leaned in to Rose with an earnest gaze. 'But I thought he was only comforting me, Rose. Because he was Andy's friend. I hope Jodie realises that now.' She fell silent for a moment, contemplating, and then blurted out 'Chris couldn't ever mean anything to me, not know that I know he's a thief.'

'A thief?' Rose frowned at the unexpected curve ball. 'What makes you say he's a thief?'

Annabel gave an earnest sniff and rolled ingenuous eyes at Rose. 'He was wearing Andy's cufflinks yesterday. I saw them.'

'Cufflinks?'

'Yes. The silver ones. I recognised them. He tried to say they were a present from his sister, but I know that can't be true. I bought those cufflinks for Andy after our first date, when I realised we had something special. And I bought them from an antiques fair in Cambridge. They were retro, nineteen fifties, the real thing.' She was becoming animated now. 'Chris said his sister bought them from Flemings in Kirkby but that can't be true. You couldn't buy these in a high street chain.' She was staring at Rose now with an expectant gaze. 'You see what this means? Chris must have stolen them. He must have taken them from Andy's bedroom after … after …' Her voice trailed off for a moment, and the doe eyes widened. 'Rose, do you think I should tell DS Scott about this?'

22

George Mulligan perched on the edge of the sofa and sniffed the stale air. The flat had been unoccupied for barely twenty four hours and already the aroma of Chris Kemp's unlaundered football kit had started to infiltrate the hallway, the kitchen, the lounge. He looked around the room with a policeman's eye and noted nothing out of place since he was last there. Well, nothing except the missing television.

Somewhere beyond the hallway he could hear cupboard doors open and close as Hector Campling took the opportunity to check the inventory of kitchenware that came with the flat. He was a snake, that Campling. Slippery as they come. Mulligan fished in his pocket and pulled out a packet of mints, popping one into his mouth. He crunched on it noisily as he thought, the strong vapours of menthol clearing his sinuses. Pity they couldn't clear his thoughts at the same time. He began to count mentally through the lies that the solicitor had already told him.

Lie number one: Andy Miller was a model tenant. And yet according to Chris Kemp's father, Andy Miller was three months behind with the rent.

Lie number two: Campling didn't have anything to do with Andy Miller. And again, according to Mr Kemp, Hector Campling was using a debt collector to chase the lad for payment.

Lie number three: Chris Kemp was a guest of Andy Miller's. If Campling didn't have any dealings with Andy on a day to day basis how did he even know that Chris

Kemp existed? He could have heard on the grapevine, possibly. But even then, why chase Chris for the rent if he was only a guest? Was he hoping to get lucky? Hoping that Chris wouldn't know his rights and think he was liable for the rent arrears?

He got up and walked over to the window, and looked out over the car park. He could clearly see the space allocated to Andy Miller's BMW, empty now except for six or seven bunches of rotting flowers, tributes from family and friends. Something out there had brought Andy out into the car park without a coat or shoes, something important enough to forget his own comfort, his own safety. Was it really just someone trying to steal the car?

Was Hector Campling, or someone on behalf of Campling, trying to steal the BMW? He shook his head. Why run the lad down if you just wanted his money? He couldn't pay what he owed if he was dead.

Behind him the lounge door opened and Hector Campling paused in the doorway. 'May I do anything else to assist you, Inspector?'

Mulligan turned to him. 'How many sets of keys are there to the flat, Mr Campling?'

'There are four. Two were given to the tenant, and two are in my possession.'

'So Andy Miller had a set, and we can assume that he gave his spare set to Chris Kemp.'

The solicitor bowed his head in agreement. 'I would assume so.'

'And the other two sets are yours.'

'Yes.'

'So you also have access to the apartment. You can come and go as you please?'

Campling bridled. 'I have not entered this flat, Inspector, since before the tenancy agreement was signed.'

Mulligan smiled. 'I'm sure.' He fished in the pocket of his overcoat and pulled out his mobile phone, and brought up the last text received from Scott. He nodded to himself and put the phone back in his pocket. 'So no one else has a set of keys?' He noted a look of impatience on the solicitor's face and put up a hand. 'Sorry to press the point, Mr Campling, but I'm trying to establish who had access to the property.'

'Very well.' Campling's tone was blunt. 'No one else has a set of keys to the apartment. I really don't see the relevance, Inspector. The young man was killed in the car park.'

Mulligan nodded. 'Indeed. And whoever was driving the car that killed him was using a spare set of car keys that were kept in a drawer in the console table out in the hallway. So anyone who had access to the flat also had access to those spare keys.' He leaned back on the window sill and folded his arms across his chest. 'Does Michael Spivey have a set of keys to the apartment?'

Campling's face turned suddenly pale. 'Michael Sp ….
I'm sorry, I don't really understand the question.'

'Well,' Mulligan smiled as he explained his viewpoint, 'I've heard a little story about Michael Spivey. He runs errands for you, doesn't he, just like he did for your father?' He watched the solicitor's face and was rewarded with a look of discomfort. 'I've heard a little story about this flat, too. I've heard that far from being a model tenant, Andy Miller was three months behind with the rent. And I've heard that you, not liking Mr Miller being three months behind with the rent, sent Michael Spivey round here to press for payment.'

'Mr Miller's rent arrears were a private matter between Mr Miller and my firm, Inspector. I cannot see they bear any relevance to his death.' He cleared his throat. 'Mr Miller's financial affairs are confidential. It would have been a breach of client confidentiality if I had disclosed the situation to you.'

'So Spivey didn't have access to the flat?'

'No.'

Mulligan smiled, and nodded towards the dusty

television stand. 'I don't suppose you would have any idea what's happened to the TV set?'

'The TV?' Campling furrowed his brow. 'We didn't provide a television set with the furnishings, Inspector. Should there be one?'

The policeman's smile broadened. 'There was certainly one here when we questioned Chris Kemp on Sunday night.' He looked around the room. 'There was a stereo, too.'

Campling's frown deepened. 'I wonder?' He glanced down at the typed inventory he was holding. 'Everything in the kitchen appears to be in order, except …' He ran a finger absently down the list. 'Yes, the coffee maker.' He looked up at Mulligan. 'We provided a coffee machine with the apartment. The terms of the tenancy are for the property to be part-furnished, and we like to ensure that our tenants have a well-equipped kitchen.'

'And?'

'It's missing.' Campling's smile was almost guileless. 'I couldn't find it anywhere.' He raised an eyebrow. 'I couldn't help wondering … well, a coffee maker seems such an unusual thing to help oneself to, but given that you've missed a TV set and stereo too … is it possible that Mr Kemp might have removed some of Mr Miller's possessions?'

'Are you accusing Mr Kemp of theft?'

'Good heavens, no. I thought perhaps he may have returned the items to Mr Miller's family.' The solicitor smiled. 'There was no suggestion at all of wrong-doing.'

Mulligan took a good look at Campling and had to suppress the laugh that was rising in his stomach. Oh there's been some wrong-doing here alright, he thought, but I'm not sure that Chris Kemp is at the bottom of it.

Reggie Croft took off his headphones and leaned back in his seat, rolling his shoulders back to ease the knot of tension forming between his shoulder blades. So far today he'd done almost double his usual quota of calls, rattling through them almost as quickly as he used to back in the day. It helped that Andy Miller wasn't looking over his shoulder now, peering at his work queue ten times a day, goading him about the amount of arrears he'd recovered, or more likely the amount he hadn't recovered.

Andy Miller. The cocky, arrogant little shit who didn't give a toss who he hurt, or who he stepped on to feather his own nest. Reggie's grey eyes narrowed. Andy Miller, always bigging himself up, breaching process to boost his own bonus payments, bullying customers to repay more than they could afford so that he could make the payments on the flash BMW that he'd overstretched to buy.

He snorted under his breath. There's no way that Andy Miller could afford a car like that, not on top of all the consumer crap he wasted money on, not on a team leader's salary. His frown lifted and his face softened with a half-smile. There was some sort of poetic justice about the way he died, mown down by the car he was always bragging about, the car he couldn't possibly afford. Reggie hoped the police were on to whoever did it, whoever it was that made the world a better place by snuffing out that delinquent. Whoever it was, they should give the guy a medal.

He gave a sigh and glanced at his watch. Four o'clock. He'd been in since seven thirty and strictly speaking it was time to go home now, but Graham Clarke had asked him to do an hour's overtime today, just an hour to help clear some of the backlog. He had no problem with that. Graham Clarke was OK.

He lifted his headset up from his desk and was just about to drop it over his ears when a girl's voice somewhere behind him caught his attention. He swivelled his chair a little to the left and took a subtle glance over his shoulder. Annabel was standing at the partition that bordered Rose Bennett's desk, her hands gently resting on the top of the panel, her head tilted to one side as she listened to something Rose had to say.

Such a pretty girl, Annabel Halmshaw. Whatever did a lovely girl like that see in a lowlife like Andy Miller? Just thinking about it made him angry and a surge of hot emotion flooded his body, making his face burn, his palms sweat, his pulse race.

It was such a long time ago. She'd grown into such a pretty girl, and she deserved so much better.

If it was her …

He took in a couple of deep breaths to calm himself.

It was her. He was sure it was. He'd been sure for a few days now. He'd only ever seen her in a photograph, a young girl with long dark hair and dark, expressive eyes. The photograph was in a newspaper, black and white, grainy and indistinct. But it was a large, large enough to imprint itself on his memory. The best part of seven years had gone by and she'd blossomed in those years, but her eyes hadn't changed.

They were still dark, still expressive, and for the most part still bewildered.

Chris Kemp turned his head towards the door and tried to focus on the female form framed in the doorway. His vision was still blurred but even through the fog he could tell that it wasn't Annabel. He closed his eyes to shut out the disappointment.

Jodie stepped quietly into the room, ignoring his silent rejection, and pulled the blue plastic chair up to his bedside so that she could sit beside him. 'Chris?' She leaned forward and whispered his name with more compassion than he deserved.

He opened his eyes slowly and looked at her. What was she doing here? Trying to make him feel worse? Could he feel worse? He didn't think so. He lay there blinking, waiting for her to speak again.

'I came to see how you are. I was worried about you.' It wasn't a lie. She looked worried. 'They told me at work this morning that you'd been hurt. I called the hospital a couple of times but they wouldn't tell me anything over the phone, so I came to see for myself.' She sniffed a self-deprecating laugh. 'I've been suspended, Chris. They won't let me back into the office.' She sniffed again. 'The police have told me I'm lucky, because Annabel doesn't want to press charges for assault.'

He cast his eyes downward and stared at the crisp, white hospital bedding. 'I don't know what to say.'

Jodie eyed him with resignation. 'There's no need to say anything. It's not your fault. We weren't right for each other, we both know that.'

Not right for each other? Not now. And never would be. Not now he'd made such a fool of himself. 'I've really screwed up, Jodie. I've screwed everything up.' He was trying to fight the inevitable slide into self-pity. 'It was good of you to come and see me. No-one else has bothered. From work, I mean.'

'Hasn't Annabel been?' It almost choked her to ask the question, but she asked it anyway.

'No.' He blinked back his disillusionment. 'She doesn't care. They gave me my phone back this afternoon. I tried to call her but she didn't answer. Didn't answer a text, either.' Truth be told, he had sent not one but six or seven texts that she hadn't responded to, but he wasn't going to admit this to Jodie. And despite the shame, there was another question he had to ask. 'I don't suppose you've heard from her?'

Jodie laughed under her breath. 'Why would I hear from Annabel Halmshaw? The last time I saw her I'd just smacked her across the mouth. I don't think I'm at the top of her Christmas card list.'

He closed his eyes. 'Sorry. It was a dumb question.' He tilted his head further in her direction and asked another. 'When will they let you go back to work?'

'I don't know. There was supposed to be a meeting about me today. How embarrassing is that? A whole management meeting just to discuss what I did to Annabel.'

'I'm sorry.'

'Don't be. Like I said, it wasn't your fault.' She looked at him with kindly eyes. Her change of mood was unexpected but he wasn't to know how exhausted he looked, the normally plump flesh of his pudgy face hanging loose around his skull, his eyes sunken into black hollows above sallow cheeks. 'You didn't deserve this, Chris.' She leaned closer still and laid a hand on his arm. 'What happened to you? Last night … who hurt you?'

Unbidden tears stung at his eyes. 'I don't know. I've been trying to remember. I remember leaving the pub and walking along the main road back towards the flat. And I sort of remember someone calling to me, down by the Mill Beck. There's a path that runs off the main road down to the water's edge. I think I went down it to see what was going on.'

'So you went to help someone?'

'I don't know. I think so. I just remember hearing a voice. I can't even remember if it was a man or a woman.'

'And nothing after that?'

He shook his head. 'No. Nothing. Not until I woke up in hospital.' He turned his head a little to look at her hand, still resting on his arm. It felt comforting. He looked up into her face. 'There's something I need to tell you.'

'Go on.'

'It's about Andy. Well, about the flat really. He … he didn't pay the rent. He'd been taking money from me, and not paying the rent with it.' He saw her take a sharp intake of breath, ready to object, ready to jump to Andy's defence. He tried to shake his head. 'I know what you're going to say. But he did, Jodie. He took the money and he didn't pay the rent. It doesn't matter. Not now.' His throat was beginning to feel tight and he coughed the tension away. 'A debt collector came to the flat, and threatened me.'

'Was he the one who hurt you?'

'I don't know. I didn't see who attacked me, but the police are going to question him.' He frowned and scrunched his eyes together, trying to concentrate. 'The thing is, I did something stupid yesterday.'

'Something stupid?'

'Because Andy took my money. Because he left me to be threatened by a debt collector.' He sighed. 'It doesn't matter what I did, but I need your help. There's a bag in my locker at work, I need you to get it for me.'

She smiled to reassure him. 'It'll be fine. Graham Clarke won't let anything happen to it.'

He nodded. 'I know. But there's stuff in there … it's important. I need it here with me. If I give you the key …'

'But I've already told you, I've been suspended. I don't know when – if – they will let me back in to the office.'

'Could you ask someone? Could you ask Reggie?'

'You want me to give the key to Reggie and ask him to empty your locker?'

'Please.' His eyes said it all. 'I know you don't have any feelings for me now, and I don't blame you. But I wouldn't ask if … if it wasn't important.' He bit his lip, losing his battle against the tears of self-pity. 'I know you don't care for me, but I can't believe you would want anything else bad to happen to me. Would you?'

23

Rose nudged Mac's rump gently with her foot. 'What's your game, then? We were only meant to be out for a walk. And you only got that because Mr Mulligan called off our meeting at The Boar.'

The terrier was curled up contentedly between her feet and a smouldering log fire burning in the grate of The Feathers' lounge bar. He lifted his head and used his one good eye to give her a knowing look, gave her shoe an artless lick, and then went back to staring into the fire.

Rose glanced over her shoulder to the bar, where Benny Bradman was picking up a couple of drinks. He looked tired, older than when she'd seen him last. Ten minutes earlier he'd blustered out of the local newsagents shop with furrowed brows, muttering angrily under his breath, and barged clumsily into Rose on the pavement outside. She'd seen his face register irritation at the collision, and then the annoyance morph quickly into delight as he realised just exactly who he had collided with.

His delight at seeing Rose had been nothing compared with Mac's delight at seeing him. The terrier had taken control of the situation and showered Benny with an embarrassment of licking and tail-wagging. As far as the dog was concerned, refusing an invitation to join Benny for a drink was out of the question.

'Red wine for Rose, a pint for me, and a packet of pork scratchin's for Mac.' Benny put the drinks down on the table and pulled open the packet, then tipped half the scratchings onto the floor next to the terrier's nose.

'Do you make a habit of that?' Rose nodded towards the dog. 'There's no wonder he was so pleased to see you.'

Benny grinned. 'He's only allowed half a packet. Lucinda gives me earache if I give him more than that.' He lifted his glass. 'Your good health, Rose.'

'And yours.' She returned the toast. 'So tell me, how's Craig getting along?'

'He's doin' well Rose, I'll tell him you were askin'. He's thrown himself into his new job, so we don't see a lot of him, him bein' down in London. He ain't got himself another girl yet, but I can understand that. It's early days.' He frowned. 'He took it hard when ...' His voice trailed off.

Rose could only offer an understanding smile. Pandora Mitchell's death had hit a lot of people hard. 'He'll get there. Just give him time.'

Benny nodded, thoughtful for a moment, then his face brightened. 'Never mind all that. What brings you back to Market Melbourne? Is it a social visit or more bankin' business?'

'The bank, I'm afraid. An assignment at the Scarborough office.'

'The seaside in December? Blimey, you get all the good jobs.' He eyed her over the top of his pint. 'Anythin' to do with this murder that everyone's talkin' about?'

'I sincerely hope not.' If there was, Rose decided, then Benny didn't necessarily need to know about it. 'Just a bit of bother with an internal process.'

'Well I'm glad to hear it. Whatever the case, it's good to see you.' There was a sincerity in his eyes that suggested they weren't just words. 'I could do with a friendly face this evenin' after the day I've had.' He chuckled to himself. 'Do you remember Michael Spivey, Rose? Scruffy little tyke that runs my errands at the shop?' The chuckle became a laugh. 'Now of course you do. The last time you were here you caught him red-handed openin' a dodgy bank account with the ENB, didn't you?'

She smiled. 'I'm not likely to forget him in a hurry. He didn't just open that bank account. He built a mock grave in Lu's garden with my name on it.'

'Blimey, I'd forgotten about that.' Benny nodded, embarrassed by the reminder. 'He tried to put the frighteners on you, didn't he? Now we know you better Rose, I can only say he underestimated you.' He grinned into his pint at some private thought, and then straightened his face. 'Well,' he fixed her with an earnest stare, 'the little toe-rag only waltzed off this mornin' with three hundred quid's worth of my petty cash to pay the newsagent's bill and he still ain't paid it, and I can't get old of him for love nor money.' He shook his head. 'He's runnin' errands for Hector Camplin' now.' He tutted under his breath. 'I've told him no good will come of it, but you just can't reason with some people.'

'Hector Campling? Is he …?'

Benny nodded. 'Henry's son. He's runnin' the family firm now.' He sipped on his pint. 'They still own those flats, you know. Bellevue Mansions.' He frowned. 'Here, that's where that lad from the ENB was murdered, ain't it?' His face became momentarily blank, as the cogs in his brain made unwelcome connections. He stared directly at Rose and was about to speak again when a girl's hand landed on his shoulder. He turned and looked up.

Vienna Fielding drew back her hand, hesitated, and then bent down towards him, enveloping him in a mist of musky perfume. 'Sorry to bother you Mr Bradman, but I've got Michael on the phone.' She looked concerned. 'He doesn't want me to speak to you, but I think he needs help.' There was a small pink phone in her left hand, and she held it out towards him with a nervous smile. 'Please?'

Benny looked at the phone, then at Rose, and finally back up into Vienna's anxious face. He took hold of it with an irritated shake of the head and pressed it to his ear. 'Michael? Where the bleedin' hell are you?' He flinched as Michael Spivey began to shout down the phone. 'Blimey,

calm down will you? You're where? At the Kirkby nick?'
He closed his eyes and went on shaking his head. 'You've
been doin' *what* for Hector Camplin'? What the bleedin'
hell are you playin' at? You're not a licensed debt
collector.' His voice was rising in volume, exasperation
building as Spivey's story unfolded from the other end of
the line. 'How many times have I told you ... Who? George
Mulligan?' He took the phone away from his ear and
turned his attention to the barmaid. 'Did you know about
this? He's in the bleedin' nick for threatenin' some bloke
over his rent.' He thrust the phone back at her. 'I can't be
doin' with this, Vienna. I've told him to stay away from
Hector Camplin' and he just won't listen. Now he's goin'
to have to learn the hard way.'

'Oh please Mr Bradman, you've got to help him.'
Vienna's eyes were pleading. She turned them from Benny
to Rose, hoping for support from any quarter. 'He hasn't
done anything wrong.'

'Of course he's done somethin' wrong. I know George
Mulligan. He wouldn't take him in unless he'd done
somethin' wrong. He's not a licenced debt collector and if
he's been stupid enough to do Hector Camplin's dirty
work ...'

'But they think he killed that bloke. At Bellevue
Mansions.' Vienna was distraught now, tears beginning to
roll down her face. 'And the other one, the one that was
hurt last night near the Mill Beck. They think Michael did
it.'

Benny froze. She had his full attention now. 'They're
tryin' to pin that murder on him?' His voice became a low
growl. 'Gimme the phone.' He pressed it back to his ear.
'Michael, keep your mouth shut, d'you hear me? Say
nothin' till I get there.' He pushed at the phone's keypad
with a stubby thumb to end the call without waiting for an
answer, and handed it back to Vienna.

'It's a good thing you've only just started that pint.'
Rose was already on her feet and slipping her arm into her

174

overcoat. 'We don't want to present Mr Mulligan with a drink driving case on top of everything else.'

'Are you comin' with me then?' Caught off guard by the gesture, Benny eyed her with amused surprise. 'I didn't think Michael meant that much to you Rose, I'm sure he'd be touched.'

Her coat buttoned, she bent down and swept Mac up, tucking him under her arm. 'He doesn't. But I'm afraid I haven't been completely straight with you.' She smiled, more than a little sheepish. 'Those lads worked for the ENB. Both of them. And they both worked for the team I'm investigating. I've got a vested interest in this turn of events.' She saw his look of incredulity and ignored it, turning instead to Vienna. 'Don't you worry about this, honey. Michael Spivey's a lot of things. He's a liar, and a thief, and if I'm honest I wouldn't trust him as far as I could throw him. But there's one thing I know he isn't, and that's a killer.'

'He's admitted to pressing Chris Kemp for the rent.' George Mulligan leaned his elbows on the table and looked first at Benny Bradman and then at Rose. 'What am I supposed to think?' He watched as Benny and Rose exchanged glances. 'I hope you two aren't cooking something up between you.'

Benny grinned. 'I can't speak for her, of course.' He jerked a thumb at Rose. 'There's no sayin' what these bankin' types will get up to. But you know me, George. I wouldn't lead you up the garden path.'

Mulligan returned his grin with some cynicism. 'I know when our paths crossed back in the summer that you promised me you'd keep Michael Spivey out of trouble if I let him off lightly. And now see where we are.'

Rose blew out a sigh. 'But Michael has an alibi. Vienna has confirmed that he was with her until eleven thirty yesterday evening. You said that Chris Kemp was attacked much earlier than that.'

The policeman nodded. 'And we'll see how that stands up when Scottie has finished taking her statement. But the fact remains he doesn't have an alibi for Sunday evening. He could still have murdered Andy Miller. He's even admitted calling at the flat on Sunday to try to collect the rent.'

Benny folded his arms and leaned back in his seat. 'I thought the papers said that Andy Miller was run down with his own car? How could Michael have done that? He would have needed the car keys.'

'He would, yes. And we believe he had access to them. You see, the spare keys to Andy Miller's car were kept in a drawer in the flat. And we believe that Michael had the opportunity to access those keys.' He watched as Rose and Benny exchanged another glance. 'According to Hector Campling, there are four sets of keys to the apartment. Two of them were in Andy Miller's possession as the tenant. The other two were kept in a drawer, in Campling's own desk in his Market Melbourne office. Michael Spivey is a regular visitor to that office and has been left alone there on more than one occasion. He could have helped himself to those keys quite easily.'

Rose leaned forward, closer to Mulligan. 'Do you have any evidence that he did?'

'Not as such. We know that Michael is light-fingered, and we know that he's been light-fingered in that office before. You both know he stole documents from Henry Campling's desk so that he could open a fraudulent bank account with them.'

'Give a dog a bad name?' Rose gave a quiet laugh. 'Is this the point where I remind you that Michael's rather pathetic attempts to defraud the ENB were actually the breakthrough you needed to find Pandora Mitchell's killer and nail Henry Campling for those money-laundering offences?'

Mulligan was unmoved. 'He's got previous.'

'It doesn't make him a murderer.'

'No, Rose, it doesn't. But when we brought him in I asked him if he would be good enough to empty his pockets out. And one of the items that came tumbling out of his jacket pocket was a set of keys to flat 2d, Bellevue Mansions.'

Benny gave a spontaneous laugh. 'You know what, George? As a bookie, I don't like placin' bets. I much prefer watchin' other people do it. But I'll lay you two to one that Hector Camplin' gave Michael those keys. And if it turns out that he did, I'll give you three to two that there are items missin' from that flat, and five to four that the sale proceeds from those items end up in Hector Camplin's bank account.'

'What makes you say that?'

'Camplin's a chip off the old block. If he's been diddled out of rent money he'll find some way of clawin' it back and he won't care how he does it. And Michael's too dim to know that you can't just walk into somebody's home and help yourself to whatever you fancy just because they owe a bit of rent. He won't ask all the awkward questions.'

Mulligan was about to reply when a door behind him opened and DS Scott's head appeared. 'The alibi's good, George. What do you want me to do?' He glanced across at Rose and his face brightened. 'Alright Rose?'

'Not bad. But I'll feel better when Mr Mulligan agrees that he can let Michael go. At least for now.' She turned an expectant gaze on the senior officer.

Mulligan's brow furrowed and his picked up his pen and twizzled it around between his fingers. 'He had the opportunity to access those keys. And he's admitted acting as a debt collector without the appropriate licences.'

'It still doesn't make him a murderer. Does it?' She glanced up at DS Scott, looking for support. 'In fact, what's to say that Hector Campling didn't access the flat himself? After all, he has the other set of keys. What's to say he didn't let himself in at some point when Andy and

Chris were at work, and help himself to those spare car keys? Perhaps he considered stealing the car to cover his losses. Maybe we're trying to over-complicate this. Maybe Andy did just run out to stop someone from stealing the car, and maybe that someone was someone he knew? Like his landlord.

'What if keeping Andy Miller quiet was more important to the thief than actually getting away with the car?'

24

Jodie rapped sharply on the brass door knocker, her heart thumping, her mouth dry with nerves. She knew she was courting trouble but she couldn't help herself. Anyway, she couldn't see how things could get much worse for her than they already were.

At the other side of the door a chain rattled as if someone was hooking it onto a latch, securing the door before it was opened, and then the lock clicked under pressure and the door swung open a few inches until the chain pulled taught. Annabel's doe eyes appeared in the gap, and she peered anxiously into the stairwell to see who was there.

Their eyes locked, and Jodie held her gaze steady. 'I haven't come to fight, Annabel. I just need to speak to you.'

There was a moment of tense silence and then Annabel pouted. 'You hit me.' It was a simple statement of fact.

'I know. And I'm sorry. You have no idea just how sorry.' Jodie's voice was beginning to waver. 'I've just been to see Chris. I thought you would want to know how he is.' She waited but Annabel didn't respond. 'I went to the hospital earlier this evening. He's quite poorly, but they say he'll make a full recovery. I thought you would want to know.'

Annabel thought for a moment then stepped back from the gap in the door. Jodie waited for the inevitable thud of the door slamming shut, and was surprised instead to hear the chain rattle off its latch. Annabel swung the door wide and gestured into the hallway. 'You'd better come in. We can't talk here on the doorstep.'

Jodie hesitated, momentarily thrown by the unexpected invitation, then followed Annabel down the hallway and into a spacious lounge. It was a far cry from the functional flat-shares of her own experience. Softly lit by an array of stylish table lamps the room was warm and elegant, its long sash windows framed by full-length drapes, and its polished floorboards covered with a heavily sculpted Chinese rug. The drapes were open, and although it was dark Jodie could see from shimmering lights in the near distance that the flat enjoyed the luxury of a fine outlook, a panoramic vista of the town's Victorian park with its flower beds, glass houses and boating pond.

Beside her Annabel gestured towards what appeared even to Jodie's untrained eye to be a Liberty sofa, and invited her sit. 'Can I get you a drink?' Her voice was hesitant. 'A coffee, or perhaps a glass of wine?'

Jodie nodded. 'A glass of wine.' It probably wasn't a good idea, but suddenly she needed the courage a drink would bring. She watched as Annabel backed out of the room and then glanced around her, taking it all in. Botanical prints, many of them in elaborate gothic frames, hung from the walls and every available surface held a flowering plant or a candle or a framed photograph. An impressive oak mantelpiece provided a home for all three, and a profusely-flowering phalaenopsis jostled for space with a collection of pretty tea-light holders and a large framed photograph of Annabel snuggled up to Andy Miller on a park bench. Jodie's stomach churned and she turned her eyes quickly away from the picture. What the hell was she doing here?

She breathed deeply to steady her nerves. She was here to find out why Annabel had made no attempt to find out how Chris was. Didn't she know how badly hurt he was? Didn't she care? She was here to find out why the girl who yesterday had been intent on seducing him had suddenly lost all interest in him.

At least, that was the original reason for her visit. But now? She had never visited Annabel's home before, never thought about where Annabel lived. She had known it was in Kirkby, away from the office, distanced from where the majority of ENB staff lived. But she had never known more than that. And she had never asked. It had never interested her.

But it interested her now.

Annabel was a graduate trainee and the ENB wasn't a generous employer. Salaries were low, grudging almost, too low to afford the rent on a place like this. And yet Jodie felt sure somehow that Annabel wasn't living beyond her means. Family money, maybe? Was it more appropriate then to wonder how someone who could afford to live like this would waste their time working in a badly-paid role for the ENB? She was in Customer Services. She was hardly likely to be doing it for fun.

Her musings were cut short by the squeak of a door opening as Annabel appeared, an open bottle of Merlot clutched in one hand, two large wine glasses hanging by their stems from the fingers of the other. She set the bottle and glasses down on a butler's tray beside the sofa, poured a generous glass, and handed it to Jodie.

Jodie took it with a polite nod. 'This is a beautiful flat, Annabel.' She bit back the desire to ask how Annabel could afford it. 'Have you lived her long?'

'Almost a year now.' Annabel picked up her own drink and sank into an oversized armchair. 'I was so lucky to get it fully furnished. I keep thinking that I ought to buy somewhere but I love this flat, I don't really want to give it up.' She gave a wistful smile. 'It has so many happy memories. Andy loved this flat almost as much as I did.' She blinked away what could have been a tear. 'I do miss him so much.' She shuddered and squeezed her eyes tight shut. 'Jodie, I'm so sorry.' Her voice softened to a whisper.

'I know you miss him too. I … I don't think I realised until this week that you were still in love with him.' She opened her eyes and stared earnestly into Jodie's face. 'You *were* still in love with him, weren't you? Even though you were going out with Chris?'

'Yes, I suppose I was.' Jodie bit her lip. This wasn't how she'd imagined a confrontation with Annabel would pan out. No anger, no incrimination, just quiet, reasoned conversation. She'd expected Annabel to be afraid of her, to refuse to speak with her, not to act as a confidante while she spilled her guts about her feelings for Andy. Annabel, a confidante? A mild belligerence rose in the pit of her stomach. This wasn't why she came here. She took a healthy swig of the wine. 'I didn't come to talk about Andy. I came to ask you to come to the hospital with me. To visit Chris.'

'I'm sorry Jodie, I can't do that.'

'But he's hurting and he really wants to see you. It's too late to go back this evening, but I think you should come with me tomorrow to visit him.'

'But I have to go to work.'

'Then come in the evening, after work.' Jodie was becoming agitated now, the wine already bolstering her confidence. 'I don't get it, Annabel. You led him on yesterday. You did something to make him believe that you cared about him. And because of that he finished with me.'

'I know, and I'm sorry.'

'Sorry? Sorry for what? For the fact that he finished with me?'

'No, I'm not sorry for that. I'm sorry that it hurt you. But you know, he really isn't the person you think he is. And neither was Andy.' Annabel sighed, and stared away from her out of the window. 'I know it hurts now, but I think in time you'll come to realise that neither of them deserved you. And I do believe that in the long run you'll come to understand that things have really turned out for the best.'

'I've checked Campling's alibi for both nights, and he's in the clear. He was playing squash with a friend on Sunday evening, and at home with the wife and her sister last night.' DS Scott laughed to himself. 'He didn't like being asked, mind.'

'I shouldn't think he would.' Mulligan put up a hand and rubbed at his forehead. 'So Campling is in the clear. If we subscribe to the view that whoever attacked Chris Kemp also killed Andy Miller, then Vienna Fielding's alibi eliminates Spivey. And taking that view also eliminates Chris Kemp, since he could hardly have whacked himself on the back of the head before he fell into the Beck.'

'There was something I forgot to mention about Chris Kemp.' Scott frowned, trying to remember. 'It was something Annabel Halmshaw said about him, about some cufflinks.'

'Cufflinks?'

'Yes. She reckons that when she saw Chris Kemp yesterday evening he was wearing a pair of cufflinks that she gave Andy Miller as a gift.'

Mulligan shook his head. 'The lad was trying to emulate Andy Miller, and he was living in his flat. It wouldn't surprise me if he just helped himself and borrowed them. He might just as easily have been planning to put them back last night and hoped that no-one noticed.' He thought for a moment. 'And even if he did steal them, being a thief doesn't make him a murderer.' He put a hand up to his face and chewed on a thumbnail, deep in thought. 'Was Annabel angry about it? I thought they were close, those two?'

'So did I. Come to think of it, she did seem overly keen to tell me about it.' He smiled. 'Maybe she's cooling towards him now she thinks he's light-fingered?'

'Maybe.' Mulligan was pensive now. 'It seems to me,

Scottie old son, that we've got a surfeit of petty thieves in this case, and a distinct dearth of murderers.' He hated this point in a case. The point where there were too many possibilities, too many suspects and motives and opportunities, and no certainties. And yet he also knew, cliché or not, that the darkest hour was before the dawn. They were so close to making the connection, so close that he could almost smell it. But not close enough. They were still one crucial breakthrough away from closing the deal. He puffed out his frustration. 'I want to take another look at that flat. Are you up for a bit of unplanned devilry?'

'What now?' Scott wasn't exactly enthusiastic. 'Rose was on her way back to The Feathers in Market Melbourne. I was hoping to follow on and join her for a drink.'

Mulligan grinned. 'Worried she's spending too much time with Benny Bradman?'

'The bookie? No, not her type at all George. I'm sure she's looking for something a bit more sophisticated.'

'And that would be you, would it?' Mulligan shook his head with a wry smile. 'Come on, we can be over at Bellevue Mansions in twenty minutes. It'll take us half an hour to look round, you can still be in The Feathers by half past nine. Send her a text and tell her to wait for you. If she's going to have anything to do with a policeman she'll have to get used to waiting.'

'And just how are we going to get into the flat? I can't see Hector Campling volunteering to turn out at this time of night, especially when we've just poked him in the eye by asking for an alibi or two.'

Mulligan smiled and fished in his jacket pocket, and pulled out a small set of keys attached to a plastic key ring. 'I confiscated these from Michael Spivey before we let him go tonight. I told him he could leave it to me to hand them back to Campling. He wasn't going to argue.' His eyes twinkled with mischief. 'I really think they ought to be returned to Mr Campling this evening. And as you're going over to Market Melbourne, you could drop them off at his home before you go to the pub.' He stood up and lifted his jacket off the back of his chair. 'But first, we have a little errand to do in Scarborough. I'd like to take another look at the spot where Chris Kemp went into the Mill Beck. We'll have to pass Bellevue Mansions on the way there, I'm sure Mr Campling wouldn't mind if we took the opportunity to do him a favour and make sure the apartment was secure.'

25

'Don't you think Rose has done enough for you tonight?' Benny Bradman shook his head. 'You'd still be in the Kirkby nick if she hadn't leaned on George Mulligan for you.'

Beside Benny's chair, Michael Spivey looked down at his feet. His normally sallow cheeks were flushed and the corner of his mouth twitched nervously. He dared to look up at Rose. 'It ain't a favour for me, Rose. It's for Vienna.' He turned and glanced towards the bar, where Vienna was serving a late customer. 'Well, really it's for her sister.' He cleared his throat and turned awkward eyes back to Rose. 'She's a real nice lady, Vienna's sister, and she's on her own with free kiddies. She needs a bit of help.'

Rose watched Michael with more than a little amusement. Six months ago, doing Henry Campling's bidding, he'd done his best to frighten her out of Market Melbourne. And now here he was asking her for a favour. Her amusement blossomed into a forgiving smile. 'What can I do to help?'

It was more than he had hoped for. His eyes widened and he glanced at Benny, who simply shook his head with a growl. 'Well, the fing is, she has a credit card with the ENB, and when she took it out they put some sort of insurance on it without asking her if she wanted it. She's complained to them about it, and she reckons they owe her some sort of compensation, but they're dragging their heels about paying out.'

She shook her head. 'I'm sorry Michael, I don't think

there's much I can do about that. They did it to thousands of people, and there's just a big backlog of claims waiting to be processed. I'm afraid she'll just have to wait her turn.'

He shook his head. 'It ain't just that. See, she's got into a bit of bother with that credit card, got a bit behind with the payments, like. The kiddies' old man, he did a runner with some other bird a few months back, and she's trying to hold it all together. She's holding down free jobs but it's a struggle. That's how she got behind with the rent.' He turned and glanced again wistfully at Vienna, and said quietly 'that's how I came to see Vienna last night. Mr Campling sent me to collect the rent arrears, and Vienna was babysitting for the kiddies.' He turned back to Rose. 'Vienna reckons that what the bank owes her would wipe out the balance on that credit card account, and she'd still have money left over for Christmas.'

Rose leaned back in her seat and looked away across the bar to where Vienna was just handing a customer his change. *Mis-sold insurance and credit card arrears?* That was the second time today she'd had reason to think about that conundrum. She turned back to Michael Spivey. 'And you say she's Vienna's sister?'

He nodded. 'She's having a real tough time. I've managed to square the rent arrears for her, but I can't do the same for the credit card.'

Benny, who had only been half-listening to the conversation, suddenly became interested. 'How much was that then? The rent arrears?'

Spivey was about to say "only free hundred quid", and then he remembered where the cash had come from. He shrank back into the collar of his shirt. 'I'll pay it back Benny, straight up.'

Benny opened his mouth to speak but Rose put out a hand and laid it on his arm. 'Never mind that now.' She turned back to Michael. 'I can't promise that I can do anything but I'm happy to talk to her.' She pulled a business card from her bag and handed it to Michael. 'Give her this and ask her to give me a call, tomorrow morning if she can.'

He took the card and stared it at. 'That's real nice of you, Rose.' Embarrassed, his voice was almost a whisper.

'You have to understand that I can't make the bank process her claim any quicker, but I might be able to find out when her case is due for review. And it's possible that something can be done to reduce her credit card payments for a couple of months until she gets straight. I can't say until I know a bit more about her circumstances.'

As Michael walked away Rose turned to Benny with a teasing smile. 'Well aren't you just an old softy, giving Michael an advance on his wages?'

'Advance? He blows my petty cash on some tart's rent bill, and you call it an advance?'

'Oh come on, you can afford it. And you must admit it's worth it just to see him all loved up like that? Vienna could be the making of him, you know … a girl of his own might be just the thing to set him on the right track.'

'I should be so lucky.' Benny didn't look convinced. 'Anyway, do you think you can do anythin'? For Vienna's sister?'

'I don't know. But I'd like to know more about it. I've been looking at an almost similar case today, as part of my investigation. A young woman called Florence Fielding has been trying to claim back mis-sold insurance premiums that would wipe out the arrears on her credit card account, and the ENB hasn't exactly been sympathetic.'

Benny's face broke into a grin. 'That ain't a similar case Rose, it's the same case.' He watched her reaction with amusement. 'You didn't know that Vienna's surname was Fielding, then?'

George Mulligan pulled his neck and chin down into the warmth of his scarf, and braced himself against the bitter cold. A brisk northerly wind chased eddies of snow around his legs, his arms, his face and he shivered as frozen flakes settled on his nose and cheeks. He pushed his hands deep into his pockets and blew out a puff of air. At his feet the icy waters of the Mill Beck streamed over pebbles and rocks on their way through a narrow strip of waste ground that ran parallel with the main road.

He turned his head and looked back over his shoulder towards the main road. DS Scott had already driven off in the direction of Market Melbourne, leaving Mulligan to survey the crime scene alone. He didn't mind that Scottie had gone. He liked it like that. Just him and the place where it happened. He liked to feel close to the crime, almost part of it, standing on the same ground as the victim, breathing the same air as the perpetrator.

He sized up the distance between the Beck and the road. It was around a hundred and fifty feet. The land inclined slightly and the top of his own car was barely visible above a stone wall that separated pavement from waste ground. There was no obvious way to cut through from the pavement to the Beck. Chris Kemp must have come over the wall.

But the lad couldn't remember why. All he could tell Scott was that he had been out with Annabel, that he was walking home alone from The Half Moon, and that he thought he remembered someone calling from the edge of the Beck. Did that really happen? Or was his brain just coming up with suggestions to fill the void where the facts should be? Did he think someone was in trouble in the water and jump the wall to see if he could help? He didn't seem the heroic type, but then appearances could be deceptive.

That crack on the head was problematic, too. Did someone lure him down here? Call out for help and then come up on him unexpectedly with a stick or a rock or some other makeshift weapon? And if so, then why? Who would want to hurt Chris Kemp?

Hector Campling was out of the frame, and so was Michael Spivey. So if it wasn't about the rent arrears, then what? Was this to do with the bank? An angry customer looking for revenge on call centre workers who stepped outside their prescriptive scripts and piled the pressure on to recover money? What were they called at the ENB? Ringers? That was the nickname, he'd heard people use it. They called them "ringers", people whose job it was to ring up strangers and politely ask them to repay their debts.

Did bank workers have to give their names when they made these calls? Was this all linked to Rose Bennett's investigation or was it just someone with a grudge targeting ENB staff, someone who didn't really care who they hurt so long as they taught the bank a lesson? He wasn't going to find the answer here. He turned away from the Mill Beck and started to climb back up the bank towards his car.

What about that tangled love quadrangle? Jodie wanted Andy, but Andy wanted Annabel. Jodie found herself with Chris, although she didn't seem to really want him, and then she discovered that Chris wanted Annabel too. And they were all "ringers", weren't they? Annabel might have been in Customer Services rather than Debt Recovery, but they all made phone calls for a living.

Andy Miller was a dead ringer now, and Chris Kemp had nearly followed him. Annabel had turned against Chris Kemp, and Jodie Pearce … well, what about Jodie Pearce? He stopped walking and thought for a moment.

Jodie Pearce was thrown over by Andy Miller for another girl. Jodie Pearce dated Chris Kemp, and had access to the flat at Bellevue Mansions, which meant she also had access to the spare set of keys for the BMW, the keys to the car used to murder Andy Miller. Jodie Pearce, thrown over by Chris Kemp for another girl. No, worse than that, Jodie Pearce thrown over by Chris Kemp for the same girl that Andy Miller had thrown her over for. Jodie

Pearce, suspended from her job for attacking the girl in question.

He glanced over his shoulder back towards the water and tried to imagine Jodie Pearce wielding a stick or a rock or something heavy in a bag, some implement that would hit Chris Kemp on the back of the head and send him swaying into the freezing cold water. He laughed under his breath. The girl was feisty and full of anger, but so were a lot of young women these days. Young women didn't resort to murder just because their pride was hurt. It was just too ridiculous to contemplate.

Wasn't it?

26

'I'm as certain as I can be that Andy Miller made that call to Robert Donovan.' Rose jammed her phone under her chin, leaving her hands free to type. 'I'm drafting you an email while we're speaking, with all the salient points. I'll prepare the full report this morning and try to have it over to you by lunchtime.'

At the other end of the line Clive Barden sounded less than impressed. 'But you have no concrete evidence, Rose. Just the word of … of …'

'A customer. Florence Fielding is a *customer*.' Her fingers continued to click on the keyboard. 'If you had given me permission I could have spoken in person to Robert Donovan and asked him to identify the voice. But you didn't want me to do that.'

'With very good reason.' He still wasn't satisfied. 'Explain to me again who this person is, and just why you set such store by her opinion.'

'Her name is Florence Fielding. She's an ENB credit card customer. I first came across her when Stan sent me some sample files of calls made to the Credit Card Recovery Team. Andy Miller made a scheduled recorded call to her about the arrears on her account. They had quite a lengthy conversation, because Florence has a claim in against the bank for the mis-selling of payment protection insurance.' She stopped typing for a moment and took hold of her phone, moving it to a more comfortable position. 'Stan later gave me documentary evidence that the rogue telephone extension used at the

Scarborough office to make the threatening call to Robert Donovan also made several calls to Florence Fielding. We don't have recordings of those calls, but we do have a recording of a call shortly afterwards made by Florence to the Customer Services department, in which she claims an ENB employee had made abusive phone calls to her. My belief is that the calls were made by Andy, using the same phone he used to call Robert Donovan. And that Florence recognised his voice.

Yesterday evening I met someone who knows Florence Fielding. It turns out that Florence lives locally, so I was able to set up a face to face meeting at short notice. I took my laptop with me, played her the recording of the original call between herself and Andy, and asked her if it was the same person who made the threatening call. She confirmed that it was.'

'With respect Rose, that's just an opinion. The caller didn't give a name.'

Rose closed her eyes and shook her head. 'Of course it's just an opinion. But you can't deny that the rogue extension used to make the calls is in the ENB's Scarborough office. We have proof of that. I've confirmed that Andy was working overtime after business hours when every call was made from that extension. And I asked Florence if she could remember when the threatening calls had been made. She didn't need to remember. She was so angry she wrote it down. The dates and times correlate to the calls Stan listed for me, the calls made by that rogue extension to Florence's number.' She opened her eyes and smiled to herself. She loved pushing Clive's buttons. 'I played her recordings of Chris Kemp and Reggie Croft, by the way. She confirmed that neither of them made the threatening calls.'

'You did *what?*'

'Oh come on, Clive, I knew you would rather I made sure that any surviving members of the Recovery Team were in the clear.' She could hear his tongue clicking in annoyance at the other end of the line. 'So I'll go in to the office later this morning and write up my report in full. Before I write everything up, can I just check whether you want me to document the content of the call Andy Miller made to Florence Fielding?'

'The content?'

'Yes. It could be deemed pretty offensive.' She glanced down at the open notebook beside her laptop. 'Apparently, after swearing at her and making deprecating comments about the Barnfield Estate where she lives, he suggested that she should go on the game to make the money to pay back her debts to the ENB.' She waited a few moments in vain for a response from Clive then adopted her best solemn tone to add 'I did apologise on behalf of the bank Clive, and she was very magnanimous about it.'

'I am aware, Rose, that you enjoy a naturally exuberant manner which at times has a tendency to border on the flippant. However, I hope that you will continue to address this matter with the seriousness it deserves.' He cleared his throat. 'The young man concerned is dead.'

Rose sucked in her cheeks and tried to stay solemn. 'I am well aware that he's dead, Clive. The question is, *why* is he dead? Is he dead because of these phone calls?'

'That is a question for the police, Rose, not for us. The question for us starts before that. The question for us is why did he make the calls in the first place? A trusted employee, a team leader, someone we relied upon to act as a role model for other employees. What did we do wrong? Was he doing it because using regulated recovery techniques wasn't generating the results we were seeking? Did we set the targets too high? Was Andy Miller stepping outside of the box to meet them? Are we as an organisation at fault?'

'All of that is possible. But unlikely, I think. I've seen evidence that both Andy and Chris Kemp were making additional calls not in their work queues, and certainly Reggie Croft knew they were making those calls. So stepping outside the box has been an accepted practice in that team. But this is more than just stepping outside the box. This is …' Rose paused, seeking an appropriate word, 'this is … well, it's demanding money with menaces.'

Clive Barden uttered an astonished laugh. 'Oh come now Rose, I think that is a little extreme.'

'Extreme? Well what would you call it? A bank employee has contacted a customer from an ENB telephone during working hours to suggest that she resort to prostitution to pay her credit card bill, Clive. Just what would you call that?'

He clicked his teeth and lowered his voice to a more temperate tone. 'I can only conclude the young man was unwell.'

'The young man was in debt.'

'I beg your pardon?'

'According to Mr Mulligan, Andy Miller was heavily in debt. He'd even taken money from Chris Kemp.'

'He stole from a colleague?'

'That's about the size of it.'

'And what does the inspector make of this?'

'He doesn't. The only explanation he has is that it's some sort of transference. That perhaps the enormity of his own debts put Andy Miller under such pressure that he was punishing other people to relieve his own guilt. It's not unheard of. Maybe he thought that punishing those customers in some way absolved him of the need to be guilty about his own debts.'

'Hmm. Hardly a satisfactory outcome.' Clive Barden clicked his teeth again. 'So what is your recommendation, Rose?'

'My view is that the call was made by an employee of the ENB who had personal issues, and was abusing his position with the company for reasons unknown. There is no evidence of fraud in relation to these calls, nor any other kind of wrong-doing. He has breached regulation around customer treatment, but not in any official capacity. In addition both he and Chris Kemp have breached company policy by making additional calls outside of the prescribed process. I recommend that you retrain to stamp out that practice, shake up the team, put in a new team leader and a couple of new faces.' She paused. 'And for goodness sake let Jodie Pearce come back to work. The girl has suffered enough.'

'That young woman has let herself down very badly, Rose.'

'She has. But who amongst us hasn't. And who amongst us hasn't been thankful for another chance?'

He thought for a moment. 'Very well. I will discuss the possibility with the management team. But I make no promises.'

'Understood.'

'I will call Robert Donovan myself today and apologise in person for the calls made to him by Andy Miller. And we will, of course, offer some financial compensation. Could I ask you, Rose, to include that as part of your report, so that we have the decision captured.'

'Of course, Clive.' There was still one thing he seemed to have forgotten. 'And what compensation will be offered to Florence Fielding?'

'Compensation? For Florence Fielding?'

'Yes. She endured two threatening phone calls from Andy Miller. And the ENB is dragging its heels about her claim for compensation.'

'Now listen, Rose …'

'I wouldn't like to think that she would share her experiences of the ENB with a third party. It would make quite a story, wouldn't it? Bank employee suggests single mother of three turn to prostitution to pay credit card bill that doesn't exist.' She paused for effect, and then added 'if she goes to the right publication she could probably sell that story for enough to pay off the whole outstanding balance.'

'Come now, Rose, on what level does the balance not

exist?'

'It won't exist when her compensation has been calculated. Looking at her credit card statements last night – she's kept them all, by the way – when the ENB upholds her claim for mis-selling the insurance policy then the refund of premiums and associated interest that the bank owes her would wipe out her arrears and put the account into credit to the tune of around two thousand pounds. So technically the ENB are harassing her over a debt she doesn't actually owe.'

'Sometimes, Rose ….'

'Sometimes, Clive, I wonder what goes on in that head of yours. Florence Fielding is in financial difficulty. She's trying to feed, clothe and keep a roof over the head of three kids. And the ENB is pursuing her for a debt that technically she doesn't owe. She should be a priority case.'

'The bank has a responsibility to deal with complaints in the order in which they are received. If …'

'Thanks to Florence Fielding, my investigation is complete. This could have dragged on for days yet, if not weeks, if she hadn't been so certain that voice was Andy Miller's. Just think of all the money she's saved you, not having to pay my fees for a few more weeks.'

Clive was silent for a moment and then asked 'Your investigation will be complete and reported by close of business today?'

'By close of business today.'

He gave a reproachful sniff. 'There are times, Rose, when I find your methods anarchic and your approach simply too difficult to comprehend.'

'Why bless you, Clive. What a lovely thing to say.'

The traffic into Scarborough was heavier than usual that morning thanks to black ice and a consequential spate of minor road accidents, and they were stationary a mile or so from the ENB's office. George Mulligan snuggled into his overcoat and folded his arms tight over his chest. He hadn't had much sleep and another early start had just added to the tiredness. Tiredness made him irritable, and he didn't like being irritable. It just made him more irritable.

This morning's news had added to his ill-humour. Evie Cooper, an obliging young officer new to the Kirkby station, had rolled up to his desk at seven fifteen that morning and presented him with a disarming smile and the CCTV footage from the bus which had carried Jodie Pearce on Sunday evening from The Half Moon pub to the stop just thirty yards away from her home. It was a journey of about two miles as the crow flies, five miles as the bus travels, and it might as well have transported her to the other side of the world as far as his investigation went.

The footage meant that Jodie Pearce had an alibi not only for the time of the attack on Chris Kemp, when she had been at home with two of her flatmates, but for the time of Andy Miller's murder.

Mulligan turned to look at DS Scott, also uncharacteristically sullen this morning for reasons which had nothing to do with the investigation. He dug into his pocket and pulled out a packet of mints and offered it to Scott. 'Rose stood you up last night, then?'

'By the time I got to The Feathers she'd gone on somewhere.'

Mulligan felt the twitch of a smile tug at the corner of his mouth. 'I warned you about Benny Bradman. He's got that "lonely widower" look about him. That trumps "lonely divorcee" every time, Scottie. You've got no chance.'

Scott grunted but didn't bite on the bait. 'Jodie Pearce is definitely out of the picture then?'

'Looks like it.' Mulligan turned his head away and stared out of the window. They were almost level with Bellevue Mansions. He unclicked his seatbelt and opened the car door. 'I'm going to get some fresh air. If the traffic picks up pull into Bellevue's car park, will you?' Outside the car sub-zero temperatures pinched at his cheeks and made steamy clouds of his breath. He dug his hands into his pockets and picked his way carefully across the icy pavement and into the car park. It was almost empty this morning, most of the residents already stuck in the gridlocked traffic on their ways to work.

He slithered over to the spot allocated to flat 2d, where Andy Miller's car had been parked the night of the murder. He hadn't been able to see much last night in the dark, just the outline of bunches of flowers scattered where Andy's body had lain jammed under the front of his BMW. He bent forward and studied what was left of the decaying flowers. A lavish arrangement of white lilies, their petals brown now from days spent in the bitter frost, carried a card from his parents, their grief encapsulated in a few heartfelt words. There were white roses from his brother and what Mulligan assumed was a sister-in-law, and children, a niece and a nephew. More lilies, pink this time, a formal tribute from the East & Northern Bank. And yet more, a large orange bouquet with a card that read simply "Miss you, Mate." He wondered if the person missing him was Chris Kemp.

To the right of these intimate tributes a collection of supermarket bunches lay heaped in an untidy pile. Chrysanthemums, carnations, shasta daisies, no notes attached, just simple offerings from friends, colleagues, probably even some from passers-by. Mulligan had learned long ago that tragedy could become a spectator sport, strangers taking the opportunity to hang their own grief on to someone else's heartbreak.

To the rear of the untidy pile someone had set up a small shrine. A framed photograph of Andy Miller, pint in hand, grinning at the camera during some noisy night out with friends, was propped against one of those plastic flower holders sold for use in cemeteries. He knew that photograph. It was the one the newspapers had used on

Monday when they covered the story. He stared for a moment, trying to think what was different about the flowers neatly slotted into their box, pink roses, their stems cut short to suit the container, their petals crisp, the soft down of their bloom undamaged by this morning's frost.

Undamaged by this morning's frost? Fresh flowers, then. All the other arrangements had been left on Monday, when news of Andy's death had broken. But these flowers were fresh. He pulled off a glove and leaned over to them, stretching out his fingers to touch the petals. They were cold, but not icy. Left this morning, then, by someone who cared more than the rest, cared enough to come back with fresh flowers? There was no card, but he didn't need to see one to know who brought them.

He straightened his back and surveyed the scene as a whole with a sudden feeling of self-satisfaction, nodded to himself, and turned to slither his way back to DS Scott's Audi, still stationary in the morning traffic. Belted safely into the passenger seat he turned to look at Scott with mischievous eyes.

Scott kept his own gaze on the bumper of the stationary car in front. 'Don't look at me like that George.' He shook his head. 'I know that look of yours. Whatever it is, I'm not doing it.'

27

Rose was finally beginning to realise why she couldn't warm to Annabel Halmshaw. The girl wasn't just a harmless flirt. There was an artfulness about her, a method to the subtle manipulations she used with men. And a corresponding lack of method to the way she engaged with women. It was more difficult, of course, to apply those manipulations to anyone not susceptible to your charms. It resulted in more than wariness, in a sort of caginess that left you sure she wasn't just sparing with the truth, more that the truth just didn't figure anywhere in the equation.

They were sitting in the small glass-walled meeting room close to the Recovery Team, one last session requested by Rose as part of the closing stages of her investigation. She looked down at her notes, freshly written during their latest conversation, and skimmed her eyes over the page again, not so much to read what she had written as to keep her eyes averted from Annabel's face.

She had been questioning Annabel about the abusive calls made to Robert Donovan and Florence Fielding for the best part of fifteen minutes, and for fifteen minutes Annabel had unwaveringly maintained her claims that she discussed the calls only with her team leader, subtly evading any attempt by Rose to drag the conversation in the direction of Andy Miller. And then with one deft move, Rose had confirmed that she'd had a positive identification of Andy's voice from Florence Fielding.

'I'm not really interested now in whether you told Andy about the calls, Annabel. To be frank, I'm not in any doubt that you discussed them with him. What I need to understand is *why* he made them.' Rose flicked her eyes up to Annabel's face just in time to see an unmistakable flash of anger in the doe eyes. She smiled at the girl. 'Did he tell you why he made them?'

Annabel paused, her face a momentary mask of inscrutability to hide the anger, and then she exhaled a sigh and tilted her head to one side. When she spoke her voice was low and slow and husky. 'Oh Rose, I wish *so much* that I could help you and say yes. But he didn't.' She rolled the doe eyes and blinked a few times for good measure. 'He *didn't*.' She folded her hands together in her lap and looked down at them. 'Of course I knew that he made the calls.' Her voice was a whisper now. 'But I don't really understand why.'

'Didn't you ask him?'

'Of course.' She looked up at Rose, the dark eyes as earnest as she could make them. 'He laughed at me, Rose. He said he did it because they deserved it. Because they'd borrowed the money and squandered it, and it wasn't theirs to spend. He said it would teach them a lesson, and if they had any sense they would stop doing it.' A solitary, forced tear rolled its way down her cheek. 'He said the bank was too lax with these people, and it was up to him to do something about it.'

'So he *did* tell you why?'

Annabel frowned. 'He gave me a reason. But a reason isn't always the same as "why", is it? He couldn't be sure the money had been squandered, and even if it had it wasn't his place to judge. He wouldn't tell me why it mattered so much, why he felt he had to punish them until they stopped doing it.' She was becoming agitated now, her voice rising with an unexpected swell of emotion, more tears beginning to flow. 'But they couldn't help it, could they? Robert Donovan had lost his wife, and Florence Fielding was struggling to make ends meet. It wasn't their fault.' The tears turned to a quiet sob. 'Why did he have to insult them? Why couldn't he have helped them instead of punishing them?' The sob became louder. 'For heaven's sake, the ENB owes Florence Fielding money. It owes her more than she owes them.' There was a pause, and then she let out an undeniably anguished wail. 'Why couldn't he leave her alone?'

Rose took in a sharp breath. Annabel *was* manipulative, but this sudden and unexpected outpouring of emotion was remarkably authentic. Was she that good an actress or had Rose finally touched a nerve? For Rose herself the question wasn't why it mattered so much to Andy Miller that these people should be punished, as why it mattered so much to Annabel that they *were* punished. She softened her tone. 'Why didn't you report him, Annabel? If the ENB had known what he was doing they would have stopped it, and then Robert and Florence and anyone else that he was abusing would have been free from his punishments.'

The girl tilted her head from one side to the other and offered up a simpering smile through her tears. 'How could I, Rose? How could I betray the person I loved?'

'Perhaps it wouldn't have been a betrayal. Perhaps it would have been a deliverance. Perhaps if you *had* reported him he might still be alive.'

The girl stiffened and a veil of hostility descended, the simpering smile turning back into an impenetrable mask. 'Please don't say that. If you say that, it … it makes me somehow responsible for his death.' Her voice was suddenly steady, measured, almost brittle around the edges. 'Andy made those calls. And if he really died because of them it wasn't my fault. It wasn't anybody's fault but his own.' She fixed Rose with the doe eyes and there was a hint of defiance in them. 'If Andy died because he made those phone calls, then he brought it upon himself.'

'The watch weren't there, Mr Campling. Not even the box.' Michael Spivey's usually-shifty face displayed an uncharacteristic innocence. 'I checked the drawer you said it was in, and I checked all the other drawers just in case.' He pouted bewilderment. 'No, it definitely weren't there.'

From the other side of his desk Hector Campling observed him with predictable suspicion. 'You collected all the other items?' He knew from his own visit to flat 2d with George Mulligan that the television, stereo and coffee maker had been removed. He still needed to know about those items secreted in drawers.

'Yes Mr Hector.' Spivey's tone was reverent. This in itself wasn't usual but there was something missing from it today that Campling struggled at first to place. 'All the other items.' He nodded with some degree of confidence.

Campling considered for a moment and then placed the missing element. Fear. He narrowed his eyes and peered at the person speaking. Where was the wheedling tone, the nervous tick, the fearful clammy face he was used to seeing at the other side of the desk? Who was this imposter claiming to be Michael Spivey? He leaned forward in his seat and steepled his fingers. 'Are you sure you didn't find the watch and just keep it to yourself?'

If the accusation was designed to provoke a reaction, it didn't work. Spivey simply frowned, thought for a moment, and then shook his head. 'Straight up, Mr Hector. It weren't there.' He sniffed. 'Was it real important?'

Important? Of course it was important. That watch was worth several thousand pounds and Hector Campling had assured himself that taking possession of it to offset his losses wouldn't be too significant a risk. He had painstakingly read through page after page of Andy Miller's credit card statements, images captured on his mobile phone, to assure himself that it was a personal purchase and not a gift. A gift may be missed by a grieving relative, a personal purchase less likely to be so. It astonished him that someone as heavily in debt as Andy Miller could justify the purchase of such a watch, but then he supposed that young people today did tend to suffer from a surfeit of entitlement and a corresponding lack of common sense. The young man had even been vain and self-indulgent enough to spend money he didn't have on a leather box for the watch embellished with his own initials.

He sighed his discontent. 'Well, if it wasn't there, it wasn't there. What have you done with the other items?'

Spivey smiled amiably. 'They're downstairs, Mr Campling. In the storeroom at the back of the office.'

'*Downstairs?*' The solicitor almost choked on the word. 'Then they have to be removed, and immediately. I can't have them on the premises.' His mind was wandering to yesterday's conversation with George Mulligan. 'I understand, Michael, that you spent some time at the Kirkby Police Station yesterday evening?'

Spivey appeared unperturbed. 'I was helping Inspector Mulligan with his enquiries.'

'Indeed?' Campling raised an eyebrow. 'Did he ask you about flat 2d?' He watched Spivey nod his agreement. 'And what did you tell him?'

'Just that I had the keys on me 'cos you'd given them to me. I said you'd asked me to check the flat was securely locked, like, 'cos you'd heard that Chris Kemp was in hospital.' If this explanation had been cooked up for Michael by Benny Bradman, his face didn't betray the fact.

'That was remarkably prudent of you, Michael. Did the Inspector accept your explanation?'

'I fink so.'

'You *think* so?' Campling didn't think so. He already knew that Mulligan had missed items from the flat and would be slowly working out what had happened to them. All the more reason, then, to have them removed from the office. He sucked in a breath. 'When we have finished our conversation I would like you to load the items in the storeroom back into your car. They will have to stay there for the time being, until they can be disposed of.'

'I'm sorry Mr Hector, I'm afraid I can't do that. Benny needs me in the shop today, there's a big meeting on at Sandown Park this afternoon.'

A refusal to accept instructions? Campling furrowed his brow and licked his lips, and wondered if this was just to do with the stolen goods, or whether this unexpected bout of disobedience ran deeper. He put a hand down to the front of his desk and slid open a drawer, and pulled out a sheet of paper, giving it a cursory glance as he laid it down on the desk top. 'Very well. If you are busy this afternoon then I shall have to make other arrangements. Assuming your busy engagement diary is free this evening, perhaps you would deal with this for me.' He slid the piece of paper across the desk. 'I have been giving the matter of Florence Fielding's rent some consideration. As you were so successful in recovering the first instalment of arrears on her rent, it occurs to me that she may have the means to pay the remainder. This is a statement of account showing the outstanding balance after deduction of the three hundred pounds already recovered, plus additional interest and charges owing. I would like you to return to Miss Fielding's address this evening and recover the outstanding balance.'

There was a momentary silence and then Spivey coughed to clear his throat. 'I'm sorry Mr Hector, I'm afraid I can't do that for you.' He sniffed with what sounded curiously like a degree of pride. 'I don't believe Flo … I mean, Miss Fielding … is in a position to pay you any more at the moment. But I'm sure that when she is, she'll pay all the arrears owing. There won't be no need to chase her for it.'

The solicitor uttered an astonished laugh. He wasn't quite sure what had come over Michael Spivey this morning, but he didn't like it. He needed a henchman, someone to do his bidding without question, not a dictator of conscience. 'I'm sure your sentiments are well meant, Michael, but we are not running a charity, we are running a business. If you are unable to perform this simple task for me, and particularly in light of your failure to recover the watch from flat 2d as requested, then the business simply will not be able to reimburse your expenses and pay for your time.'

Across the desk Spivey gave a deferential but acquiescent smile. 'That's alright, Mr Hector, sir. As it happens, Inspector Mulligan has got wind of the collections work I was doing for you.' He put up a hand to reassure the solicitor. 'I didn't give nuffing away, Mr Hector. I ain't a snitch. But he weren't having it, and he says if he catches me at it he'll nick me for being unlicensed.' He sniffed an afterthought. 'And he says if that happens, it won't just be me that's in bother, he'll nick the person what asked me to do the collecting as well.

28

It was late morning by the time George Mulligan finally arrived at the ENB's office to meet with Rose. She ushered him swiftly and silently into the small glass-walled meeting room and pointed to a large black leather holdall which lay open on the table.

Mulligan peered into the bag. 'And you say this was found in Chris Kemp's locker?' He dipped a hand into the bag and pulled out a black leather box bearing Andy Miller's initials. He opened it up, examined the watch inside, and nodded to himself. 'This must be a worth a bit.' If he sounded disappointed it was because he was. He'd hoped that reports of Chris Kemp wearing Andy Miller's cufflinks had been nothing more than a mare's nest, that maybe he had just borrowed them, was even wearing them in remembrance of his friend.

The contents of the leather holdall could only contradict his hopes. The watch, in its tell-tale box, was only one of a number of items that had belonged to the late Andy Miller. He looked up at Rose. 'Tell me how Jodie Pearce fits into all this?'

Rose glanced out through the glass wall to where a chastened Jodie Pearce was sitting at her desk taking a customer call. 'I persuaded Clive Barden to let her return to work and she jumped at the chance. She was so keen when Graham called her this morning that she asked if she could come back today.'

Mulligan raised an eyebrow. 'And what about Annabel?'

'Unlikely though it sounds, the two of them seem to

have come to an uneasy truce.' She smiled at the policeman. 'Annabel says she had no intention of bringing charges over the assault, and has accepted an apology from Jodie. And Jodie has promised to keep her temper in check, on the understanding that if she steps out of line again it will be instant dismissal and no going back. We have no idea how long the peace will last but for now, at least, the ENB are prepared to take Jodie back and see how it goes.'

'And the bag?'

'Mm, I was coming to that. It seems that Jodie visited Chris in hospital yesterday, and while she was there he gave her the key to his staff locker and asked her to empty it out and bring the contents to him at the hospital. Of course she couldn't, because at the time she was still suspended. As I understand it, Chris tried to persuade her to involve Reggie in this bit of subterfuge.'

'And did she?'

Rose shook her head. 'I don't think so. I'm not sure what she was planning to do with the key before Graham called her this morning. Perhaps being invited back to work swayed her in favour of doing the right thing. She turned up here with it and gave it to Graham. He asked me to open the locker with him, by way of witness, and this is what we found.' She nodded in the direction of the bag. 'According to Jodie the bag belonged to Andy, as did most of the contents. We thought we should at least let you know about it. It didn't seem right to send it on to Chris.'

The policeman dropped the box gently back into the bag and zipped it up. It would have to be examined and then returned to Andy Miller's family, but not until he had discussed it with Chris Kemp. He turned an inquisitive eye towards Rose. 'Doesn't it seem strange to you that he gave the key to Jodie and not to Annabel? I thought they were finished? Isn't that what the catfight was all about?'

'Yes, I've been thinking about that. Apparently Chris hasn't heard a thing from Annabel since he was attacked.

She hasn't returned any of his calls or texts. Jodie tried to get her to visit him but she refused. Annabel is making out that it's because she saw Chris wearing Andy's cufflinks. Because she thinks he's a thief.'

Mulligan chuckled and pointed to the leather holdall. 'We can't say she was wrong about that, Rose.'

'No, we can't.' Rose had to share a smile, but her eyes were still troubled.

He watched her for a moment, amused by the transparency of her thought processes, some cause for concern reflected in a frown, a decision mirrored in an almost imperceptible nod of the head. 'Come on Rose, spit it out.' He grinned at her with good humour and was rewarded by a self-deprecating shake of the head.

She leaned her elbows on the table and rested her chin on her hands. 'I've been speaking to Annabel this morning. About the abusive calls.'

'And?'

'Truthfully? I think the girl is unstable.' She nodded to herself. 'Oh she's flirtatious and manipulative and all the rest of it. She puts on a good act. But there's something, something running very deep that's troubling her. I can't tell you what. I can't even hazard a guess. But she got very, very upset when we talked about Andy Miller making those calls.'

'You told her that he was responsible?'

'I didn't have to. She already knew.' She saw surprise register on his face and shook her head. 'Oh, I was never in any doubt of that, even though she denied it. Nor that she discussed it with him. I thought she denied it because she was trying to protect him. But now I'm not so sure.' She leaned closer to Mulligan and stared into his face, looking for understanding. 'She wasn't upset for Andy, she was upset for his victims. Upset that he had judged them. She kept going on about how they didn't deserve to be bullied. I don't know what that means, Mr Mulligan, but it means something.'

It was the vaguest of statements and yet he felt again the unmistakable sensation of hairs prickling at the back of his neck. 'There's a link, isn't there Rose? Between the calls and Andy Miller's death?'

'I want to say yes, but I can't tell you why.' Rose was troubled. 'The thing is, I can't see a link between Chris Kemp and the calls. Surely if the person who murdered Andy also attacked Chris, then there must be a connection?'

Mulligan disagreed. 'Not in the way you mean. You're suggesting that the motive for both crimes has to be the same. But that doesn't have to be the case. Plenty of second murders have been committed to stop a witness speaking out about the first.'

'You mean Chris could have been attacked because he knew who killed Andy Miller?'

'Because he knew, or because he suspected. Or simply because he asked the wrong questions of the wrong person.' He smiled at her with knowing eyes. 'That's the thing with some murderers, Rose. Even though they only set out to commit one murder, they just don't know when to stop.'

'Another piece of chocolate cake, Sergeant Scott?' Marion Halmshaw had already cut another wedge and it hung precariously in the balance atop a small silver cake-slice.

Scott smiled at her and held up a hand. 'No, very kind of you. It was delicious but I don't think I could manage another.' It had been delicious, too, a small compensation for the ridiculous four hour goose-chase George Mulligan had sent him on.

She tipped the slice of cake onto her own plate. 'Oh well, if you're sure. I can never resist a second slice.'

That explained the curves, then, the softly rounded hips and the ample bosom. His eyes skimmed over her as she started to eat, sizing her up. She was a homely woman and somehow sexy at the same time, as warm and round and substantial as her niece was ethereal. Her honey-coloured hair was immaculately bobbed, and her skin glowed with a lethal combination of inner well-being and very expensive face cream.

She was generous on the inside, too. So far since he'd arrived she had empathized with him over the length of his drive from Scarborough, the inclemency of the weather, the driving conditions, and the dire state of his blood sugar and caffeine levels once he'd arrived in Cambridge. The latter she had rectified with the chocolate cake and a double-shot Americano fresh from the most complicated home barista machine he'd ever seen.

Across the table from him she was enjoying the orphaned slice of cake with a slow deliberation, using a small pastry fork to deconstruct its component parts, savouring each in turn. He pursed his lips to suppress a laugh and looked down at his hands so that she couldn't see the amusement in his eyes. He liked to see a woman enjoy herself, he found it sexy. That was probably what went wrong with his marriage, his ex-wife's determination to have a miserable time. He put a hand up to his mouth and coughed to clear his throat. 'I suppose we'd better get back to business.' He pulled a small notebook and a pen from his jacket pocket. 'I just need to confirm those timings with you again.' He flipped open the notebook. 'Like I said, it's only a matter of procedure, there's nothing to worry about. It's purely to eliminate Annabel from our enquiries.'

Marion paused with the fork halfway to her lips and gave an understanding nod. 'Anything we can do to help her, Sergeant.'

'I believe she was staying with you at the weekend, that she arrived on Friday evening and stayed with you until Sunday?'

'Yes, that's quite correct.' She put the fork down and beamed at him. 'We're always so pleased to see her. She's very special to us.'

It was an opening and Scott took it without hesitation. 'She isn't just your niece, is she? Annabel told me that you adopted her.'

'Yes.' Marion gave a sad smile. 'She's my sister's girl. An only child. We didn't have any children of our own, Peter and I.' The smile became momentarily wistful. 'Annabel lost both her parents within a very short space of time, not much more than a year. We were already very close. My sister was a very generous woman, Sergeant Scott. She knew I couldn't have children and she shared her daughter with me. It was only natural that Annabel would come to us.'

'You must be worried about her.'

'Oh, we are. When she called us on Monday evening to tell us Andy had been murdered, I was beside myself. We'd only met him once, you know. When we went up to Kirkby to visit Annabel. He didn't seem to be her usual type. But she seemed very fond of him.'

Scott blinked. 'Not her type? Why was that?'

'Annabel is such a quiet girl. She usually goes for the quiet type to match her own temperament.' She smiled. 'Not that she's had many boyfriends, of course. She's not that sort of girl.'

Not that sort of girl? 'I see.' Scott thought back to Monday and the way Annabel Halmshaw had pouted at him as he'd interviewed her, twirling strands of her hair engagingly around her fingers while they spoke. Just before she threw herself at Chris Kemp. He brushed the thoughts away. 'So you thought Andy was … what? A little more outgoing than her usual boyfriends?'

'Well, speak ill of the dead and all that. He seemed nice enough, a bit cocky maybe but then what young man isn't these days? Of course Annabel's taken it very badly, but she just won't countenance the idea of coming home.' She rolled her eyes. 'Oh, we've tried to get her to come home, Sergeant Scott, but there's no talking to her. I can't bear to think of her up there alone in Kirkby, dealing with this awful thing. She won't even let me come up there and keep her company. I've offered to, you know, Peter would manage here without me.' She sighed. 'But what can you do? Young people will have their own way, won't they?'

He nodded. 'It must be difficult for you. Tell me, did she speak to Andy at all while she was here at the weekend? Did she call him or take a call from him at all?' He gave a smile of encouragement. 'I only ask because it might help us form a picture of where Andy was at the weekend.'

'Of course.' She frowned, considering. 'There were a few calls, I think. She called him on Friday evening to let him know she'd arrived safely. And then on Saturday teatime, just to chat. I seem to think she said he was going out on Saturday evening with his flat mate. Chris, is it?'

'Yes, Chris Kemp.'

She nodded, satisfied at her own recollection. 'Yes, that's right. Chris.' She thought for a moment. 'Then there was the call on Sunday, just before she set off.' She gave a gentle laugh. 'She wanted him to know that she was setting off in plenty of time, because she didn't want to get held up by the weather. She wanted to be back by seven o'clock.'

'Seven?' He felt his pulse miss a beat. 'So what time did she leave?'

'Oh, I should think it was about two o'clock. It usually takes her about four hours door to door, she left an hour earlier because of the weather. They were planning to go the cinema.' Marion was chuckling to herself. 'They live such fast lives these days. If I'd done a four hour drive at that age I would have wanted to put my feet up afterwards.'

A few hours ago, with the Audi tucked safely into the inside lane of the slush covered A1 southbound at a steady sixty miles an hour, Ian Scott had cursed George Mulligan for sending him on a pointless expedition to Cambridge.

He'd even gone so far as to imagine Mulligan sitting safe and snug with Rose Bennett in the staff restaurant at the ENB, sharing a coffee and a joke at his expense, Rose laughing as she asked Mulligan if he'd really despatched Scottie all the way to Cambridge because of a bunch of flowers.

But it wasn't a joke. He'd just written proof of that in his notebook. He had to hand it to Mulligan. He didn't know how he did it but when the old man got that prickle in the back of the neck he was always right on the money.

29

'I don't know what to make of it, Rose. I called Robert Donovan this morning only to find that someone from the bank had already called him. I have queried the matter with the Head of Customer Services, and she has assured me that no such call had been scheduled.' Clive Barden's tone was querulous. He didn't make a habit of humbling himself in front of individual customers, and lowering himself to do so only to find that a junior member of staff had beaten him to the punchline had been a curiously humiliating experience.

Rose tried to sound sympathetic. 'Did the caller leave a name?'

'No. All he could tell me was that it was a young woman, calling on behalf of the bank. She called him yesterday evening.' He sniffed his disapproval from the other end of the line. 'Apparently she apologised to him on behalf of the ENB, and said that the staff member who made the call had been identified and disciplined. She told him that she could promise him unequivocally that the person responsible wouldn't trouble him again.' He paused, then asked "what on earth does it mean, Rose?'

'I suspect, Clive, that someone took it upon themselves to make an apology to Robert Donovan. Probably Annabel Halmshaw.'

'Annabel? Why on earth would she take it upon herself to make such a call?'

'Well, she does work in Customer Services, and she was originally responsible for Donovan's complaint. She

216

probably just wanted to put his mind at rest. You should be pleased that she takes her responsibility to the customer so seriously.' She hoped her explanation would placate him, at least until she'd had the chance to discuss it with George Mulligan. If it was Annabel who made the call she had used an unusual turn of phrase. Perhaps murder *was* the ultimate discipline. 'Would you like me to have another word with her while I'm here?'

'Thank you Rose, that would be appreciated.' He thought for a moment. 'Perhaps I am over-reacting a little, but there has been so much deception over this issue. I thought we had everything under control.'

'Did Robert Donovan accept your apology?'

'Yes, he was most magnanimous about it. I have agreed that the bank will make a donation to a charity of his choice, in memory of his wife. He seemed … most touched.' Clive sounded almost wistful.

'Well, that's a good outcome then, isn't it?' She paused, and then asked 'and what about Florence Fielding? Have you called her yet?' He didn't respond. 'You are going to call her, aren't you, Clive?' She didn't have to see him to know that he was squirming at the other end of the line.

'I won't be dealing with anything else today until the Robert Donovan affair is completed to my satisfaction.' He cleared his throat. 'After that then, yes, I will call Florence Fielding.'

She smiled to herself. 'Well I'm glad to hear it.' She glanced down at her watch. 'Listen Clive, I don't mean to be rude but I promised you that I would complete my report today and I'm working against the clock. Why don't I go now and make a few enquires about this latest call to Donovan?' She began to click at her keyboard, framing the briefest of queries to Stan Wilkins as Clive ended the call.

Stan's response arrived within seconds. 'We have no way of checking calls made from a phone until at least twenty four hours have passed. When do I get my banquet at the Spice Garden?'

Trust Stan to cut to the chase. She hammered off a reply with a wry smile. 'When I've finished my investigation'. She needed to finish that damned report but she would have to speak to Annabel about the call first. She swivelled round on her seat and made to stand up. In front of her Reggie was seated at his desk, his headset resting gently between his fingers, his eyes focused away somewhere in the distance as he pondered some private thought. Rose sank back onto her chair and swivelled back to her keyboard. There was something else she'd been meaning to ask Stan for days now, and it kept getting pushed down to the bottom of the pile. She clicked quickly at the keyboard and tapped the send button, then without waiting for his reply got to her feet and headed off in search of Annabel Halmshaw for what she hoped would be the last time.

George Mulligan had never been in any doubt that he could smell guilt on Chris Kemp. But it wasn't the guilt of murder, it was the guilt of theft.

The lad was looking better today and was sitting up in bed, pillows propped around him, an oversized bandage still swathed around his head. At the sight of the policeman a healthy flush of colour had spread across his unshaven cheeks, an indication of … what? Embarrassment? Shame? A mixture of both?

Mulligan pulled up a plastic chair and placed it next to the head of the bed so that he could sit and look the young man in the face. 'I'm glad to hear you're feeling better, Chris. I imagine there are a few things you'd like to get off your chest.' He watched as the healthy flush deepened into an unmistakable blush. 'There's nothing to worry about, lad. I know about the rent, and I know about Michael Spivey.' He chuckled to put the lad at ease. 'I don't think you were ever at risk there, you know. Michael likes to think he's a hard man, but he hasn't had much practice.'

'He threatened me. He pushed me against the wall and threatened to take stuff from the flat.'

'I know he did. He's told me all about it. And he's very sorry.' Mulligan wasn't sure that Spivey was actually sorry, of course, but he wanted to put Chris Kemp's mind at rest and move his thought process past flat 2d onto what happened on Tuesday evening. 'I don't want you to worry about anything that happened at the flat, Chris. Spivey's been spoken to, and I'll deal with Hector Campling. We'll have your belongings removed from the flat and returned to you.' He focused his eyes on Chris Kemp's face. 'And we'll have all of Andy's belongings removed and returned to his family.'

He watched with some satisfaction as Chris Kemp looked away sharply, stung by the reminder of his crime. 'It's alright lad, I know you took Andy's stuff. We've got the bag.' This brought a different reaction, one of surprise. 'Yes, I know you gave the key to Jodie. She's a decent young woman, she handed it to Graham Clarke, and he passed it to us.' It wasn't quite the way things had happened, but it would do for now.

Chris Kemp looked squashed now, deflated by the exposure of his crime, the pettiness of it all beginning to dawn on him. He made a vague stab at justifying has actions. 'Andy stole from me. He took the rent money I gave him and he didn't pay the rent.'

'I know he did. And I suppose you just thought you were redressing the balance by helping yourself to some of his stuff by way of compensation.' Mulligan nodded. 'But it didn't really make it better, did it?' Chris Kemp didn't respond, except to frown sullenly. Mulligan pressed on with his line of questioning. 'Listen Chris, I have some questions I need you to answer for me. I know you're still not a hundred percent, so just do your best.'

Chris nodded his agreement.

'Have you spoken to Annabel Halmshaw?'

'No. She hasn't returned any of my calls.' He looked

down at his hands, avoiding Mulligan's gaze. 'I suppose she's been busy.'

'So you haven't spoken to her since Tuesday evening?'

'No.'

'And she left you in the pub when? Nine thirty?'

'I think so. She was tired after the fight with Jodie. She just wanted to go home.'

'And you weren't ready to go home? You wanted to stay in the pub a bit longer?'

Chris Kemp blushed. 'I was avoiding Michael Spivey. I thought he was going to come back for the rent.'

Mulligan nodded in understanding. 'But when she offered you a lift home, you weren't ready to go?'

This threw Chris Kemp. 'Offered me a lift? I don't remember that?' He frowned, trying to remember. 'Maybe she did and I just can't remember. All I remember is staying to have another quick half with the landlord, and then setting off walking. I walked slowly, like I said I wasn't in any rush.'

'Were you drunk?'

'Drunk? I don't think so.' He tried to remember. 'I'd had a couple of glasses of wine in the restaurant, a couple of pints and another half in the pub. Nothing more than that.'

'And then part of the way home, something happened to draw your attention to the Mill Beck. Can you remember what that was?'

Chris Kemp shook his head. 'I can't be sure. I thought I heard someone calling for help.'

'A girl?'

'I don't know.'

'Can you remember the attack yet, Chris? What happened when you were hit on the head?'

Chris Kemp folded his face into a frown of concentration. 'I sort of remember the pain at the back of my head, and putting up my fingers and they were sticky. I suppose it was blood.'

'So the blow wasn't hard enough to knock you out straight away? You were still conscious?'

'I suppose I must have been if I can remember feeling the blood.' Chris Kemp shivered. 'There was only one blow. I think I turned round to look where it came from. There was someone there but I couldn't make out who it was.'

'A man or a woman?'

'I don't know. Everything was blurred. I tried to stay upright, stay on the land. But ...' His face crumpled, distressed by the memory, 'whoever it was kept pushing at me with something. I don't know, it must have been what they hit me with.'

'They pushed you into the water?'

He nodded. 'I can't remember anything else. I'm sorry.' His lip began to quiver, pushed almost to the point of tears. He blinked them back. 'Mr Mulligan, why would anybody want to hurt me like that?'

'Truthfully Chris, I don't know. But I can promise you that I'll do whatever I can to find out.' Mulligan gave a half-smile of reassurance. The lad was getting anxious now and it wouldn't be right to push him. He leaned forward in his seat and spoke as gently as he could. 'You've been really helpful, Chris, but there's one more thing I need to know before I leave you in peace.' He fixed his eyes on Chris Kemp's face. 'Can you remember what you and Annabel were talking about before she left the pub?'

30

Rose read the brief email over again to make sure she hadn't misunderstood the tone. 'Why do you need to know about Reggie? Can't you leave the poor bloke in peace?' Nope, she hadn't misunderstood. She cast a glance over her shoulder at the poor bloke in question. Reggie was taking a customer call, his head nodding away in kindly agreement at whatever tale of woe was being related.

She clicked a brief response into her keyboard. 'Who rattled your cage?' It wasn't like Stan to be so abrupt. 'I wouldn't ask if it wasn't important.' Within seconds her mobile phone danced into life and she swept it up and pressed it to her ear. 'Stan? Why am I in the dog house?'

Stan's voice was as curt as his email. 'Hell Rose, everyone has a right to be forgotten.'

'Of course they do. Always supposing they've done something in the first place that might require forgetting.' She blew out a breath of frustration. 'What is it that you don't want to tell me?'

'Why do you want to know?'

'Because I think it might be material to Andy Miller's death, and to the attack on Chris Kemp.'

'Yeah, right.' He sounded belligerent. 'If you want to know about Reggie, ask Clive Barden.'

'He'll only tell me what he wants me to know. And I want to know the truth.' She turned again and looked at Reggie. He looked so unremarkable. And yet …

She'd seen another side to him, a temper that flared when she probed too deeply into his motivations. She put her lips close to her phone and whispered into it. 'Andy Miller and Chris Kemp were chasing Reggie's customers for extra payments. He wasn't meeting his collections targets and they were rubbing his nose in it.'

'So?'

'So he had a motive for getting his own back on them.'

Stan snorted a disparaging laugh. 'You're way off the mark, Rose. I've known Reggie for years. He wouldn't hurt a fly.'

'Then prove it.'

There was a long silence. Eventually he said 'OK, I'll give you a hint about Reggie. Get a pen and write this down. I'm not prepared to put it in an email.'

She grabbed at her pen and scribbled as he spoke. 'Alan Simmonds. 2007.' He fell silent, and she read the words over. 'Alan Simmonds, 2007. What does that mean?'

'That's for you to work out. And you didn't get that from me. Clive Barden promised it was dead and buried, that no one would talk about it again.' He paused and then said a little more kindly 'I don't want to fall out with you over this, Rose. Don't rake things up that are better off forgotten. People could get hurt.' He hung up on her without another word.

Rose stared at the disconnected phone, silent and disappointed. She didn't want to fall out with Stan either, and she certainly didn't want to hurt anyone, but it was a bit too late for Andy Miller for anyone to take the moral high ground on that one.

She went back her laptop and clicked determinedly at the keys, typing the words Stan had dictated to her into an internet search engine, along with the words "East and Northern Bank". The screen responded with a list of possible matches and she scanned each in turn, hoping for an obvious fit. Halfway down the screen a headline caught her eye, an entry from the archives of a national newspaper, and she clicked on the headline to bring up the detail.

She didn't have to skim too far through the content to realise that Stan was right. People *could* get hurt. But it was too late to worry about the consequences now. People already *had* been hurt.

Reggie Croft joined the sandwich queue in the staff restaurant with little more on his mind than what to have for lunch. His usual choice was a plain baguette with ham and cheese, an unexciting combination that he'd been enjoying every day for as long as he could remember. But the morning had been a difficult one, and the temptation was growing to compensate by indulging in the more exotic option of a ciabatta roll filled with coronation chicken, preferably with a side order of chips.

There was no rush to make a decision. The queue was a long one, maybe a dozen people in front of him, plenty of time yet to make up his mind. A little further ahead of him Jodie Pearce was gazing over the counter at an array of sandwich fillings. He hadn't expected to see her back at work so soon. In fact, he hadn't expected to see her back at work at all. Not that he minded her being back in the team, she was a good worker. He just hoped she wasn't going to try to use him as a confidante again.

He glanced around idly, enjoying the empty headspace that an hour away from his desk afforded. He'd handled a number of difficult calls in the last couple of hours and the effort had left him drained. He tried to be sympathetic to every customer he handled, whether they deserved his sympathy or not, but it wasn't easy. He'd made himself a promise, many years ago, that he would treat every customer with compassion, and never stand in judgment, but it wasn't an easy promise to keep.

It had been easier with Andy Miller and Chris Kemp in place, of course. If he handled a call from a dishonest customer, some chancer with the means to pay his debts and the inclination to spend the cash on something else, then he could keep his promise and show as much compassion and understanding as he liked, safe in the knowledge that Andy or Chris could be relied upon to make a follow up call and chase the scheming bastard for a payment. He frowned to himself. He definitely deserved the ciabatta.

The queue was moving forward now and he shuffled a few steps with it. To his left a shorter queue was forming at a salad bar and he smiled to himself. Who eats salad in December? Skinny girls, of course. His smile deepened. He didn't need to examine the queue too closely to know who would be in it. Isabel Pritchard from Accounts. She always looked like she needed a good feed. And Megan from the mail room, permanently on a diet since setting the date for her wedding. She'd been engaged for two years now and the wedding wasn't until next August. That was a hell of a lot of lettuce.

And Annabel Halmshaw.

She was leaning, pale and ethereal, against the chrome runners that skirted the salad bar, spooning something cold and unappetising into a clear plastic box.

Reggie hesitated, undecided for a moment between the food he wanted to eat and an alternative choice that would put him closer to Annabel, and on impulse plumped for the latter. Behind her in the short queue he could smell her perfume. It was musky and sensual, a curious choice for a young girl. And she was tall for a young girl, even without heels. What was he thinking? She wasn't a young girl any more, was she? She was a young woman now. If it was her.

Of course it was her. He still had the photograph, clipped from a newspaper, and he'd examined it again yesterday evening. There was no mistake. Older, a little taller perhaps, but definitely her. She'd even grown to look like her mother. That poor woman.

His mouth was suddenly dry, his feet rooted to the tiled floor, his hands clammy. Someone behind him coughed and he turned his head to see a thin, dark-haired girl, impatient for her turn to pick up a plastic box and fill it with cold pasta and tasteless watery tomatoes. When he turned back to the bar Annabel was gone. His eyes scanned the restaurant and he saw her again, walking over to the coffee bar to pick up a drink. She was getting away from him.

He stepped out of the queue, ignoring discontented mutterings behind him, and strode over to the coffee machine next to her. He pulled a paper cup from a dispenser and set about pouring a white coffee, no sugar, twisting his head slightly to look with a smile at the girl beside him. Annabel looked away, and it occurred to him that she was avoiding any sort of engagement.

Did she know, then? Did she know already? Surely not. Surely there would be an acknowledgement? Anger, rage, frustration, even just the simple desire to know *why*?

If she knew.

Unable to help himself, he shifted all his weight onto his left hip and feigned a stumble, knocking into her with his elbow. 'Annabel, I'm so sorry.' It was a clumsy subterfuge, and he showered his own fingers with burning hot coffee in the process. He dropped the cup onto the counter and began to lick the liquid from his fingers, his eyes darting over his hands to her face, searching for a reaction.

She did turn to look at him, but with only the barest recognition. 'These machines are so awkward, aren't they?' She didn't even use his name. The briefest of exchanges, detached and unsympathetic, and she was gone. Gone over to a till to pay for her lunch, leaving him to lick at his scalded fingers.

He wanted to dash after her, to pay for her lunch, to sit and talk to her. But it wasn't going to happen. He could see that now. The absurdity of his thoughts suddenly hit home and he turned back to the machine and carefully poured himself a second coffee. What the hell was he playing at? Did he think he could just treat her to a canteen lunch and everything would be alright? Was he really foolish enough to think that he could befriend her, talk to her, explain it all away?

Of course not. He clamped a lid onto to the coffee and turned towards the tills. There was no sign of Annabel, gone now back to her desk or some other corner to eat her lunch. He threw a scattering of coins onto the counter to pay for his drink and strode off down the restaurant, only to catch sight of her in the distance, making her way into the lift with a crowd of other colleagues.

He paused and looked around for an empty table. He'd lost track of time, bought a coffee he didn't want, and completely forgotten about lunch. He was out of his routine, anxiety catching his breath, guilty thoughts fraying at the edge of his nerves. He sank down onto a chair at an empty table for two and put the coffee down in front of him, then rested his elbows on the table and covered his face with his hands. He was as sure now as he'd even been that it was her. Calling herself Halmshaw wasn't enough of a disguise.

What the hell was she doing here? Why was she here, in this office, working here? Co-incidence? Was co-incidence really that cruel? He'd kept it together all these years, put it all behind him, done his best to forget. And now here she was, the starkest reminder he could ever have that he was never going to escape the legacy of his actions, the consequences of just doing the job he was instructed and paid to do.

There wasn't going to be any forgiveness. Not for him. He tried to keep his nose clean these days, stay away from the sort of tricks that Chris and Andy had used to put pressure on a customer. If Annabel had known just what sort of a lowlife Andy Miller was, she would never have got involved with him. If she'd known he was a bully, if she'd known that he was systematically threatening customers, tormenting them about their debts, she might …

He didn't want to think about it. If Annabel had known the sort of things Andy Miller was up to, well God only knows what she might have done.

31

'Come on then Rose, what have you got for me?' George Mulligan leaned his elbows on the table and stared into her face. She looked troubled, not a state of mind he associated with Lu Aylesbury's niece.

They were sitting in the Riverside Café, a rendezvous of her choice, well after the lunchtime rush had died down and beyond any risk of a stray ENB employee overhearing their conversation. Rose pulled her laptop out of her briefcase and propped it on the table, and opened the lid. 'It doesn't matter how I know about this. I need to tell you something about Annabel.'

Mulligan's eyes narrowed. Somehow today all roads led to Annabel.

Rose pulled her chair closer to him and lowered her voice, even though the café was empty. 'Back in 2007 an ENB customer called Alan Simmonds got into financial difficulty. He had a number of business accounts with the ENB, including a significant overdraft and a credit card account, and a credit card in his own name as a personal customer. Earlier in the year his business had suffered cash flow problems, and it seems he'd used his credit cards to fund what he thought was going to be a short-term issue for the business. Only it wasn't a short-term problem. He ran out of credit both for the business and on a personal level, and he couldn't meet the contractual payments.'

'Were the bank sympathetic?'

Rose replied with a withering look. 'This is the ENB we're talking about. What do you think?' She smiled at his reaction. 'Anyway, the failure of his business hit him very hard and caused him a great deal of stress. I'm sorry to say that … well, he committed suicide, Mr Mulligan. It's terrible to think of, a man being under such financial stress that he feels there is no way out.' She paused and sighed. 'At the inquest, his widow claimed that he'd been hounded by the ENB over his debts, particularly his personal debts. She went so far as to suggest that they were partly responsible for his death, that the harassment he received had tipped him over the edge. There was one particular individual who called him regularly about his credit card accounts, eight, nine, sometimes ten times a day, and those calls went on for weeks and weeks. She described the calls as relentless bullying.

'Clive Barden attended the inquest on behalf of the bank and pitched a very tight case. The ENB were criticised for their tactics in applying undue pressure to a customer in difficulties, but the coroner found that they couldn't be held responsible for the death because other factors had to be taken into consideration. His widow continued her campaign against the bank alone, but her grief got the better of her. Four months after the inquest she died from a heart attack. She was just thirty nine years of age.'

Mulligan frowned. 'This is all very sad, Rose, but I don't see what it's got to do with the case.'

'You will.' Rose sighed. 'The Simmonds left a fifteen year old daughter. She wasn't without family, and the reports I've seen say that she went to live with her aunt and uncle.' She leaned a little closer to Mulligan and held his gaze. 'In Cambridge.'

In Cambridge. In Mulligan's brain the wheels and cogs began to turn. 'And the aunt and uncle were called Halmshaw.' It was a simple statement. No need for it to be a question.

Rose turned her laptop towards Mulligan and pointed to the screen. 'This is one of the newspaper reports of the inquest.' She had zoomed the screen to home in on an indistinct photograph, a grainy image of Alan Simmonds, his wife and his daughter. The picture was blurred, but there was no doubt. 'Annabel Halmshaw is Alan Simmonds' daughter.'

He took hold of the laptop and pulled it towards him. 'Have you told anyone about this?'

'No, not even Clive.' She sounded anxious now. 'There's something else. Someone made an unplanned call to Robert Donovan yesterday evening. A girl, claiming to be calling on the bank's behalf. According to Clive, whoever made that call didn't just call to apologise. She told Robert Donovan that the person responsible had been disciplined.'

'Disciplined?' His frown deepened. 'Was it Annabel?'

'I don't know yet. I went looking for her earlier but she'd gone for lunch. I didn't want to follow her to the restaurant, it's not something I want to ask her about in public.'

Mulligan was grave now. 'Rose, I'm going to need your help. The reason Scottie isn't with me is because I sent him to Cambridge to see the Halmshaws. I wanted to confirm Annabel's alibi for Sunday evening. He won't be back for a couple of hours yet.' He shook his head. 'I need you to keep my confidence on this, Rose. There's doubt over her alibi for Sunday night. According to her aunt she left Cambridge hours earlier than she claimed. We're trying to verify that now, but it could take some time.'

'You think she could have killed Andy Miller?'

'I don't know.' He shrugged. 'But I fear so. Could Andy Miller or Chris Kemp have been the ringer who made those calls to Alan Simmonds?'

'Unlikely. Neither of them would have been in the Recovery Team at the time. And you have to understand that banking regulation wasn't as tight then as it is now. Whoever made the calls, the bank couldn't be held responsible for Alan Simmonds' death.'

'Can we find out who it was?'

Rose was uncharacteristically cagey. 'It might be possible. But is it really necessary?'

Suspicion rose in Mulligan's eyes. 'You already know, don't you?'

'No, I don't know. Not with any certainty. But I do believe that the person responsible was exonerated and promised anonymity going forward. If it's in any way possible, I'd like to think we can deal with this in a way that won't expose that individual. He's been trying to put it behind him for seven years now.' She thought for a moment, uneasy at the arrival of some unbidden thought. 'Is there any evidence to point to Annabel as Andy Miller's killer?'

'Hard evidence, no. Circumstantial evidence … I wouldn't know where to start.' Mulligan put his head in his hands. The girl had access to the flat and to the spare car keys. She lied about her alibi, she could have arrived back in time to kill the lad and then drive around killing time until eleven o'clock, making it look as though she'd just arrived back from Cambridge. She was with Chris Kemp in Scarborough on Tuesday evening, she left him just before he was attacked, and she knew exactly which route he would be taking to walk home. She lied about him being drunk and about offering to give him a lift home. She could easily have driven ahead of him, parked up, and gone down to the edge of the Beck to lie in wait. All she had to do was call to him, make some commotion to get him down to the water and hit him with something heavy enough to knock him out, something also long enough to push him into the Beck with when he became dizzy. The blow to the back of the head didn't kill him. It wasn't hard enough. It could easily have been delivered by a girl, even one as slight as Annabel.

Worst of all he realised now that there was a chilling detachment about her, as if once the crime was committed she could cast all thoughts of the victim from her mind.

She'd made no attempt to visit Chris Kemp in hospital, ignoring his calls, ignoring his texts, latching on to notion that Chris was a thief to justify her coldness towards him. And as for Andy Miller ... easy to weep over a dead man, easy to play the grieving girlfriend when you can't be called upon to validate the depths of your affections for a warm, living, breathing human being.

But a bit of a giveaway when you don't even bother to mark his passing by leaving flowers at the place where he died.

A walk in the fresh air was supposed to clear your head, especially after lunch. That's what Marion always said.

Annabel leaned against the wall, resting her forearms on the coping stone, and stared across the waste ground. Not too far in the distance she could see the Mill Beck, glistening as it hurried around moss-covered boulders, too shallow today to cover more than the smallest cobbles.

Why hadn't the water been deeper?

Too late to do anything about it now. She took in a deep breath and turned back to the pavement. A few yards further along there was a curve in the wall, a viewing point where railings replaced bricks, and a thoughtfully placed bench where wildlife lovers could sit and observe the spot where urban foxes were known to sometimes play, and where Chris Kemp had been struck too feebly on the back of the head.

She hadn't expected the blow to kill him, but she had at least hoped it would knock him out, render him senseless enough for the icy waters of the Beck to finish him off.

But he was still alive, calling her mobile hour after hour, sending text after text, asking her to visit him, asking if she could remember exactly what happened on Tuesday evening, asking her if she was OK. She squeezed her eyes tight shut. Of course she wasn't going to visit him. Of course she could remember exactly what happened. Of course she wasn't OK.

He was still alive, wasn't he? How could she be OK?

He was supposed to die. That was the whole point of hitting him on the back of the head. The baseball bat had just been too heavy. She'd swung it with all her strength but she couldn't get the height, couldn't lift it high enough for the blow to land with enough force to shatter his skull, couldn't muster enough hatred for him to do the job properly. At least the bat had been long enough to push him without getting too close, to skew him off balance enough to topple into the Beck.

She felt a sudden surge of shame. Uncle Peter had bought her that baseball bat. Keep it in the boot of your car, he'd said. A young woman driving around on her own should have something handy, something to defend herself with. You won't ever need to use it. A girl like you wouldn't know how. But if it's there in the boot, a part of me will be there with you. It'll make you feel safer.

Poor Uncle Peter. What would he think if he knew she'd tried to kill with it, that she'd tried to use the thing he'd given her for self-defence to take another's life? What would he think if he knew it was in the North Sea now, stained with Chris Kemp's blood and floating away with all the other flotsam and jetsam, carrying her guilt away with it?

He loved her. He would understand. And so would Marion. They wouldn't blame her for what she'd done. She could hold on to that thought, keep it safe, nail her sanity to it. But they mustn't know. She must protect them from that. She'd lost one set of parents, she mustn't lose another.

There was no need for them to know. No one suspected. Why would they suspect her? No one knew who she was. To all the world she was a grieving girlfriend. She had no obvious motive for killing Andy, or for hurting Chris. No one at the ENB knew she was Alan Simmonds' daughter, no one would suspect that she'd taken a job at the bank just to get at the truth, to see for herself whether they really did hound customers to their deaths, pushing ruthlessly for money without regard to circumstance. She had to know the answer.

And to get the answer, she'd had to get as close to the truth as she could. No bank process was ever going to reveal what really happened above and beyond acceptable behaviour. There were no training sessions in how to threaten a customer. She'd scoured every file and document, every internal web page within her rights of access, and found nothing. But then a bank is just an entity.

A bank can't think, can't feel, can't decide for itself. Only individuals can do that, think of other methods, feel the temptation, decide to act outside the rules. The truth wouldn't be found in the process, only in the people who worked the process.

Only in those who stepped *outside* the process.

Andy Miller stepped outside the process. She knew that from the day she met him, the day she went down to the Recovery Team to ask about a customer account. She'd asked if nothing could be done to help the woman and Andy had laughed, showing all his little ratty teeth, and asked why she should be helped. She'd borrowed the money, she had to pay it back. Just another scrounger.

To him, she was just another scrounger. Is that what he thought of Donovan, and Florence, and her father? He stepped outside the process when he hounded Robert Donovan and Florence Fielding, and God knows how many others who didn't deserve it. Just as he'd hounded her father, calling him hour after hour, day after day, week after week, taunting him about his debts, torturing him about the burden he could never repay.

She shivered. It was turning colder, the winter sun already sinking into the mid-afternoon, taking her heart with it. It was hard playing the long game but she'd played it this far, she was almost home and dry. If she could just stick it out for another week or so she could resign, blame her grief at Andy's death, go back to Marion and Peter, find a job in Cambridge, forget it ever happened.

Andy was dead. He couldn't tell anyone that she came back from Cambridge early to see him, that she took his spare car keys from the drawer in the hall while he was making a coffee. He couldn't tell anyone that she'd left the flat and let herself into the BMW, that she called him from the car to tell him that she hated him, to tell him that he was scum, tell him that she was going to drive his precious car into a brick wall. Couldn't tell anyone how he'd looked out of the window, phone in hand, as she flashed the BMW's headlights to show she wasn't joking. How she'd waited until he ran out of the door, watched him slide across the icy car park in his socks, watched him throw his hands over the bonnet of the car, his eyes wide with bewilderment as she'd put her foot on the gas. Couldn't tell anyone how she'd closed her eyes tight shut as the car had lunged forward crunching over his body once, twice, three times, crushing his bones as she crushed the life out of him. How she'd flung open the door and slithered between parked cars and the boundary wall back to the sanctuary of her own car, tucked into the safety of the side street that flanked Bellevue Mansions.

Her heart was beginning to pound. She had to stop thinking about it. It had been easy at first, pretending that it hadn't happened. She'd managed to blank it out. But she couldn't do the same with Chris. Chris wasn't dead. He hadn't realised it was her, she was sure of that. He was in too much pain when he turned to look at her, and his eyes had looked queer, like frosted windows into an empty soul. He'd looked at the baseball bat, but not at her. And what if he had? She was wearing an old coat he'd never seen, a coat with fur around the hood, a hood so deep it had shrouded her face so well you would swear there was no one in there.

No, Chris didn't know it was her, and yet all the same it

made her feel afraid, knowing that he wasn't dead. There was a risk to him being alive, a tiny, fragile risk that one day someone might say "who hit you, Chris?" and instead of saying "I don't know" he might say "it was a girl". And then people would begin to wonder which girl …

The sky was darkening now, threatening a winter shower. She cast her gaze back towards the office. She'd have to go back and brazen it out for the rest of the day. If she could get through today, keep a low profile, she could call in sick tomorrow. Yes, that would work. She could call in sick tomorrow, get the doctor to sign her off with stress, maybe even submit her resignation. Then she could go home to Marion and Peter. She needed to see them now. She needed to talk to Marion, tell her that she was wrong.

She needed to tell Marion that taking a walk in the fresh air didn't always clear your head.

32

'I absolutely forbid it.' Clive Barden raised himself to his most pompous height and gave George Mulligan the full force of his authority. 'I will not permit such activity on bank premises and I will not, absolutely not, have you put my staff at risk.'

Two hundred and fifty miles away in Scarborough, unable to witness Clive's physical posturing from the end of a phone line, Mulligan was impervious to the display. He closed his eyes and thought for a moment, choosing his words carefully. 'Mr Barden ... Clive ... I'm not actually asking for your permission. I ...'

'Then what the hell are you doing?'

'I'm trying to keep you informed.' The policeman rolled his eyes in frustration and brought them to rest on Rose, sitting quietly beside him in the glass-walled meeting room. Rose for her part was avoiding his gaze, her face the serene mask of someone clearly more accustomed to riding out Clive Barden's tantrums than Mulligan himself. He blew out a breath. 'We have strong grounds to suspect that Annabel Halmshaw knows something about the murder of Andy Miller and the attack on Chris Kemp.' He fell short of sharing his own suspicion that she was responsible. 'I don't believe there is a risk to anyone's safety but we believe that the girl may be unwell, and that she may not react well to being questioned. I'm waiting for a female officer to join me here so that there is an appropriate officer on hand to support Annabel, if needed.'

'Why have you asked me to provide support from our

security staff if there is no risk to safety?'

'It's a precautionary measure. We understand that Annabel left the building at lunchtime, but she's back at her desk now. We would prefer her not to leave the building again until we've spoken to her. But Rose believes she may be a little … fragile. Given the events of Tuesday, and the fight with Jodie Pearce, we think it's in everyone's interests – Annabel's included – for there to be someone on hand.'

'Given the events of Tuesday? Good God, you're not expecting another fight to break out?'

Mulligan was momentarily at a loss how to answer. Expecting it? No. Insuring against it? Maybe. 'Look Clive, all I'm asking is that there are some security personnel on hand for up to an hour until my officer gets here. Rose is going up to Customer Services now, to ask to speak to Annabel, and she's going to take her to the staff restaurant for coffee. That will keep her occupied and on site until my officer appears.'

'Absolutely not. I forbid it, Inspector Mulligan. You are not to put Rose in a position of risk.'

'You forbid me to put Rose in a position of risk?' Mulligan turned to Rose with a wry smile and a raised eyebrow. He knew that repeating Clive's words would get her attention. She turned to look at him, nodded her agreement, and quietly let herself out of the room. Alone with his phone, Mulligan smiled. 'I'm sure Rose would be gratified to know that you have an eye on her safety.' He watched through the glass as she walked away from the Recovery Team, heading in the direction of Customer Services, and realised with some curiosity that he wasn't alone in watching her.

Reggie Croft was also watching her, and Mulligan observed as he took off his headset and placed it down on his desk, leaning back in his chair, his eyes fixed on her back as she exited through a nearby doorway. Mulligan wondered what Reggie's interest was, even more so when

Reggie turned to glance at him through the glass wall of the meeting room, and then turned quickly away with a blush on realising that he was not only watcher, but himself being watched.

The policeman got to his feet and lowered the blind above the glass wall, shielding himself from prying eyes. 'Clive, there's something I need to tell you about Annabel Halmshaw.' He slipped a finger between the slats of the blind and peered through the gap at the Recovery Team. Reggie had vanished. He let go of the blind. 'But before I do that, there's something I need to ask you. How long has Reggie Croft worked for the ENB?'

Rose smiled and sipped on her coffee. 'I promise this will be the last time I bother you, Annabel. My work completes today, but there were just one or two things I needed to cover off with you before I leave.'

Across the small restaurant table Annabel forced a smile of her own. The bloom had gone from her cheeks now, and dark hollows curved beneath the once-innocent eyes. 'Of course. Whatever I can do to help.' It was the right thing to say but there was insincerity in her voice. She didn't look directly at Rose, but turned her head to look out of the window, avoiding eye contact. There was a small formal garden below, a place of contemplation provided by the ENB for staff to enjoy during the summer months, and she appeared to be studying it, its winter emptiness illuminated by the glow of surrounding office windows.

'Did you use the garden in the summer?' Rose bent her head to follow Annabel's gaze. 'Clive thinks it's a shameful waste of money and ought to be turned into a car park.' She gave a deprecating laugh. 'Typical banker, every penny has to earn its keep.' She had brought a notebook with her and she flipped it open and scribbled the date at the top of a clean page. 'One of the reasons I wanted to speak to you was to thank you for calling Robert Donovan yesterday.'

Annabel stiffened and turned a questioning eye towards her. For a moment Rose thought she was going to challenge the assumption, and then her face showed an unexpected acceptance and she nodded. 'Yes, I did call him. I suppose you think that was wrong of me?'

'Not at all. I think you did it with the best of intentions.'

'How did you know?'

'Clive called him this morning to apologise on behalf of the bank, and he wasn't too pleased that you beat him to it.' She leaned towards Annabel. 'Between you and me, it made my day. It does Clive good to have the wind knocked out of his sails every so often. It keeps him on his toes.'

'You're not angry then?'

'Of course not. The bank needs people who care about the customer, Annabel. And you care about the customer.' Rose thought for a moment and then asked 'how did you come to work here? For the ENB, I mean? You're not from this area, are you?'

A faint hint of colour flushed into Annabel's pallid cheeks. 'Oh, there was no real plan. You know how it is these days. I left university with a degree in Business Studies and there just weren't enough exciting jobs to go round.' She gave a hollow laugh. 'Well, there weren't enough jobs to go round, period. The university encouraged us to apply for graduate trainee roles wherever we could, whether we wanted them or not. I was lucky. People with better degrees than mine are flipping burgers.'

'Was that this year?'

'No, last year.'

'Are you enjoying it?'

Annabel shrugged, and looked the least Rose had ever seen like someone who was enjoying her job. 'As a trainee I get to move around a lot. I enjoy the variety of moving from department to department.'

'Is that how you met Andy?'

The flush in Annabel's cheeks deepened. 'Yes. In a way. I'd been moved to Customer Services and had to field a query about an outstanding debt. My team leader sent me to the Recovery Team to ask Andy about it.' Her cheeks dimpled into a smile that was almost genuine. 'We hit it off straight away. I bumped into him a few times in the restaurant, and then one day he asked me out for a drink. We were more or less inseparable after that.'

Rose put down her pen and wrapped her hands around her coffee for comfort. It was warm in the restaurant, the heating turned up against the winter cold, but she needed something to cling to, something to hold on to. She felt suddenly out of her depth. Not unsafe, but unqualified, unprepared for the turn in direction that the conversation was about to take. No going back now. 'It must have been very difficult for you.'

'It is. I still can't quite believe that he's gone.'

'I didn't mean Andy's death. I meant learning that someone you loved didn't share your values.' Rose stared into her coffee as she spoke. 'Because he didn't, did he? I mean, you had every reason to root for the customer, to want the customer to be treated fairly, with sympathy, and with dignity. But Andy didn't sing from the same hymn sheet, did he?'

The challenge hung in the air for a moment, and then Annabel's face morphed into an impenetrable mask. 'I don't understand the point, Rose.' She spoke very quietly now. 'Could you please explain to me?'

Rose turned to look at her. 'Well, Andy didn't care about the customer, did he? At least, that's the impression he gave. He didn't think twice about pressurising people to make payments they couldn't afford. And he didn't think twice about making threatening phone calls. Whatever the reason for such behaviour, it must have troubled you. There must have been times you thought about ending the relationship?'

Annabel had turned away again, and was staring out of

the window. 'I didn't really think about it.'

'Florence Fielding will be compensated, you know. For the calls Andy made to her. I've leaned on Clive, and he's agreed to address her complaint as soon as possible. She'll be well compensated for what's happened.'

There was a prolonged silence and then Rose asked 'Tell me, Annabel, did you apply to other banks when you were looking for work, or just the ENB?'

'Like I said, we were encouraged to apply anywhere we could.' It was almost a whisper.

'So it was just a random application, then? And nothing to do with finding the person who hounded your father over his debts?'

The last remnants of colour drained from Annabel's cheeks and she closed her eyes, and for a moment Rose thought the girl was going to pass out. Then her lips curled with a smile and she gave the slightest nod of the head, a gesture of surrender. 'I did find him.' She opened her eyes and turned them directly on to Rose. 'It was Andy.'

33

'It wasn't Andy, Annabel.'

'Of course it was.' Annabel was becoming animated now. 'I only suspected at first, but when I asked him about the Robert Donovan call he laughed about it. He admitted it to me. He was a bully, Rose. He bullied people over their debts.' She gave a quiet contemptuous laugh. 'He found it funny. He said it was funny to hear the customer squealing and squirming under his telephone threats. Even funnier when the customer had some claim against the bank.'

'Like Florence Fielding?'

'Yes. When I told him about her call, he said how funny is that, that I can bully her to pay money back to her account when the ENB probably owes her more in compensation than she owes on her credit card? And she can't do a thing about it.'

Rose tried again, her voice as gentle as she could make it. 'It wasn't Andy, Annabel, he wasn't the one. He wasn't the person who harassed your father.'

Tears had begun to stream down Annabel's pale face, hot angry tears that smeared her cheeks with melting mascara. 'What do you know about my father? Who are you to judge what happened to my father?' She rubbed at her face with the back of her hand, trying to wipe the tears away. 'My father was a good man. A kind man. He didn't deserve what happened to him. He just had bad luck. Do you know what happened to him, Rose? I mean, do you really know? He had his own business, all those people working for him, depending on him, and then one day an invoice doesn't get paid and everything begins to slide. Thirty thousand pounds that customer owed him. It doesn't sound much, does it? These days people pay that for a car. But for my father it was everything. It was the wage bill. Cash flow was already tight, so he borrowed the money from his credit cards. He said he couldn't leave the staff without their wages.' She closed her eyes and swallowed.

'I know what happened Annabel, and I am truly sorry. I know your father was trying to do right by his staff. And I don't for one minute condone the way the ENB behaved towards him.' Rose spoke quietly. 'But you can't blame Andy. Or Chris. Neither of them worked in the team at that time. And punishing the innocent for something they didn't do ...' Rose suddenly felt sick, her own eyes beginning to fill with tears she could only ascribe to shock. Had this ordinary young girl really committed those crimes? She looked away, hoping to see Mulligan or some other rescuer, but there was no one. She took in a deep breath. 'Is that why you struck up a friendship with Andy? To get close to him, because you thought he was responsible for your father's death?'

'No. I just wanted to ... to know. To understand why they treated customers so badly. To understand what gave them the right. It was only after I got to know him that I realised he was responsible. He was so cruel, so judgmental.'

'But he wasn't responsible for what happened to your father. He didn't work in the Recovery Department when your father received those calls.'

'That's not true. He told me himself that he'd been working recovery calls since 2007.'

'Yes, but he started in that team in August 2007. The calls made to your father stopped in June when ... when he took his own life.'

'You can't know that.'

'I can. I do. I've checked the personnel files.'

Annabel closed the doe eyes tight shut and her face crumpled into a mask of pain. When she spoke again her voice was low and calm. 'I don't care. I don't care which one of them it was. They're all guilty. Every one of them. Day after day, hurting people, taunting them, making fun of them. Making them suffer.' Her eyes flicked open and she held Rose's gaze. 'People who have done nothing wrong. People who owe money because of the hand that life has dealt them Rose, just because of life.' She scowled. 'He called them losers. That's what he thought of my Dad, Rose. That's what he was thinking when he harassed him, and hounded him, and drove him to his death.'

Rose leaned over the table and took hold of Annabel's hand. She wanted to comfort the girl but there were no words, nothing she could say would be enough to salve the suffering. When the silence was finally broken, it wasn't Rose who broke it.

'You can't blame Andy for what happened to your father, Annabel. Andy didn't make those calls. If you have to blame someone for what happened to your family, then maybe you should blame me.'

They turned as one to see who had spoken. Reggie Croft was standing behind them, his grey eyes heavy with regret, his face drawn and haggard. He quietly pulled a chair up to the table and sat down next to Annabel, and swallowed hard. He kept his eyes downcast, unable to look at her. 'I've spent seven years trying to forget about your father, Annabel, but it won't go away. I can't undo what's been done, but I can help you try to understand. It's not right that you blame Andy for something he didn't do.'

Annabel shook her head. 'You hated Andy. I know you did. Andy told me. Why would you try to defend him now?'

'I'm not trying to defend him. Maybe the reason I hated him was because he reminded me of myself.' He smiled sadly. 'When I dealt with your father's accounts, it was at a time when there were no limits on the behaviours we could use to recover money from a customer. The kind of thing that Andy was doing, threatening customers, pressing them for money they didn't have, that was all OK back then. In fact, it wasn't just OK. It was expected of us. Anything we could do, they said, to recover the bank's money.'

'You could have refused.'

'It wasn't that easy. It was what I was paid to do. And I needed my job.' He shook his head. 'You know, Andy and Chris used to laugh at me. Poke fun at me for not meeting my targets. And I couldn't even fight my corner, fight back and tell them that I knew all about pushing customers, that they were amateurs compared with some of the tactics I had used.' He hung his head. 'No blame was ever attached to me over your father's death, Annabel. As far as the court was concerned I was just carrying out my employer's instructions. But I've carried the guilt every day of my life since your father died.'

Annabel was listening intently. She put a hand gently on Reggie's arm and leaned her face closer to his. 'Why didn't you tell them? Why didn't you tell them about my father? They might have stopped. Andy might not have made those calls.'

He looked ashamed. 'I didn't want them to know. The bank could have hung me out to dry after it happened, made a scapegoat of me, but Clive decided to take a different approach. I think he felt responsible, for pushing staff too far in the name of profit. He said it would never be mentioned again, that he wouldn't tolerate anyone in the bank mentioning it, there was to be a fresh start. He said I had a right to anonymity. How could I say anything about Andy and Chris, and the way they were behaving, without drawing attention to myself? I had to make a choice between keeping my anonymity and making them stop.'

'It was the wrong choice.' Annabel shook her head firmly. 'The wrong choice.' She was becoming agitated again. 'Andy's paid the price now. He's paid the price for hurting my father, and he was only a bully. If what you say is true, he was only a bully, and he didn't have to die.' Her face began to crumple with a dawning, painful understanding, and her grip on Reggie's arm began to tighten. 'He didn't have to die.' She turned to look at Rose now, her face full of fear, the doe eyes widening with panic. 'Oh God, Rose, he didn't have to die.'

Rose felt her mouth turn dry and her body prickle with a rush of adrenalin. When she spoke, it was a whisper. 'Is that what you meant, Annabel, when you told Robert Donovan that Andy had been disciplined?'

The silence between them hung in the air and then Rose turned troubled eyes to Reggie. Reggie had begun to shake, his hands trembling against the table, his face suddenly clammy with the horror of realisation. 'My God, it should have been me.' He drew his arm back, freeing himself from Annabel's grip, and finally turned his gaze towards her face. 'Annabel, you didn't … kill Andy … because you believed he … oh sweet Jesus, no. No, not another death because of me?'

34

'They're from me and Vienna. For helping Florence, like.'
Michael Spivey thrust a large, elaborate box at Rose with
unceremonious inelegance. He nodded at it. 'They're
Belgian truffles. Handmade. Proper posh.' He sniffed with
more than a little pride. 'Vienna knows about that sort of
fing.'

Rose took them with an appreciative smile. 'That's very
kind of you Michael, but there was no need. I was happy
to help.'

Spivey cast a defiant glance at Benny, who was eyeing
him over a pint of bitter with a cynical amusement. 'Nah,
it's only right. It's made Flo's Christmas. And the kiddies.'
His eyes were still fixed on Benny, and they glowed with
determination. 'Vienna says you should always show
people you appreciate what they've done for you.'
Following Vienna's value system didn't come easy to him
and it showed in his face. He blew out what sounded like a
sigh of relief and turned on his heel, and scurried back to
the bar, the ordeal over.

Benny leaned in to Rose. 'I'm havin' trouble dealin'
with him now he's got love on his side. He keeps makin'
grand gestures and apologisin' for things he hasn't done.'

'He's making up for the past.' Rose held the box of
chocolates out towards him. 'These aren't really for me,
you know. They're for you.'

'Me?' He sat back in his seat.

'Of course. Why do you think he was looking at you
when he made that little speech about showing people you

appreciate what they've done for you?'

Benny looked uncomfortable and gulped at his pint. 'He needn't start that game. I prefer it when he's a lyin', deceitful little git. I know where I stand then.' He turned to look at the bar where Vienna was teasing Spivey with some private joke, and his voice softened. 'But I won't deny she's good for him.' He drained his glass and gestured with it towards the bar. 'Time for another, Rose?'

'Sure, why not.' She settled back into her seat as he lumbered off to the bar. It felt good to unwind with someone a million miles away from the ENB, and she deserved another glass of wine after today. A large one. More than one. She regretted for a moment not asking him just to bring her the bottle.

If she closed her eyes she could still see the tears cascading down Reggie Croft's cheeks as he sobbed out seven years of repressed guilt, only to see a life-sentence of survivor guilt rising up in front of him as he realised that Annabel's blow for justice had missed him by inches and landed instead on Andy Miller. She could still see the anguish on Annabel's face, the panic in the doe eyes as George Mulligan had gently led her away to a waiting police car, his arm reassuringly around the girl's waist for support and for comfort.

Annabel Halmshaw wasn't her problem, but somehow she couldn't shake off the feeling that she wished she was, that there was something she could do to make up for what the girl had suffered, for what she was still to suffer. There was no question that the girl would have to pay the acceptable price for her crimes, there was no avoiding a custodial sentence of some sort, even if a good brief was able to introduce the idea of mental instability. A jury might take one look at the evidence and call it a revenge killing. But Rose didn't believe it was.

There was a fine line between killing in retaliation, and killing to avenge a perceived wrong. Rose was in no doubt that Annabel had killed Andy Miller and attempted to kill

Chris Kemp to avenge her father's death, and her mother's. That she had been motivated by a grief so deep it had driven her to dispense her own justice. And Rose, for whom justice mattered so much, could understand that, even if she couldn't condone the outcome. Just as well, she thought, that Annabel had no idea about the payment protection insurance wrongly sold to her father along with his debts. If claims were lodged now, she mused, the debts would be wiped out with plenty to spare. Just as they had been for Florence. The debts might never have existed.

If the debts had never existed Alan Simmonds might still be alive. His wife might still be alive. Andy Miller most certainly would be alive, Chris Kemp wouldn't be lying in a hospital bed, and Annabel wouldn't be looking at a lengthy prison sentence.

If … if … if …

Somewhere deep inside her bag her mobile phone vibrated with a text, and she pulled the bag up onto her lap and fished it out. They had finished questioning Annabel for the day, and Scottie was on his way over to The Feathers to join her for a drink. Over at the bar, Benny was enjoying some joke with Vienna as she pulled him a fresh pint. She smiled to herself. Sometimes the odd "if" was a handy thing to have around.

If Scottie found Rose in The Feathers with Benny, he might be disappointed. If Benny knew Scottie was on his way over, he might not be in any hurry to leave. If Mike knew she was enjoying a drink with Benny Bradman, and mischievously looking forward to seeing how the evening would pan out with Detective Sergeant Ian Scott thrown into the mix, he certainly wouldn't be too impressed.

But then if she could persuade Lu that she needed a couple of weeks at the cottage to recover from her latest assignment, she wouldn't have to dash back to Hertfordshire to find out.

ABOUT THE AUTHOR

Mariah Kingdom was born in Hull and grew up in the East Riding of Yorkshire. After taking a degree in History at Edinburgh University, she wandered into a career in information technology and business change, and worked for almost thirty years as a consultant in the British retail and banking sectors.

She began writing crime fiction during the banking crisis of 2008, drawing on past experience to create Rose Bennett, a private investigator engaged by a fictional British bank.

Dead Ringer is the second Rose Bennett Mystery.

www.mariahkingdom.co.uk

Printed in Great Britain
by Amazon